The Secret of
Willow Inn

By
Pat Nichols

THE SECRET OF WILLOW INN BY PAT NICHOLS
Published by Guiding Light Women's Fiction
An imprint of Lighthouse Publishing of the Carolinas
2333 Barton Oaks Dr., Raleigh, NC 27614

ISBN: 978-1-946016-77-5
Copyright © 2019 by Pat Nichols
Cover design by Elaina Lee
Interior design by AtriTex Technologies P Ltd

Available in print from your local bookstore, online, or from the publisher at: ShopLPC.com

For more information on this book and the author visit:
https://patnicholsauthor.wordpress.com/

Brought to you by the creative team at Lighthouse Publishing of the Carolinas: Jennifer Slattery, managing editor.

Library of Congress Cataloging-in-Publication Data
Nichols, Pat.
The Secret of Willow Inn / Pat Nichols

Printed in the United States of America

Praise for *The Secret of Willow Inn*

The Secret of Willow Inn, by Pat Nichols, captivated me from the first page and held me rapt far into the night until I finished it. I couldn't put it down! A story of longing, heart wrenching sorrow, forgiveness and restoration, all set in a small town you will love.

~Ane Muligan
Bestselling author of the Chapel Springs series

It takes a really good book to let me be a reader again, and *The Secret of Willow Inn* did. It lifted my spirits. I loved it!

~Haywood Smith
New York Times and USA Today bestselling author

Pat Nichols' debut will appeal to fans who love cozy mysteries wrapped in small town quirkiness and accented with big city lights. A sweet, funny read for anyone who has ever dared to dream a crazy dream.

~Lindsey Bracket
Author of *Still Waters,* Selah 2018 book of the year

The small town of Willow Falls in the North Georgia mountains is faltering. Yet three strong women--virtual strangers to one other--are drawn to save it through the development of a winery and an inn. Unbeknownst to them, their lives are inextricably linked through secrets that when disclosed will blow the reader away. I fell in love with this charming town and its wonderful citizens and cannot wait for author, Pat Nichols, to invite us to spend more time in Willow Falls with sequel after sequel.

~Sherri Stewart
Author of Sleeping Through Christmas

The Secret of Willow Inn is a beautifully written story. The many twists and turns kept me guessing until the very surprising and suspenseful climax. It is a great balance of mystery and faith with a touch of Southern charm. The characters are well developed and I felt as if I had made new and interesting friends as I devoured each chapter.

~ **Maria Sutej**
Former Executive Vice President, Avon Products, Inc

Acknowledgments

The road to publication is not traveled alone. It is paved with inspiration and insight from many. To all my friends, thank you for your encouragement and kind words.

To my friend Sherri Stewart, an accomplished author who edited my first manuscript, thank you for helping me transition from novice to published writer. To my beta readers, Pat Davis and Beverly Feldkamp, your insight and feedback helped take my work from draft to polished manuscript. To Eva Marie Everson, thank you for providing my first professional critique with so much grace and wisdom. You inspired me to continue writing and learning the craft.

A special thanks to Lighthouse Publishing of the Carolinas and Eddie Jones, for the opportunity, the amazing support, and blessed inspiration. To my editor, Jennifer Slattery, thank you for taking my work to new levels. I will forever be grateful for all you have taught me.

To members of American Christian Fiction Writers, North Georgia Chapter, thank you for your education and friendship. To Word Weavers International, Greater Atlanta Chapter, thank you for helping me perfect my writing.

To our beloved small group, thank you for your inspiration, prayers, and praise.

Thank you to my amazing family who believed in me from the moment I began this journey. A special thank you to my daughter Shelley Jordan. Your support and inspiration mean the world to me.

Above all, I thank God for His grace and unconditional love. He planted the seed and gave me the courage to water it.

Dedication

To Tim, my husband and the love of my life. Thank you for believing in me and always encouraging me to move beyond my comfort zone and reach for the stars.

Chapter 1

As far back as Emily Hayes could remember, her heart yearned for a sister. She directed her earliest requests to Santa Claus, which made Christmas mornings a confusing blend of excitement and disenchantment. Later, she bargained with God. He disappointed her too. When she learned where babies came from, she petitioned her mom with promises to keep her room clean and be the best sister in the whole wide world. Nothing worked. At some point the pleas stopped, but the lingering desire left a hole in her heart.

Thursday morning, Emily stepped outside the white-columned home converted to a hospital and traced her ultrasound image with her finger. It wasn't at all what she'd expected. She pressed her hand to her chest to ease the fluttering sensation, slipped the photo in her jeans pocket, and texted her husband. *Have results. Meet me in the park in five.*

A cool breeze nipped her cheeks and rustled the new crop of leaves on the mature willow oaks lining Main Street. She dropped her phone in her purse, pulled her sweater tight, and crossed the two-lane road to the sidewalk fronting a grand estate. White columns extending from a railing supported the roof over the wide, front porch. The home was weeks away from final transformation to the Willow Inn, thanks to her parents' first effort to save their town from a slow, painful death.

The second stood next door—an abandoned, four-story, brick hotel. All they needed to bring it to life was a boat-load of money. If everything fell into place, their ship would come before they returned home. A bird fluttering to a nest in a tangle of ivy summoned images of new beginnings and eased Emily's tense shoulders.

She wandered past the hotel to the adjacent lakeside park and settled on the foot-high retaining wall at the water's edge. She gazed across the street at the picturesque, century-old Main Street storefronts. Pepper's Café's faded awning flapped in the breeze and triggered memories from her childhood. Picnics in the park with her friends. Hiking with her dad to the waterfall. Begging her mom for a sister.

From the corner of her eye, she spotted Scott exiting his store and heading her direction. He sat beside her and kissed her cheek. "How'd your appointment go?"

"When I was a little girl, Mom brought me to town so I could put my letters to Santa in that red box." Emily pointed to the vintage, cast-iron mailbox on the corner. "Afterward, she'd treat us to dessert at Patsy's. It's a miracle her store and the café are still open."

"At least for now. Enough about Willow Falls' problems. What'd you find out?"

She handed over the ultrasound photo.

As he studied the image, his brow furrowed. "Tell me what in the heck I'm looking at."

"Answers to all my pleas and prayers for a sister skipped me and went straight to our babies."

His eyes opened wide. "Are you saying—"

"Twins. Both girls."

Scott pivoted and propped a knee on the wall. "Are you sure?"

"Positive."

"Wow. Two babies to feed and dress. Two cribs. Two of everything." He ran his fingers through his thick, brown hair. "Did you tell your mom?"

Emily shook her head. "I wanted to tell you first." She dug her phone from her purse and pressed the number. Her mom's recorded voice forced her to leave a message and shove the phone in her pocket. "I'm surprised she didn't answer. She knows I scheduled the ultrasound."

"If your parents are meeting with their potential investor, they most likely turned their phones to silent."

"Or they're out of range. Who knows what cell service is like in Savannah?"

Scott locked eyes with Emily and brushed a stray lock of curly hair from her cheek. "How are you taking the news?"

"I'm thrilled our girls will never yearn for a sister." She pressed her thumb into her palm and massaged the back of her hand. "At the same time, I'm worried about the expenses. Plus, my plate is already full. There's my part-time job at the paper, and you need my help at the store. As soon as Mom and I finish the inn, I plan to focus on my novel. You know I want to complete a first draft before my due date." She patted her belly. "I have no idea how difficult this pregnancy will be, and caring for two infants is way more than a full-time job. How can I possibly handle it all?"

"First, I don't want you to worry over money, I'll find a way to make our finances work. About the babies, you know your mom will help you take care of them." Scott grinned and tapped the tip of her nose. "I hope our daughters look exactly like you, strawberry-blond hair, green eyes, freckles, and all."

His touch, the musky scent of his cologne, and his smile eased her anxiety. "And miss out on your adorable cheek dimples? Not a chance. I want them to take after their father."

Scott held the ultrasound image close to his hazel eyes. "Nope. They're gonna look like you."

"I think your imagination is on overdrive."

"I'm just stating the facts, ma'am. Tell you what. How about we hightail it across the street and grab a bite while we wait for your mom to call?"

"Might as well. I'm as hungry as a lady pregnant with twins." She pocketed the picture.

"What are you in the mood for?"

"Chocolate ice cream would hit the spot. Maybe with two dill pickles on the side." Emily chuckled. "I better not joke around with Pepper. She'd figure out what I'm talking about and broadcast the news to everyone within earshot before I have a chance to tell my parents."

Emily linked arms with Scott and ambled across the street to the chalkboard displaying Pepper's daily special. "Meatloaf and mashed potatoes. Not as enticing as ice cream and pickles, but it'll do."

She glanced through the café windows at the four booths hugging the partially-exposed brick wall on the left and the five Formica-topped tables lined up in the center. "It looks like we're the first lunch customers."

Scott opened the door and nodded toward the right. "Except for one."

Inside, Pepper Cushman stood behind the counter, drumming her fingers on the surface and glaring at Maribelle Paine, the town's number-one purveyor of mail and gossip.

Emily leaned close to her husband. "I think we're interrupting a serious discussion."

"It looks more like an all-out war. Do you want to leave?"

"And miss all the drama? Not a chance." She settled on the stool beside Maribelle. "Hey, ladies. What's got y'all in such a tizzy?"

Maribelle propped her fists on her ample hips. "Sadie Liles gets released from jail tomorrow and Pepper's bringing her here. That woman has no business coming back. Most everyone knows she's why our population keeps dwindling and our town's in trouble."

Pepper swept dark-brown bangs away from her eyes. "You can't lay all the blame on Sadie."

"Why not? Because of her, Willow Falls isn't a popular north Georgia tourist destination." Mirabelle shifted her weight. "Think about it. Helen is modeled after an alpine village, and Dahlonega has a goldmine. But neither has a fifty-foot waterfall and scenic trails a mile from town. And don't forget Willow Falls is Naomi Jasper's hometown."

"Are you kidding?" Pepper shook her head. "The woman moved to Charleston years ago after a wealthy collector discovered her paintings and sponsored a show at some fancy art gallery."

"It doesn't matter. She still owns her family home and studio on Main Street. The point is, our town had something to offer. All we needed to attract tourists and keep our one celebrity from moving away was a first-class place for people to stay. Building the hotel made Robert Liles our hero, but he never got a chance to finish the place and welcome the first guest."

Pepper's cheeks flushed. "Did you forget? The man's failure to leave a will, along with his mountain of debt, led to the foreclosure."

Mirabelle huffed. "Neither would have mattered if Sadie hadn't shot him dead."

"Well, we'll never know, will we?" Pepper's tone oozed sarcasm.

"All us clear-thinking residents do know we can't let her dredge up the past and sabotage the Redding's plan to get the money to finish the hotel."

Emily tossed her purse on the counter. "Hold on a minute. The investor is Dad's old college buddy, and he lives in Savannah. I doubt a three-decade-old crime, miles from anywhere, will keep him from making a sound investment decision."

Scott settled beside his wife. "Emily's right."

Mirabelle shook her finger at him. "I can't believe you don't agree with me. I mean, you've got more at stake than most everybody. Open up your thick skull, young man, and think about North Carolina's Mast General Store. Your place has a way better story. But, without tourists looking to experience hundred-year-old history, how do you expect to keep your great-granddaddy's store open?"

Scott's jaw tensed. Emily patted his knee and reflected on his decision to abandon his career to manage the store when his father passed away. He knew the hotel offered a last-ditch effort to keep Willow Falls from becoming a ghost town and his family's business from going under.

Maribelle shifted her attention to Pepper. "If you bring Sadie back, she'll ruin everything—again."

"You have to understand, she's been my friend since she and her mom moved to town. Besides, Mitch and I have been visiting her in prison for years, so it makes perfect sense for her to move in with us until she gets her feet on the ground."

Mirabelle guffawed. "A murderer living with the sheriff and his wife. That's rich. Hey, Emily, do you think your boss will let you write an editorial about the law harboring a fugitive?"

"You know good and well Sadie's not a fugitive." Pepper crossed her arms. "What's more, she's done her time and the parole board believes, following thirty years behind bars, she deserves to live free like every other law-abiding citizen."

"Well, I say let her become a fine, up-standing resident in someone else's back yard, not mine." Mirabelle slid off the stool.

"It doesn't matter what you or anyone else thinks," said Pepper. "I'm picking her up in the morning. So give it a break and get used to the idea."

Scott flicked a crumb off the counter. "Who'd have guessed we'd come in for lunch and get a belly full of controversy?"

Maribelle slapped a five-dollar bill on the counter. "Which is going to ramp up big time the second word gets out about Sadie returning to the scene of her crime." She stomped toward the door. "Don't say I didn't warn you if plans to open the hotel fall apart because of you and your ex-con buddy."

Pepper filled two glasses with sweet tea and pushed them to her new arrivals. "It makes me angry folks think they know everything about the day Sadie shot her stepfather."

Emily's eyes widened. "Are you trying to tell us something?"

"I'm just saying there's another side to the story."

"And?"

"I'm not at liberty to say more."

Emily propped her elbows on the counter and laced her fingers. "You do understand, dropping a story snippet on a newspaper reporter and an aspiring novelist—without promising a conclusion—is akin to triggering an incurable itch and an out-of-control imagination."

Pepper removed Mirabelle's plate from the counter. "It's not easy listening to people disparage my friend when they have no idea what really happened. Still, I should have kept my mouth shut and not got caught up in the moment."

"How do you know something we don't?"

"Years ago, she told me the truth and made me swear to never repeat it. Until today, I didn't utter a word to anyone except Mitch. So please, do me a favor and forget about this conversation."

"Easy for you to say. Impossible for me to do. You know I started writing a story based on our town's history and Scott's store."

"And your point is?"

"A mysterious murder would make a great hook."

"All the same, her story will come out when and if she wants people to know." Pepper pointed to two ladies approaching the door. "It looks like lunch won't be a total bust. Before I take their order, what can I get for you two?"

Emily watched the new arrivals move to a booth. "Are you still pulling double duty as chef and server?"

"Yeah, but not for long. Sadie starts waiting tables for me Saturday."

Scott let out a long whistle. "Talk about swatting a hornet's nest."

"Crazy, huh. I'm counting on controversy and a big dose of curiosity to boost business. But my real objective is to give Sadie a chance to start over. And maybe the good people in our town will find it in their hearts to forgive her and make her feel welcome."

Scott shook his head. "Based on Mirabelle's reaction, that's a tall order."

"No kidding. Back to your lunch."

Emily grinned. "I had a hankering for a sweet and salty dessert. However, I'll settle for your daily special."

"Make it two."

"Two specials coming right up." Pepper moved to the kitchen.

Emily sipped her tea while combing through her memory for details about the town's most notorious crime. Like every other resident, she knew the real scoop—or at least thought she did.

Scott nudged her arm. "I can tell something's rumbling around in your pretty head."

"Facts about Robert Liles' murder. The sheriff found him with a bullet in his chest at the top of the grand staircase in his home. Sadie pleaded guilty and refused to go to trial. After a judge announced the sentence, her mother hightailed it out of town."

"Didn't she die a few months later?"

Emily nodded. "Cancer. Although some folks believed she died from a broken heart. Following her death, Robert's home went into foreclosure."

"If your parents hadn't stepped up to give it new life, the house would still be empty. Which makes them Willow Falls' newest champions."

Pepper returned from the kitchen carrying two plates. "The meatloaf is a new recipe I'm trying out. Let me know what you think."

Emily breathed in the woody scent and savored the minty taste. "It's delicious. What's your secret?"

"A pinch of sage."

The sound of chimes emanated from Emily's pocket. "It's Mom." She slid off the stool and pressed the phone to her ear. "Hey."

"Hi, sweetheart. I can't wait to hear if we're going to welcome a grand-daughter or grandson?"

"Hold on a sec." Emily walked across the street to the park and settled on a wrought-iron bench. "I slipped away so no one can hear me."

"Why? Is something wrong?"

"Everything's fine. I wanted you to hear the news before the rest of the town." She relayed the ultrasound results.

"Are you sure?"

"One-hundred-percent positive." Emily shifted her phone to her other ear. "At first, I thought the nurse was kidding until she showed me the pictures."

Silence.

"Mom, did I lose you?"

"I'm trying to take it all in. You've wanted to get pregnant for such a long time, and now to find out you're having twins … God has given you a wonderful blessing."

"I can't wait for you to get back home so we can celebrate. Oh, I almost forgot to ask, how's everything going with the deal?"

"I don't know yet. We'll make our pitch tonight."

"Everyone's counting on you to come through with the money."

"Believe me, we feel the pressure."

"I have faith in you and Dad. When are you heading back?"

"If everything goes as planned, we'll play tourist tomorrow and leave for home Saturday afternoon. I love you. Say hello to Scott."

"I love you too." Emily pocketed her phone and strolled back across the street to the café.

Scott set his fork down. "How did your mom react?"

"I think shocked. And excited."

Pepper removed Scott's plate and wiped the counter. "Why'd you leave to talk to your mom? Is everything okay?"

Emily pulled the ultrasound photo from her pocket and pushed it to Pepper. "Take a look and tell me what you see."

Pepper pulled her reading glasses from the top of her head and studied the image. "I'm no expert, but it looks like two little people."

Emily smiled. "Both girls."

"Wow. Do you know the last time twins were born in our little town?"

"I don't have a clue."

"Neither do I, which means it's been longer than anyone remembers." Pepper scurried to the center booth and placed the photo on the table. "Ladies, meet our town's newest residents."

Emily thumped Scott's arm. "Which news nugget do you suppose will top tomorrow's gossip list, Willow Falls' notorious criminal or our twins?"

"No way two babies five months from showing up can compete with an ex-con returning to the crime scene."

His comment sent a question skating along the edge of Emily's mind. Was it possible a thirty-year-old crime could destroy her parents' plan to save the town?

Chapter 2

Rachel Streetman strolled past the high-dollar paintings and plush furniture to the window. Located on the thirty-eighth floor in a downtown Atlanta high-rise, her father's office offered a spectacular view. She gazed down Peachtree Street toward the renowned Fox Theater. A smile curled her lips as she imagined standing center stage, ready to entertain an adoring audience. Her mind drifted back to her senior year in college when she played Peggy Sawyer in *42nd Street*. The accolades fellow students showered on her remained as the last trace of a lifelong dream to act.

Greer Streetman breezed into the room, stood behind his daughter, and put his hands on her shoulders. "It's a great view from up here with the rest of the world at our feet."

Her mental image vanished, along with her smile.

"In your new position, I expect you to play a major role in expanding my business."

While her mind urged her to tell him it wasn't the role she was born to play, her heart compelled her to swallow the comment. She spun around and looked up into her father's brown eyes. "I understand."

"There's enough undeveloped land in north Georgia to keep us busy for decades and add millions to our bottom line. Start by checking out some of those obscure little towns."

"I'll begin researching next week."

"Naomi Jasper comes from somewhere up there."

"Who's she?"

"A highly-rated artist. I bought one of her pieces a few years back." He glanced at his watch. "It's time to bring the staff up to speed. Are you ready, Strawberry Girl?"

She tensed and told him what he wanted to hear. "Of course I am."

He fingered his salt and pepper moustache and eyed her designer suit. "Emerald green is a good color for a redhead. Matches your eyes."

"Thanks."

"Everyone's waiting for the big announcement." She cringed as he clasped her elbow and escorted her to the conference room.

Chatter among the associates ceased the moment her father moved to the head of the long table. He stood ramrod straight and held his head high. "Thirty-five years ago, I stepped into my father's shoes to take over this business. In my hands, Streetman Enterprise experienced explosive growth and became the most successful real estate development firm in the Southeast."

He nodded toward his daughter. "When Rachel graduated from the University of Georgia seven years ago, I began preparing her to one day carry on the family tradition. Today I'm announcing an important step in my strategy, her promotion to Executive Vice President of Acquisitions, reporting directly to me."

Rachel flinched at the polite applause. She knew a half-dozen associates who were far more qualified for the job and suspected everyone in the room knew as well. As she moved to her father's side, she scanned the faces staring at her. To ease her anxiety, she pictured her audience as fans waiting for her to perform. "I'm humbled and comforted knowing I am surrounded by an amazing team of men and women who make our company great. I'm counting on you to help me as I transition to this new role. Together, we'll continue to strengthen our business and make our boss proud."

She stepped aside and watched her father move a tray of gold-rimmed champagne glasses from the console behind him to the table. His assistant moved from the back of the room carrying two bottles of chilled Dom Perignon. Greer twisted the corks from the effervescent wine, filled the flutes, and distributed them to his staff. "Stand and join me in a toast to our future leader, Ms. Rachel Streetman."

He took a sip and clapped twice. Four white-gloved waiters, balancing trays of appetizers, promenaded into the room.

Facial expressions and body language spoke volumes about her father's over-the-top antics. Rachel's face flushed as associates moved away from the table, mingled, and made their way to her. She attempted to mask her embarrassment by countering their congratulations with compliments and praise. By the time the celebration ended and the conference room cleared out, her feet hurt and her jaw muscles ached.

Eager for solitude, she escaped to her office, closed the door, and gazed around the massive space she'd occupied for the past six years. At least her new position made her father's decision to move her into the second largest office less obnoxious. A touch of nostalgia compelled her to pick up her mother's photo from her desk and carry it to the window. She kicked her shoes off and peered down at the twenty-story Skyview Ferris Wheel. She imagined climbing on board and discovering at the pinnacle that the exit door had disappeared, leaving her trapped on an endless trip to nowhere.

She traced her mother's face with her finger. "Why did you have to die?" Tears erupted and spilled down her cheeks. "If you were still alive or if my father didn't cling to a one-child-per-family concept, I'd be rehearsing for a leading role in a new musical. Instead, I'm moving up the chain of command in a business I struggle to tolerate."

A tap on the door disrupted her mental pity party and forced her to wipe her eyes with the back of her hand. She grabbed her shoes, placed the photo back on her desk, settled in her high-back executive chair, and invited the intruder to enter.

Brent Walker sauntered past the couch facing the window and propped his hip on the corner of her desk. "Has the big promotion sunk in yet?"

In addition to being ambitious and easy on the eyes, the man possessed a ton of talent. Second to her, Greer tagged him as his favorite rising star. Rachel propped her elbows on the desk and laced her fingers. "My father should have put you in this position."

"How about sharing your opinion with the boss the next time he moves you up another rung in the ladder."

"No need. You're already on his radar."

"Good to know." He winked. "But it helps to have his gorgeous, smart-as-a-whip superstar pulling for me."

She shook her head, thinking the guy was less subtle than a hungry lion ready to pounce on a stray gazelle. "You have more than enough talent to get to the top without any help from me."

"I know, but it'd be a whole lot more fun climbing up with you."

She dismissed his comment with a flip of her hand. "What's on your mind?"

"A bunch of us are heading to Cut's Steakhouse around six. You have to join us so we can cozy up with the new VP."

The thought of another late dinner-and-drink get together to politic, gossip, and play the game of one-upmanship churned her stomach. She wanted to decline, yet knowing her father expected her to participate obliged her to accept the invitation. "I'll do my best to break away and meet you over there."

"We'll all pitch in and buy your dinner."

Rachel shook her head. "After my father's little champagne caper, I don't need any more recognition."

"At least let me buy you a glass of wine."

"I'll think about it. In the meantime, I have a ton of work to do."

Brent hopped off the desk and winked. "Got it. I'll see you in a couple hours."

Moments after Brent left, Rachel's father strolled in and dropped onto a leather chair facing her desk. "Hey, Veep Girl, your acceptance speech was spot on."

"Thanks, boss. I have to say, Veep—without the girl—is a more appropriate nickname for your second-in-command than the one you tagged me with all those years ago."

"Is a name change your first executive decision?"

"I suppose it is."

"In that case, the boss approves. However, you're still my Strawberry Girl." He pulled a slim, black box from his jacket pocket and pushed it across the desk. "To commemorate today."

Rachel untied the white ribbon, pulled off the cover, and removed a white, gold-trimmed Montblanc pen engraved with her name—her father's favorite success symbol, an outrageously expensive writing instrument. "It's beautiful."

"I trust you'll use it to sign a ton of contracts and lucrative deals."

"I'm glad you have more confidence in me than I do."

He propped an ankle across his knee and fingered his Louis Vuitton shoe. "My faith in your ability is well founded. After all, you're a natural, like me."

She stared at her mother's photo as a question formed on the tip of her tongue. Why did her father refuse to recognize who she was at her core? She dropped the pen in the box and swallowed the comment before it could escape. "I promise to put everything you've taught me to work and make you proud."

"I expect nothing less. By the way, I want to treat you to dinner tonight."

"I told Brent I'd join the troops at Cut's, but I can cancel."

"No. You need to socialize with the associates. Besides, the guy's crazy about you."

Exasperation bubbled up from the pit of Rachel's stomach. Although she succumbed to her father's wishes for her career, she drew the line when it came to her personal life. "Brent's ambitious and eager to flatter the boss's daughter. Nothing more."

"Your brains and beauty would attract him even if you weren't related to me. Lucky for you, he's a darn good catch."

"For someone else, maybe. Definitely not for me."

"Don't strike him off your list before giving him a chance."

"Are you kidding? I'm way too busy with work to even have a list. And if I did, believe me, it wouldn't include Brent. Getting back to your dinner invitation, how about tomorrow night?"

"Works for me. I'll make reservations at Bones."

Greer's administrative assistant poked her head in the office. "Mr. Streetman, your four o'clock appointment is here."

"Duty calls." He planted both feet on the floor, pushed up, and patted Rachel's hand. "Enjoy your evening with Brent and gang."

She clenched her jaw and waited for him to saunter from the office before tossing the boxed pen in her desk drawer. Eager to escape into her private world, she hurried to close the door and returned to the window. She closed her eyes and dreamed she was standing behind deep-red, velvet curtains as they opened to the roar of applause in a theater packed with enthusiastic fans.

Chapter 3

H er parents' golden retriever whimpered and nudged his cold nose against Emily's cheek. She forced her eyes open, swung her legs over the side of the bed, and covered her mouth with her hands until a wave of nausea subsided. "Hey, Cody. Are you my wake-up call?"

The dog panted and wagged his tail.

She pulled her body upright and strolled to the kitchen. Cody padded close behind.

Scott held a chair away from the table. "Good morning, sleepyhead. Have a seat and I'll bring you a cup of decaf."

"With honey and vanilla creamer?"

"You bet." He filled her favorite mug and handed it to her. "Did you sleep okay?"

She breathed in the rich scent before taking a sip. "I dreamed Sadie's dead stepfather showed up alive. Worse, he forced Mom and Dad to give the inn back to him before setting fire to the hotel and burning it to the ground. Sadie found out and shot him again. A judge sentenced her to life without parole and Willow Falls turned into a ghost town."

He laughed. "It sounds like your writer's imagination shifted into overdrive, or you're dealing with a bad case of indigestion."

"Maybe I'm suffering from an attack of out-of-control hormones. If I'm this whacky now, how am I going to act when my belly looks like I swallowed a gigantic balloon and I waddle around like an overfed duck?"

Scott pulled a chair beside her. "You'll waddle with so much grace and charm, all the other ducks will hide their heads in shame."

She patted his cheek. "Your comment deserves your favorite breakfast."

"Flattery still works." Scott stretched out his long legs while she whipped up a batch of blueberry pancakes. "What's on your agenda for today?"

"Shopping at Nathan's. I have to select furniture and accessories for the inn. As soon as I help Mom finish the decorating, I'll have more time to devote to writing my novel."

"Did you finish your first chapter?"

"You bet I did. In fact, two days ago, I emailed it to the critique group I joined."

"The what?"

"A group of writers who give each other feedback on their work. Everyone's published except me, so I'm fortunate they let me in." She stacked three pancakes on a plate and smothered them with blueberry syrup. "Here you are, Mr. Hayes. A breakfast fit for a father of twins."

"You're not having any?"

"It's too heavy for my queasy tummy." Emily held her finger in the air. "I hear a call coming in."

"Sit tight. I'll get it for you." He hurried to the bedroom and returned with her phone. "It's Nora."

Cody's ears perked up at the mention of his owner's name.

"Hi, Mom. I'm putting you on speaker. How did your meeting go last night?"

"It's good your dad's college buddy has a ton of confidence in his ability to get the job done. I'm convinced he's on board with our proposal because Roger's in charge."

"Are you saying you have the money?"

"We have a verbal agreement. The money will come next week, as soon as the guy's attorney puts his stamp of approval on the contract."

Scott leaned close to the phone. "You and Roger are batting a thousand. If people ask, is it okay to put their minds at ease and tell them it's a done deal?"

"I know everyone's on pins and needles, but I think it's best to wait. In case the lawyers don't like the deal and we have to renegotiate. Besides, I suspect the uproar over Pepper bringing Sadie Liles back to Willow Falls will keep questions about the hotel to a minimum."

Emily's jaw dropped. "How did you hear about it?"

"Maribelle left a message on my phone. She wants me to side with her and force Sadie to leave town before she has a chance to settle in. I understand why she's upset. Nevertheless, Sadie deserves a second chance."

Emily nodded. "When work on the hotel gets underway, all the hullabaloo about our resident ex-con should fade away."

"We can hope. Anyway, your dad and I have a couple of touristy things planned in the morning, before we hit the road early afternoon. We should make it home by nine, in time to take our pup off your hands. I hope he hasn't been too much of a nuisance."

Emily reached over to pet Cody's head. "Not at all. In fact, I'm going to miss having him around. I can't wait for you and Dad to get home so I can show you the ultrasound photos."

"Yesterday I bought the cutest little dresses and bonnets for our grandbabies. Oh, and a couple of pink teddy bears. I'm already loving being a grandparent."

"You mean a doting grandma."

"Doting and proud. I have to go. I love you guys."

"Love you, Mom. See you tomorrow night."

Emily laid her phone on the table and refilled her coffee mug. "I can see it now. They'll spoil our girls rotten."

"Yeah, and whip out their phones with dozens of baby pictures to show everyone in a five-foot radius." Scott's smile faded. "It's sad my parents can't join them."

"I know. They passed away too early." Emily tilted her head toward the ceiling. "In my mind, they're our babies' guardian angels. I'm picturing your mom dancing on a cloud, flapping her fluffy, white wings, telling everyone about our twins."

"Not Dad. He's sitting in a fancy pickup making newcomers feel welcome before telling them stories about Willow Falls and Hayes General Store."

"That sounds like him."

Scott gobbled the last bite of pancakes, rinsed his plate, and put it in the dishwasher.

"Wow. You normally leave your dirty dish in the sink. I'm beginning to think being pregnant with twins comes with unexpected benefits."

He laughed and kissed the top of her head. "Prepare to be pampered, pretty lady."

"Pampered, you say. Do you want to begin tonight?"

"What do have in mind?"

"Dinner at Pepper's. I know money's tight, especially with twins on the way. But she's expanding her hours to serve dinner Friday and Saturday nights. Like every other surviving business, she's trying to keep her doors open. I want to support her."

Scott closed the dishwasher. "Do I detect an ulterior motive in your noble gesture?"

"What motive?"

"Curiosity about the notorious released prisoner."

She carried her mug to the sink. "Hey, buddy, I write for the local paper, and I'm gathering material for my novel. So, I have to stay tuned to all the goings-on in town."

"You mean the local gossip."

"Doesn't matter what it's called if it has the potential for a good story. How about it? Do you want to meet me there at five?"

"Why not? I'm up for some crazy hometown drama."

Emily kissed him goodbye, moved to the nursery, and plopped down on the oak floor. Cody lay beside her and rested his head in her lap. She ran her fingers over his silky fur and reimagined the room for two little girls.

"What do you think, Cody? Pretty pastels and frills fit for princesses? Maybe some iridescent stars on the ceiling and a Cinderella castle painted on the wall. And I must have a comfy rocking chair by the window." His tail thumped the floor. "I'm glad you agree."

She closed her eyes, let the sun streaming in caress her cheeks, and pictured her babies growing from infants to toddlers, to preschoolers. She imagined them going off to first grade, hand in hand—companions forever. Although their letters to Santa would be far different than hers, she'd take her girls downtown to deposit them in the vintage mailbox.

Cody's bark disrupted her reverie. She blinked and caught sight of a cardinal pecking at it's reflection in the window. "Crazy bird." She pulled her body up and stretched her arms over her head. "Guess I better get ready to go shopping."

Emily showered, dressed in jeans and a button-down pink shirt, and drove to Nathan's Antique and Furniture Emporium. The owner, who pulled triple duty as pastor for the local church and town mayor, greeted her with a hug. "How's Willow Falls' mother of twins feeling this morning?"

"Amazed at how fast the news spread."

"Only one way to keep a secret in our town—don't tell anyone."

"You've got that right. I suppose you also know about our infamous criminal returning to the scene."

"Along with the controversy it's stirring up." Nathan glanced at his watch. "Pepper picked her up a couple hours ago."

Mirabelle's comments about Sadie popped into Emily's mind. "I hope she's not making a mistake coming back here."

"One thing's certain. She'll need a lot of support and prayer." He pushed his glasses up and smiled. "What brings you in this morning, furniture for your nursery or the inn?"

"Both."

"Your timing is perfect. A truckload of quality antiques came in earlier this week." He glanced around and leaned close to Emily. "They're from Robert Liles' home."

"Are you serious?"

"Yeah. After Sadie shot her stepfather, a Greenville dealer bought everything in the house. A few months back the man passed away, and the crazy thing is, his will directed his heirs to return the items he kept for himself to be sold in Willow Falls."

"How odd. I wonder why?"

"Maybe guilt over darn near stealing everything for pennies on the dollar. Whatever the reason, I don't want word to get out, because people like Maribelle will cause a ruckus. Business is bad enough without added controversy."

"Thanks for trusting me with your secret."

"I know you're level-headed. Besides, your parents deserve first crack at the items since they rescued the house before it deteriorated to the point of collapsing. There's a lot of merchandise to choose from. The estate items are all marked with new-arrival tags."

"Is there room for negotiation?"

"For you, tons." He handed her a clipboard and a pen. "Take all the time you need."

"Thanks, I will." Emily moseyed to the first aisle, eager to wander through the decorative displays and imagine the stories behind each treasure. Pieces from the Liles estate added intrigue to her musings. Did Sadie sleep in the four-poster bed or use the roll-top desk? Did Naomi Jasper's original watercolor hang in a room on the first floor? What about the still-life? Was the claw-foot chair Robert's favorite? What was the real story behind the murder?

By late afternoon, she'd selected a rocking chair for the nursery, filled a two-page list for the inn, mentally fabricated a fictional story about Robert coming back from the dead, and haggled prices with Nathan. "It's a pleasure doing business with you, sir."

"Likewise. How's progress on the inn coming along?"

"We're on the home stretch. For a while, we couldn't decide between tearing down the garage behind the house or turning the upstairs storage area into a guest apartment. The second option won out. Now, it's Mom's favorite spot."

"I can't wait to see the transformation."

"Before we officially open, we'll invite you over for a personal tour."

Nathan smiled. "While I'm there, I'll pray for God to pour out his blessings on the building and all future guests who walk through its doors."

"We'll take all the help we can get."

Emily left her car parked at the store and walked along Falls Street, surprised to see vehicles filling every parking space. She stopped beside the cinema's boarded-up ticket booth. Going to the movies to watch Disney films had been a special treat. She remembered celebrating her fifth birthday sitting on the front row with six friends watching Princess Jasmine fly on a magic carpet. For weeks, she climbed into bed and pretended to soar over Agrabah with Aladdin. So many good memories. When the seventy-five-year-old venue closed its doors for good, a dark cloud descended on Willow Falls. Like too many small towns, technology outpaced funds. The owner couldn't afford new equipment to adapt to Hollywood's switch from celluloid to digital.

She moved past, rounded the corner at Main, and halted. "What the heck?" She yanked her phone from her purse, punched Scott's number, and stared past the crowd at Hayes General Store, which stood perpendicular to the block-long section of Main. She tapped her foot on the sidewalk until he answered. "Have you looked out your window to see what's going on?"

"You mean Willow Falls' version of a protest?"

"What are those people thinking?"

"They're not. They're reacting. I haven't seen a single customer since Mirabelle and her sign-waving warriors lined up outside the café."

She tucked her purse under her arm. "I'm heading over to give Pepper moral support."

"Nothing's going on here, so I might as well close up shop and join you."

Emily stuffed her phone in her pocket and approached Patsy Peacock, owner of Patsy's Pastries and Pretties next door to the café. She adored the senior citizen who lived in the apartment above her shop. "You're the sweetest lady in town. Why are you siding with Mirabelle?"

Patsy adjusted her peacock-feather-adorned hat and waved her *Keep Our Town Safe* sign. "I'm not trying to cause trouble, but I have to think about my little store. I'm too old to start over somewhere else and I can't leave the home where I've lived with the love of my life."

Emily touched the petite woman's shoulder. "With the only dessert and gift shop in town, your business is in better shape than most. Besides, when Mom and Dad come through with the money and the hotel opens for business, tourists will flock to your door. I hope you change your mind and come over to our side."

Patsy blinked and lowered her sign. "I have to think about it."

"I know you'll do what's right." Emily moved past the protestors, stopped at the plate glass window, and gawked at the standing-room-only crowd inside Pepper's Café.

Scott joined her. "I haven't seen this many people downtown since last year's July Fourth picnic."

"Crowds show up for fireworks … both kinds."

"I guess we better go on in." Scott held Emily's hand as he pushed through the throng to reach Pepper. He bellowed above the noise. "Looks like you need your husband to get things under control."

"Mitch is on the way. I can't remember the last time I served more than twenty people at one sitting."

Emily's gaze swept the crowd. "Is Sadie here?"

"No, she's hiding out at our house."

"I imagine she's jittery as a mouse caught in a cat's claws."

"You have no idea." Pepper glanced over Emily's head. "Mitch is coming in the door now and those pesky sidewalk protestors are right behind him."

At six-foot-four, Sheriff Cushman stood out in a crowd and commanded attention. Folks moved aside to let him through. Arguments stopped mid-sentence and heads turned as he took center stage. He faced his audience and grinned. "Well now. It seems Sadie Liles has ruffled some of our fine citizens' feathers. Tell me what's on your mind."

A woman carrying a protest sign stepped forward. "We don't mean to sound disrespectful, Mitch. But it just doesn't seem right for her to come back and dredge up old memories."

A fellow protestor stepped forward. "Yeah, and how do we know she won't get it in her mind to shoot one of us?"

"He's got a point," said a man at the counter. "Being in jail for thirty years most likely made her more dangerous."

Emily bristled at the barrage of comments his comment unleashed.

"Who made you people judge and jury? It's a free country. Sadie has a right to live where she chooses."

"And we have a right to protect our town."

"From what I hear, she's gonna live under the same roof with Mitch and Pepper. How much safer do you think we gotta be?"

"Safety's not the issue. Sadie's a jinx. It's her fault Willow Falls is dying."

"Which will change when the inn and hotel open up."

"That will never happen if word gets out we've got a killer on the loose."

Pepper leaned close to Emily. "It's all I can do to keep my mouth shut about the truth."

Mitch gave a two-finger whistle. When the diatribe stopped, he massaged his neatly-trimmed beard. "What we have here is a difference of opinion. No matter which side of the debate you're clinging to, Sadie has a right to live and work in our town. And I assure you, she's no more dangerous than Patsy or Emily or anyone else in here. Tomorrow, she'll begin waiting tables for Pepper, so I suggest you come on in and see for yourself how harmless she is."

"I'll come in all right, to keep an eye on her." Mirabelle flapped her sign over her head. "This isn't over, Sheriff. We have every right to protest."

"Yes, you do, if you keep it peaceful and don't block access to anyone's business. For now, there are way too many people in here. The fact is, we can only seat forty. If you want to order dinner, pick your spot. Otherwise, go on home or take your debate across the street to the park."

Neighbors scrambled to fill the seats. Those who missed out grumbled and filed out the door.

Emily nudged Pepper. "You're right, Sadie's great for business."

"And she's not even in the building. I suspect people are sticking around to let us know what they think."

Mitch strolled over to Pepper. "I hope you have enough food."

"I'll manage, if folks aren't too picky. My challenge is not having any help."

"You don't think I'm going to leave my wife alone with this bunch, do you? Get me an apron, Chef, and tell me what to do."

"I'll help wait tables." Emily smiled at Scott. "How about you, honey, do you want to join the fun?"

"How can I turn down such an irresistible offer?"

Pepper pressed her palms together. "You guys are amazing."

Scott rolled his sleeves up. "You might change your mind when we mix up orders, spill drinks all over your customers, and drop stacks of dirty dishes."

"I forgive all mishaps in advance."

"Well then, it's time to get to work." He nudged Pepper. "We need order pads, boss."

Pepper stepped to the counter and returned with pads and pens. "I'll let you know when I run out of specials." She and Mitch rushed to the kitchen.

Emily quickly discovered diners were more eager to ask about her twins and voice their opinion about Sadie's return than they were to order dinner. She dug deep for the patience to keep her comments neutral and redirect her customers to the task at hand. By the time the last customer finished eating and left the café, exhaustion overwhelmed her. She collapsed onto a chair, pulled her shoes off, and massaged her aching feet.

Scott finished clearing tables and joined her. "I have newfound respect for people who wait tables. It's a ton of hard work." He reached into his pocket and pulled out a handful of ones. "For a few bucks in tips."

"You're not kidding. I hope customers are more generous with Sadie."

"Based on the comments I heard, I suspect she'll need a second job if she's going to make it on her own."

Mitch and Pepper strolled in from the kitchen carrying four plates. "I hope sandwiches and potato salad are okay, with lemon-meringue pie for dessert."

Scott grabbed a fork. "Right now, I'm hungry enough to eat day-old oatmeal smothered in hot sauce."

Pepper laughed. "By contrast, this meal qualifies as fine dining. Thanks again for all your help. I don't know what I would have done without you two."

Scott dug his fork into the potato salad. "I can't believe we got through the night without any spills or crashes."

"We did mix up a bunch of orders." Emily laughed. "Which might explain why customers were stingy with tips."

Mitch untied his apron and wiped the sweat from his forehead. "All I've got to say it's a good thing we don't have more than forty seats."

"No kidding," Scott said.

Pepper plopped onto a chair. "I hope folks didn't give you too hard a time."

Emily swallowed a bite. "No one hesitated to give us a piece of their mind. Based on the comments I heard, I'm guessing people who want to boot her out of town outnumber Sadie supporters two to one."

"I hope more supporters than naysayers show up tomorrow." Pepper shook her head. "She's already having second thoughts about working here."

Mitch pulled his phone from his pocket. "It looks like we're in for heavy storms. Maybe nasty weather will keep the troublemakers away."

"Or fire them up." Emily wiped her mouth with a napkin. As a writer, she was eager to meet Sadie. But as a resident who loved Willow Falls, she feared the woman's return would wreak havoc on a town struggling to survive.

Chapter 4

Relieved her father's bi-weekly staff meeting ended before lunch, Rachel gathered her notes and fled from the conference room. His agenda never varied—review active projects, discuss potential new business, and update progress on financial and growth goals. He ignored her suggestions to praise employees' efforts. In his opinion, generous compensation and annual bonuses provided more-than-adequate recognition.

She stopped at her assistant's desk. "Is this a good time?"

"Perfect."

"Okay, come on in." Every Friday, Nancy shared tidbits of office intel with her boss. The insight to employees' collective pulse helped Rachel compensate for her father's dispassionate approach to business. The two women settled on the beige couch facing the window. Rachel kicked off her shoes, pulled a knee up, and rested her arm across the back. "I love your new hairstyle. Very chic."

"I hope it makes me look younger than forty-two."

"Are you kidding? You look years younger than your age. In fact, I suspect you have to show ID every time you order a cocktail."

Nancy grinned. "Flattery will get you an extra dose of news. Starting with an interesting comment I heard following the meeting."

"I suspect it wasn't a compliment about the agenda."

"Hardly. Mr. Streetman's newest hire said, 'If *died of boredom* was more than a catchy phrase, the boss would have to replace his entire management team twice a month.'"

"That's a good one, and downright accurate. His meetings are about as exciting as watching ivy creep along the ground in search of water."

"Thank goodness I don't have to sit through them. The second-best comment came from Brent. He claimed to have mastered the art of napping with his eyes wide open."

Rachel ran her fingers through her hair and smiled. "I imagine half the people required to show up are perfecting that skill. Including me. As long as our staff feels valued, I suppose boring meetings aren't worth fretting over."

"Good point. You might find this interesting. I overheard two ladies in the break room debating whether or not you and your father are related." Nancy leaned close. "To tell you the truth, the same question has crossed my mind more than once."

"Because I don't look like him?"

"It's way more than appearance."

"How so?"

"Mr. Streetman is crazy ambitious and hard-nosed to boot."

Rachel rested her cheek on her knuckles. "And I'm not?"

"Everyone knows you work your tail off. But you also take time to listen to people and let them know they're appreciated. Believe me, your efforts make a huge difference to company morale. I know a dozen associates who swear they'll leave if you ever bail. I admit I'm one of them."

"I hope you know how important you are and what a good job you're doing."

"I do, thanks to you. And don't get me wrong. I respect your father's business skills. It's just ... you two seem so different. I suspect you take after your mother in more than the looks department."

Rachel glanced at the photo on the corner of her desk. "Yeah, otherwise I might believe a stork with defective GPS got lost flying over downtown Atlanta and dropped me on the Streetman doorstep by mistake." She caught sight of the sun peeking through the clouds, like a secret escaping from the dark recesses of a mysterious mind. "Did I ever tell you I grew up dreaming about making it big on Broadway?"

"You mean like Bernadette Peters?" Nancy smiled. "She's one of my favorites. I watched her perform in *Follies* last summer during my trip to New York. I even got her autograph after the show. She kind of reminds me of you."

"Wow, thanks for the compliment. Anyway, I had my future figured all out before I finished fifth grade. Following high school, I'd graduate from Julliard School of Performing Arts—"

"In New York?"

Rachel nodded. "Then I'd get discovered by a famous Broadway talent agent and soar straight to stardom." She broke eye contact and shifted her gaze back to the window. "Mom was my biggest fan. Every time my friends and I made up little plays and performed for her, she smothered us with compliments and encouraged us to come up with more."

"She sounds like the perfect mother."

"I still miss her."

"What about your father, did he watch?"

"When he was home. Much of the time he was too busy building the business."

"Too bad for him. What happened to your dream?"

"Cancer. It stole my mother from me. I always hated how her skin and clothes smelled like a dirty ashtray. So, did my father. At least we had that in common." Rachel swallowed the fist-size lump in her throat. "He called my aspiration to act the unrealistic musings of a naïve child. Needless to say, I never made it to Julliard. Instead, I ended up at his alma mater. The day I graduated, I tossed my dream onto the trash heap of unrealized child-hood fantasies."

"To follow in your father's footsteps?"

"Something like that."

Nancy stared at her boss for a long moment. "In my book, you're an exceptionally talented actress."

Rachel's brow furrowed. "How would you know? You never watched me perform. "

"I beg to differ. Tell me, did your desire to walk onto a stage and bring joy to a theater full of adoring fans ever go away?"

She envisioned her invisible audience watching. "You have no idea how often it bubbles up and consumes me."

"Yet every day you come to work with an upbeat attitude and pour your energy into your job."

"I try."

"In my opinion, your performance makes you a top-notch actress. Not to mention an Oscar nominee for best-supporting role."

"It's not exactly what I had in mind. But I suppose it's the best I can do, given my father's expectations." Rachel gave Nancy's hand a squeeze. "Now you know my deepest secret. I admit it's liberating to share it with someone. But no one other than you and I can know the truth."

Nancy ran her thumb and index finger across her lips. "Mums the word." Her head tilted to the side. "I don't mean to pry, but do you mind if I give you some advice?"

"About work?"

"Not exactly."

"I'm listening."

"I have a pretty good singing voice."

"Really?"

"Yeah. Not like Bernadette Peters, but good enough to do solos at church. It satisfies my love for singing. My point is, you don't want to wake up thirty years from now and regret throwing all your dreams away. You should find a way to make acting a reality."

"I appreciate your suggestion, but I work sixty plus hours a week. No way could I squeeze any more into my schedule."

"I'm just saying you shouldn't let your father, or anyone else, dictate your life."

Rachel grimaced. The truth hung in the air like a rancid odor. Did the entire staff think she was nothing more than her father's puppet?

Nancy reached across the couch and touched her arm. "I'm sorry, I didn't mean to upset you."

"It's okay. I appreciate your honesty."

"Well, if you ever do pursue your dream, I promise to become your number one admirer. Heck, I'll even start a nationwide fan club for you."

Rachel forced a smile. "You're a true gem, my friend." A knock on her door compelled her to lower both feet to the floor and slip her shoes on.

Brent charged in before she could respond. "I hope I'm not interrupting anything important."

The spicy scent of his cologne floated around him in an invisible cloud. "Nancy and I are in the middle of important business. What's up?"

"A bunch of us are heading out to lunch. How about coming with us?"

"Sorry, way too much work is piled on my desk to take a break. A VP's curse, so to speak."

"Too bad. Maybe dinner with the gang again next Thursday night?"

"I'll think about it." She stood and dismissed him with a wave of her hand. "In the meantime, enjoy your weekend."

Rachel waited for Brent to stroll from her office. "He's more annoying than an itch from a dozen mosquito bites."

Nancy pushed up from the couch. "I suspect you being nice to the biggest brownnoser in the office qualifies as another award-winning performance."

"Definitely worthy of a nomination." Nancy's comment about her father dictating her life tumbled from her mind to the tip of her tongue. "One of these days I'll find a way."

"To do what?"

Shocked she'd verbalized her thought, Rachel tugged on her earlobe. "Tell my father the truth about my dreams."

Chapter 5

Emily forced her body out of bed, plodded into the kitchen, and plopped down at the table.

"Good morning." Scott poured a cup of coffee, added vanilla creamer and honey, and brought it to her.

"When did you wake up?"

He dropped two pieces of bread into the toaster. "Half hour ago."

"I had no idea waiting tables was so exhausting." She took a sip of coffee before pulling her computer close.

"The forecast calls for rain, so it's a good day to work on your book."

"I'm way too tired to think. Besides, I want feedback on the first chapter before I start the second." She scrolled through her emails. "Hey, I got a message from a critique partner. The author with the most published books."

Scott buttered the toast and carried them to the table. "What does she say?"

"My writing shows excellent potential. She wants me to take her feedback as constructive." Emily stared at the screen. "What do you suppose she means?"

"I think she's giving you a compliment."

"Or she's preparing me for bad news. You know this is the first time anyone has commented on my writing."

"You mean, other than me."

"Of course. The thing is, I want to know what she thinks. At the same time ... it took me weeks to finish the chapter. What if it isn't good enough?"

He swallowed the last ounce of orange juice and pushed his glass aside. "Tell me, why did you join this group?"

"What do you mean?"

"Were you looking for accolades or did you want professional feedback?"

"I suppose some of each."

"Good, because a worthwhile critique partner will give you both."

She breathed deep and opened the document. "You're right." She pressed the page-down key and chewed on her fingernail until she reached the end of the chapter.

Scott stared at the screen. "Wow. That's a lot of red strikethroughs and underlines."

"There are deletions and additions in more than half the paragraphs. She says tightening up my writing and using stronger verbs will keep readers engaged. I feel like I'm back in college and my professor gave me a D minus on a final exam."

"Hold on a minute." He tapped the computer screen. "What does it say in that first bubble off to the right?"

"I did an excellent job pulling the reader into the story."

"In my book that's an A-plus comment. Besides, this is the beginning of a semester, so to speak, not final exam week."

"True. It's just ... I guess it's unrealistic to expect excellence right out of the gate."

Scott patted her knee. "Think about it in a professional sports context. All athletes, even the best, have coaches to help them improve."

"I see your point."

"So, what are you going to do?"

"I suppose I should put my ego aside, toughen up, learn from my mistakes, and become a top-notch novelist."

"That's my girl." He stood and carried his glass to the dishwasher.

"But not now, because I'm heading over to Pepper's to meet Sadie."

"In a couple of hours, can you help me out at the store?"

Emily nodded and closed her laptop. "If you can wait twenty minutes for me to get ready, I'll ride into town with you."

"You've got it."

Scott pulled up to the curb in front of Pepper's Café. Emily kissed his cheek, reached for her umbrella, and scurried under the awning. Inside, she found Pepper at the counter wrapping spoons, knives, and forks in paper napkins. "It looks like a slow day."

"Lately, they're all slow." Pepper placed the stack of wrapped utensils in a wire basket. "I'm surprised to see you here. Are you hungry?"

She shook her head, pulled her purse off her shoulder, and laid it on the counter.

"Have you recovered from your waitress gig?" Pepper filled a glass with orange juice and pushed it to Emily.

"Are you kidding? I didn't wake up till nine and I'm still worn out."

"I know what you mean. We served more customers last night than I normally serve in two weeks. At least I'm closed every Sunday, so I'll have a chance to rest tomorrow."

"Did Sadie start work this morning?"

"Reluctantly. The good news is—at least for her—the three people who came in for breakfast treated her with respect." Pepper pointed to the middle booth. "Those four ladies make up the entire lunch crowd."

"Maybe folks are coming to their senses."

"Or, like Scott suggested, the weather's keeping the rabble rousers away. The real test comes in a couple hours. If I don't get good dinner crowds every Friday and Saturday … I don't know how I can keep my doors open."

"Scott and I'll be here tonight."

Pepper tightened the lid on a salt shaker. "Dinner's on me. Payment for last night."

"Thanks. Your cooking beats tips by a mile."

The kitchen door swung open. A short, thin woman—her gray hair pulled into a ponytail—made her way to the booth and distributed checks.

"I assume she's Sadie."

Pepper smiled. "In the flesh."

Emily spun her stool and watched the ladies pull bills from their purses and lay them on the table before sliding out of the booth and heading for the door. Sadie stashed the money in her apron pocket and carried a stack of dishes to the kitchen.

Emily swung back toward Pepper. "It looks like she's handling the job okay."

"Looks are deceiving. She's less confident than a mouse cornered by a twenty-pound tomcat, so promise me you'll go easy on her when I introduce you."

"You mean ignore my journalist role?"

"And your writer's curiosity."

"Sadie's fortunate to have you as a friend."

"That goes both ways. I remember the day my homeroom teacher introduced sixteen-year-old Sadie from Thomasville, Georgia. Her mother's marriage to Robert Liles was the talk of the town, so, needless to say, I was eager to find out more."

"Maybe you should have become a writer?"

"Not a chance. My curiosity doesn't translate to writing skills. Anyway, we hit it off right away and became best friends. I was devastated when she was arrested, but something deep down kept me from abandoning her." Pepper pressed her palms together and touched her fingertips to her chin. "I think it was God's doing, because Mitch and I have been her only connection to the outside world for thirty years."

"Are you serious? No wonder she's struggling."

The kitchen door swung open again. Pepper motioned to her friend. "Come on over and meet Emily Hayes. She's helping her mom transform Robert's house into the Willow Inn and her husband Scott runs Hayes General Store. He took over after his father passed away."

Emily extended her hand and gazed into Sadie's blue eyes. Crow's feet and wrinkles on her forehead made her look years older than Pepper yet didn't diminish her pretty features. "It's a pleasure to meet you."

Sadie stared at Emily's hand and kept her arms clamped to her sides. "Your daddy-in-law always treated me and Mama like hometown folks."

"He was a charmer, all right." Surprised by her refusal to make contact, Emily withdrew her hand and took a sip of orange juice.

"Emily is going to become our town's most famous celebrity, besides Naomi Jasper."

"Robert had one of her paintings." Sadie pulled the cash from her apron. "He claimed she'd hit it big someday."

"He had a good eye. Anyway, Emily plans to write a novel."

Sadie moved to the cash register and opened the drawer. "I bet she's itching to know what it's like to live behind bars." She transferred the money.

Heat crept up Emily's neck and warmed her cheeks. She glanced at Pepper and shrugged.

Sadie pushed the drawer closed. "I learned how to read people years ago. It's an important skill for jailhouse survival." She crossed her arms and glanced at Emily. "The answer to your unasked question, at least life in the joint was predictable. What do you plan to write about?"

"Our town's history. Facts spiced up with a big dose of fiction."

"About real people?"

"Yes and no."

Sadie nodded toward the café entrance. "It looks like we've got another customer."

Mitch moseyed over and settled on the stool beside Emily. "What's up, ladies?"

"Not much." Sadie pushed a menu to him. "What can I bring you?"

"The board out front says apple pie is the dessert special. I'll have mine à la mode."

"Talk about predictable," said Pepper. "Bring him a salad and low-cal dressing. They're both in the fridge."

"It seems my wife's number one mission in life is to keep me from eating all the good stuff, like cheeseburgers and fries." He propped his forearms on the counter. "I hear in Italy, salads are served following the main course. Sadie, bring my pie with the green stuff on the side."

"Yes, sir." She strode to the kitchen.

Pepper thumped his arm. "Since when is pie considered a main course?"

"I'm sure it's written down somewhere. Besides, it's healthier than donuts."

Sadie returned with his order. "Here you go."

Mitch shoveled a bite of pie in his mouth and pointed his fork at Sadie. "Did you know Emily's pregnant with twins?"

"She does now." Pepper grinned at Sadie. "In addition to your return, it's the biggest news around here."

"At least babies are good news. Can't say the same about me coming back."

A crack of thunder echoed in the distance. "We've got a nasty storm brewing out there." Mitch took another bite of pie and nudged Emily. "Any word from your parents about the money?"

"They're still working on it."

"If I know Roger, he's got the deal wrapped up and the money in the bank." Mitch's radio squawked. "This is why I started with the pie." He pulled it off his shoulder and stepped away from the counter. Moments later, he returned and grabbed his hat. "I've gotta go. There's a serious situation out on County Road." He made a beeline for the exit.

"Be careful, honey." Pepper shook her head. "So much for getting him to eat a healthy lunch. It's a good thing the dressing is on the side. He can eat it tomorrow. How about you, Emily? Are you sure you're not hungry?"

"Positive. Besides, before I head over to give Scott a hand at his store, I want to order some maternity clothes. In a couple more weeks, a shoe horn won't help me squeeze into anything hanging in my closet." She reached for her purse and hopped off the stool. "We'll see you tonight for dinner."

"Make it early, in case a crowd shows up."

Emily retrieved her umbrella and headed two doors down to the town's one remaining clothing store. She flipped through a catalogue and selected two pairs of pants, a skirt, and one top.

The owner frowned. "Four pieces aren't enough to get you through the end of your pregnancy."

"True, but money's tight."

"I know what you mean."

"I'm counting on finding some oversized shirts at the church thrift shop." Emily pocketed her receipt and headed toward the door.

"I'll call you when your order arrives."

"Thanks." Outside, she opened her umbrella and turned right toward the bank that anchored the corner where Main Street turned ninety degrees to the north. She crossed the street to Hayes General Store. The bell over the glass door jangled, announcing her arrival.

Scott nodded to her and continued chatting with a customer while scooping old-fashioned candy into a bag from one of the dozen glass jars lined on the check-out counter.

Emily closed her umbrella and propped it against the wall. Grateful for a few minutes alone to wander through the store, she tuned out the customer's comments about the town's financial woes.

The ancient wood floor creaked and moaned as she admired the hundred-year-old tin ceiling and exposed brick walls. The barrels, cabinets, and wooden shelves displaying an array of old-fashion tools, housewares, and country style accessories stimulated mental images of colorful characters pulling up in Model T's. She imagined ladies wearing fancy hats and dresses with long skirts, carrying parasols to protect their skin from the sun.

She reached the steps leading to the second floor, half the size of the first. Scott had converted the space to an arts and craft consignment shop in an attempt to increase revenue when dwindling profits forced him to lay off his last employee. The thought of the family business shutting its doors forever triggered a sigh. She sent up a silent prayer for her parents' success at their Savannah meeting.

The jangling doorbell drew her attention. She twirled around and smiled as Scott sauntered toward her. "My customer's gone."

"How's business?"

He rubbed the back of his neck, his jaw muscles tense. "Don't ask."

"That bad, huh?" She stood on her toes and planted a kiss on his cheek. "I met Sadie."

"Oh yeah? What's our hometown villain like?"

"Not what I expected after hearing Pepper sing her praises. She was standoffish and wary, even distrustful. She wouldn't shake my hand."

"I don't know why you're surprised. The woman lived more than half her life locked up with criminals. She probably spent most of her waking hours watching her back."

"I suppose you're right. Which means she has a lot to get used to."

"Uh oh. Your expression tells me your writer's curiosity is getting the best of you."

Emily pulled a bar of lavender-scented soap from a barrel and held it to her nose. "If I can get her to trust me, maybe she'll spill the beans about her stepfather's death."

"Don't count on it. I suspect she has a darn good reason to keep it a secret."

"I know it's a long shot, but not impossible. Anyway, right now, I'm here to help you. I assume you want me to work the front while you get some stuff done in the back."

"You got it."

"Can we close up early and head over to Pepper's?"

"Might as well. I'm not expecting enough sales this afternoon to pay today's light bill." He slipped around her and headed toward the back. "At least you're here if a stray customer happens to wander in with a couple of bucks to spend."

Scott's despondent tone triggered a tightness in Emily's chest and unleashed the fear he was losing his struggle to remain optimistic. Although the town's troubles weren't his fault, she knew he'd consider the store closing a personal failure. A thunder clap made her jump and disrupted her mental anguish.

She strolled behind the counter, climbed up on a stool, and let the sound of rain pummeling the metal roof ease her tension and summon childhood memories of visits to the store. Playing hide-and-seek with Scott while her mom shopped. Her sixth-grade crush when he found her crouched behind a barrel of kitchen gadgets and kissed her for the first time. Too much history lingered inside these brick walls to let the store fail.

Emily propped her elbows on the counter and rested her chin on her knuckles. From the front window, she had a perfect view of Main Street. A warm sensation flowed through her as she gazed beyond the hotel and caught sight of the white Willow-Inn sign with black letters. For nearly a year, it had served as a beacon of hope for residents who called Willow Falls home. Now, weeks before she and her mom finished the interior, a new beacon was on the verge of appearing. She suspected her parents had names in mind for the hotel and planned to put up a sign before the end of next week.

Lightning dancing across the clouds caught her eye. She reached into a jar for a lemon drop and watched the downpour move across the lake. It left behind a gentle drizzle and a dazzling rainbow, a sign all was right with the world. Eager to talk to her mom, she pulled her phone from her pocket and pressed the number. The call went straight to voicemail.

Chapter 6

Surprised to see every parking space on Main Street filled, Emily slipped her hand in Scott's as she sidestepped a pollen-filled puddle. "I guess we should have headed to the café an hour ago."

Inside Pepper's, they headed for two of the four stools at the far end of the counter that remained empty.

Emily set her purse on the floor. "Obviously, bad weather didn't dampen neighbors' curiosity."

"It goes to prove controversy and juicy gossip trumps mother nature."

"Good news for journalists and novelists." Emily elbowed her husband. "It gives us more to write about."

Mirabelle strolled in and plopped on a stool beside Scott.

"Welcome to the counter crowd. You're lucky there's a spot left for your husband."

"He's not coming." Mirabelle shrugged. "Atlanta Braves are playing tonight. He never misses a game."

"He's a loyal fan. Have you talked to Sadie?"

"No, and I don't intend to."

Emily tilted her head and gazed at Mirabelle. "You do know she's our waitress."

"It doesn't matter. I'll wait for Pepper to take my order."

"Based on the crowd size, I suspect you'll have to wait a long time." Emily spun around and spotted four customers turning their backs on Sadie.

Nathan and his brother Jacob—the Willow Post editor, Emily's boss, and part-time laborer for her parents' business—along with their wives, occupied the table beside the cold-shoulder diners. Nathan motioned Sadie to his table. "We're honored to let you take our order."

One of Pepper's morning regulars spoke up. "She can come to our booth next."

"She's not coming to our table. We'll wait for Pepper." The middle-aged woman sitting close to the window crossed her arms.

Two tables down, a man snapped his fingers. "Same goes for me and my family."

Sadie slipped her order pad in her apron pocket and scooted to the kitchen.

Mirabelle thrust her thumb over her shoulder, toward the kitchen door. "We don't want that convict working here and bringing more bad luck to our town. Without a job, she'll have to plant her butt someplace else."

A young woman sitting at the other end of the counter shook her head. "Why don't you people grow up and stop behaving like narrow-minded adolescents?"

"You weren't born when she killed Robert Liles, so you don't have a clue," said Mirabelle.

Nathan pushed up from his seat, lifted an open palm in the air, and cleared his throat. "It sounds like some of our fine upstanding citizens have forgotten about Jesus' second great commandment. You know, the one that tells us to love our neighbors as ourselves. Now I doubt anyone in here suffers from self-loathing." He pointed to the empty stool beside Mirabelle. "So, imagine for a moment the Son of God is sitting right over there watching how we treat one of His children."

Eyelids lowered, bodies shuffled, throats cleared.

"So, if you're here to eat some good food and enjoy a pleasant evening, I suggest you let Sadie wait on you. On the other hand, if you're looking to give her a hard time, please leave and make room for neighbors who have a bit more love in their hearts."

Emily cringed as she watched half the customers grumble and shuffle out the door. "It looks like some of our residents need a good lesson on brotherly love."

Scott spun back toward the counter. "What about you, Mirabelle? Since you're sitting next to invisible Jesus, are you gonna play nice with Sadie?"

She thrust her chest out and shook her finger at Scott. "If you think his little speech is going to make me give up, you've got another think coming. Sadie doesn't belong here any more today than she did yesterday. I'm sticking around to keep an eye on things."

"You're one stubborn woman."

"I do what I have to do."

Nathan approached the counter and touched Emily's shoulder. "I'd appreciate it if you go tell Sadie we want her to come back."

"I don't know if she'll listen to me, but I'll try." Emily hurried to the kitchen and breathed in the mingling culinary scents. She spotted Pepper with her arm around Sadie's shoulders and paused before approaching them. "The troublemakers are gone and the rest of us are ready to order. How about it, Sadie, will you come back?"

"I've a good mind to bail." She wiped her cheeks with the back of her hand. "But no way I'm leaving Pepper stranded."

"You're a strong woman, my friend." Pepper smiled. "Don't let them get under your skin."

"At least I don't have to worry about any of them pulling out a knife and stabbing me in the back."

Emily watched Sadie walk out of the kitchen and head straight to Nathan's table. On the way back to her stool, she stopped beside Mirabelle. "I hope you change your mind and let Sadie wait on you."

"Don't need to, I'm not hungry."

"Suit yourself."

When Emily sat, Scott whispered in her ear. "I'll bet you ten bucks she gives in and places an order before the evening ends."

"You're on."

Emily propped her elbows on the counter behind her. As she watched Sadie engage with customers and move back and forth to the kitchen, her curiosity heightened. "I have to get on her good side."

"Sadie's or Mirabelle's?"

"Very funny. There's so much I can learn from her."

"I suppose we all can."

As Emily continued to watch Sadie work the room, she mentally compiled a list of questions to ask—if she ever got the chance.

Fifty minutes passed before Sadie made her way to their end of the counter. "Sorry for the long wait."

"Not a problem. I want you to meet my husband Scott."

He lifted his hand and quickly withdrew it. "The pleasure's all mine."

Sadie tilted her head. "I knew your daddy. He was a decent man. It's good you kept his store open."

"You should come in and check the place out. It hasn't changed much in the past thirty years."

"I will, if I stick around. What can I bring you two?"

Scott glanced at the menu. "Any chicken left?"

"Enough for one, but there's plenty of meatloaf."

"Bring us whatever you've got."

"I'll fix you up a nice plate." Sadie tapped the counter in front of Mirabelle. "What do you want to order, ma'am?"

Mirabelle shrugged and elbowed Scott. "Tell her to bring me a bowl of soup. And a piece of apple pie."

"No need. I think she heard you."

Sadie stuck her pen behind her ear and scurried to the kitchen.

Emily pulled a ten from her purse and slipped it to Scott. "Glad you didn't bet a hundred."

He pocketed the cash. "I'm sorry I didn't."

"What are you two mumbling about?"

Scott grinned at Mirabelle. "A little bet about the menu."

She pursed her lips and squinted. "Are you sure?"

"Hey, don't you trust me?"

"You two are sitting over there whispering like two crazy people. Who knows what you're talking about."

Sadie delivered Mirabelle's soup and pie before returning with Emily and Scott's dinners. "The meatloaf is the best I've ever tasted. Even better than my mama's."

Mirabelle swallowed a spoonful of soup and guffawed. "I bet it is. Especially after eating prison food for thirty years."

"Hey." Emily pointed her fork at Mirabelle. "Why don't you ease up?"

"It's okay." Sadie crossed her arms and glared. "Because she's right. Jailhouse grub is crappy. What's worse, if jailbirds don't treat the cook with respect, they end up with some nasty stuff in their chow. I learned that lesson early on. But it ain't about to happen here, cause me and Pepper got too much respect for people in this town." Before Mirabelle could respond, Sadie turned on her heel and marched back to the kitchen.

Emily's eyes opened wide as she choked back laughter. "I guess she set you straight."

Mirabelle pushed her plate away. "That woman is a menace."

"Give it a break already." Scott speared a slice of zucchini.

Emily savored a bite of garlic mashed potatoes, blocked out the noise, and let her mind wander. When she swallowed the last bite, she leaned close to Scott and breathed in his aftershave's woody scent. "In spite of the challenges we face, I'm fortunate to have some amazing blessings in my life."

"Like what?"

"I'm married to the most wonderful man."

He grinned and winked. "Glad I top the list. What's second?"

"My life-long desire for a sister became instant reality for our babies."

"That's a good one."

"There's more." She held her thumb an inch from her index finger. "I'm this close to helping Mom finish the inn."

"And then you can finish writing your book?"

"You've got it."

Gratitude washed over her and filled her heart with joy.

Startled by a hand on her shoulder, Emily spun around and locked eyes with Sheriff Mitch. His pained expression shattered her euphoria. "What's going on?"

He leaned close. "You and Scott need to come with me."

Chapter 7

Emily cringed and swallowed the bile erupting in her throat. "I don't understand. Why do we need to come with you?" Her voice trembled. "What's wrong?"

Scott held her hand and helped her down from the stool. "Tell us what's going on, Mitch."

"Not here. We'll talk in Pepper's office." He led them away from the counter, stopped, and whispered in Nathan's ear. The man dropped his fork, sprang to his feet, and fell in line behind Emily and Scott.

Conversations throughout the café ceased.

Mitch held the office door open and stepped in last. He closed the door behind him and pointed to a chair. "Please sit down, sweetheart."

Why did he bring us in here? Did our house burn down? Did something happen to the store or Cody? "No, I want to stand. Tell me why you dragged us in here. Why you couldn't talk to us out there. Now, Mitch."

The sheriff sucked in air. "It's your parents." He shifted his gaze away from her. "When I left Pepper's earlier today … there's been a fatal accident."

Emily gasped. Her knees buckled. Her husband caught her and guided her to a chair. Nathan knelt beside her.

"What happened?" Scott's voice quivered.

"A drunk driver hit them head-on at Devil's Curve. Their car plunged down the embankment." Mitch blinked. "It took us a long time to get to them. Based on the damage, I believe they died on impact."

Emily shook her head. "It's not possible. They weren't supposed to leave Savannah until this afternoon." She jumped up and clutched Mitch's arm. "Don't you see? You made a terrible mistake. It's not their car. They couldn't have been anywhere near here." She dropped back onto the chair. "It's not them."

Scott dropped to his knees and wrapped his arms around her.

She pushed him away. "No. It's not true. They're not gone. They're our babies' only grandparents. God wouldn't take them from us. Not now. Not when everything is falling into place."

Her eyes pleaded with Nathan. "Tell me He wouldn't let something bad happen to them. Please, tell Mitch he got it wrong. Tell him my mom and dad are still alive."

Nathan held her hand in his. "I'm sorry, child."

Pepper stepped into the room. "Sadie told me you four stormed back here. What's going on."

Mitch relayed the tragedy and pounded a fist against the wall. "Why didn't I force the county to do something about that curve? A bigger warning sign. A wall. More guardrails. Anything."

"It's not your fault, honey," Pepper said.

"Then whose fault is it?" Emily yanked her hand away from Nathan's and bolted to her feet. "Why did God let a worthless drunk slam into my parents' car? Tell me, why did they have to die?"

Scott wrapped his arm around her shoulders. "It was an accident."

She wrenched her body away and thrust her fist toward the ceiling. "An accident He could have stopped." Her jaw clenched. "Take me home. Now, Scott. I have to get away from here."

Pepper touched Scott's arm. "Pull your car around back. We'll bring her out to you."

Emily glared at her. "No. I'm walking out with my husband, but not out front by all those people."

"I understand." She held the door open.

Scott led Emily through the hall. He pushed the rear door open and guided her into the alley. The stench of garbage mingling with humid air accosted her. Nausea gripped her. She doubled over and vomited until nothing remained except bitter sorrow.

Chapter 8

Rachel slipped her feet into fuzzy slippers, tied the sash on her robe, and plodded to the front door. She lifted the newspaper off her stoop, headed to the kitchen, and popped a cappuccino pod in her coffee maker. She guarded her Sundays. No phone. No work. No overbearing father. No pretending.

With the newspaper clutched under her arm, she carried her coffee to the deck. She brushed a layer of yellow pollen off the chaise lounge, settled down, and conjured up memories from her childhood. Faith never played a role in her parents' lives, so they attended church once a year to mingle with friends and flaunt the latest fashions. That didn't bother her. As far as she was concerned, God was distant and irrelevant. Perhaps He brought comfort to some, but He did nothing to impact her world.

Images of Sunday picnics, trips to parks, and educational outings played in her mind. Following her mother's death, her father attempted to continue the tradition, yet frequently gave in to the lure of work. At least he let her hang out with him in his home office.

A warm breeze caressed her cheeks and ruffled her hair. She sipped her coffee, wiped a milk moustache from her lip, and watched two squirrels scamper up a tree trunk in the wooded area behind her townhouse. Their antics reminded her of her father's response when she begged for a puppy. *Animals belong in zoos or the woods*, he'd said. *Not in professionally decorated, multi-million-dollar homes. If you want a pet, get a goldfish or go outside and play with the squirrels.* Rachel added one more item to her bucket list of unrealized dreams—a big dog, maybe a golden or chocolate lab.

The resident hawk circled, landed on a limb, and scanned the ground below. She pointed her finger at him. "Do you have any idea how fortunate you are to have the freedom to fly when and where you choose, seven days a week?" The hawk's head turned toward her before it blinked and took flight.

"Oh yeah, you know. But enough with the mindless musings, Ms. Streetman. You're fortunate you have one unencumbered day to do whatever you choose." She mentally ticked off her agenda. Spend the morning catching up on the news. Attend an afternoon play. End the day watching TV or losing herself in a romance or mystery novel.

She opened the paper to scour the arts and culture sections and entertainment reviews before moving on to hard news. One headline—buried on the last page of the front section—grabbed her attention and made her wince.

North Georgia Couple Killed by Drunk Driver. A man with a suspended license plowed head-on into another car. Following a third DUI arrest, a judge released him without bail. The drunk's failure to appear for his court date triggered an arrest warrant.

Rachel dropped the paper on her lap. Other than the fact the drunk should have been in jail, not behind a wheel, why did a fatal accident in a place she never knew existed have such a strong tug on her heart? Something about the story gnawed at her. She read it again and noted the victim's hometown. Her mind drifted back to Friday's staff meeting and her father's review of a client's bid on a land tract a couple of miles outside the town. He planned to start a vineyard and open a winery. As far as she knew, no one other than Greer Associates, the buyer, and the seller knew about the pending sale. Was Willow Falls one of the obscure little towns her father wanted her to research? Unwilling to let work disrupt her private time, she forced the thought aside and carried the paper and coffee cup inside.

Following a hot shower, Rachel drove into the city, pulled into the underground parking garage, walked upstairs, and entered the Alliance Theater lobby for the first time since its dramatic renovation. The white-haired usher handed her a playbill and checked her ticket. "Second row." The woman leaned close. "You're sitting beside one of Atlanta's best television reporters."

"Good to know."

She moseyed down the aisle and sidestepped her way to the middle of the row.

"Second-best seat in the house." The pretty young woman with flawless skin, the color of milk-chocolate, extended her hand. "I'm Alicia Adams. Doesn't the theater look spectacular?"

"The transformation is amazing. My name's Rachel. I recognize you from TV. Are you critiquing the play?"

"Unofficially, for my blog. Live theater is my passion, so I write about performances for my fans. I'm also part of a little improv group. How about you?"

Rachel pulled her purse off her shoulder and placed it on the floor. "I did some acting in college. Nothing since."

"I guess the bug didn't bite you too hard."

If she only knew. "My work got in the way. But I'm a big fan. I'm partial to musicals and comedies."

"In that case, this play is right up your alley. It's about a small, Southern town and a mysterious murder. The actor playing the lead female role is a friend of mine." The lights flickered. "We can talk more during intermission."

Rachel pushed her thoughts aside and focused on the set and performance. The dialogue and actor's timing triggered bouts of laughter and filled the theater with joy.

At the end of Act One, Alicia nudged Rachel. "What do you think?"

"The dialogue is brilliant, dense with wordplay, and the cast is top-notch. I love the pace and how the quirky neighbors interact like a big, meddlesome family." Rachel pictured her neighbors. She knew a handful by name but nothing about their personal lives. "I wonder if the writer's depiction of small-town life is anywhere close to reality?"

"Based on some of my reporting, I'd say it is. I love it when my followers respond to my critiques, especially if they're actors." She pulled a business card from her pocket. "If you get a chance, check out my blog. It posts every Tuesday."

"I will."

"And if you ever get a hankering to act again, give me a call. Our little improv team welcomes new talent."

Nancy's suggestion to pursue her dream played in her head. Was meeting this woman a coincidence, or fate knocking on her door? She dismissed the question as ridiculous and slipped the card in her slacks pocket.

At the end of Act Two, the two women strolled into the lobby. Alicia slung her purse over her shoulder. "I'm parked down the street. How about you?"

"In the garage."

"I enjoyed talking to you and I suspect we'll see each other at some future venue. In the meantime, don't forget to call if the acting bug manages to get under your skin. Oh, and please post your impression of tonight's performance on my blog."

"Thanks, I'll think about it."

While driving down Peachtree Street, past the Fox Theater, Rachel considered Alicia's invitation. Maybe hanging out with amateur actors would satisfy her penchant to perform. "Who am I kidding? I don't have time to play at life."

She stopped at a deli to order takeout, returned home, poured a glass of Chardonnay, and settled in front of the television. Flipping through channels, she landed on an old *Murder She Wrote* rerun. Intrigued by the small town, engaging characters, and mysterious murder, she was eager to binge watch.

She climbed up to her second-story bedroom. When she undressed and tossed her slacks across her bedroom chair, Alicia's business card fell on the floor. She picked it up and let her imagination roam before reality smacked her down. "Forget about your dream, Rachel." She dropped the card in her purse, dressed in pajamas, and climbed into bed. To soothe her soul, she watched amateur detective Jessica Fletcher solve four more murders.

As she drifted off to sleep, the desire to visit Willow Falls and see firsthand what it was like living in a small town edged into her consciousness.

Chapter 9

The Reddings' accident struck Willow Falls with the force of an EF5 tornado. The tragedy devastated morale and intensified the uproar over Sadie's return. Flowers, candles, cards, and a variety of items from friends and neighbors filled Willow Inn's front porch and spilled onto the front lawn but did little to ease the grief.

For three days, Emily refused to take phone calls or accept visitors. Her emotions alternated between devastating grief and gut-wrenching anger at God. The endless roller-coaster ride rendered her incapable of making a single decision. As if sensing her sorrow, Cody remained by her side with his tail tucked between his legs.

Pepper and Patsy came to Scott's rescue and helped him make final arrangements for his in-laws.

The morning of the funeral, Emily stared into her open closet. Her hands hung to her side, her body refused to move. Other than jeans, she didn't own any dark clothing. Her wardrobe resembled a psychedelic rainbow of bright colors. What would people think if she didn't wear black, or at least something dark? Did it even matter?

Cody lay at her feet, his head resting on his paws.

Scott moseyed over. "Why don't you wear last year's Easter dress, the blue one with the polka-dot skirt?" He pulled it from the hanger.

She bought the dress during her annual mother-daughter shopping trip to Atlanta. Little did she know it would be their last. Tears trickled down her cheeks as images of trying on dozens of outfits, stopping for lunch, and indulging in a decadent chocolate dessert played in her mind. She wiped her eyes and pulled the dress over her head. "At least I can still squeeze into it." She turned her back toward Scott and pointed to the zipper. "Will you pull it up?"

"Glad to. You know your mom and dad are up there smiling down on their beautiful daughter."

Emily's jaw tightened. "It's all wrong. They're supposed to be here, making plans to spoil their grandbabies. But they're not. Because a criminal—who had no business driving in the first place—tore around a curve on the wrong side of the road. I don't understand why they left Savannah early. If they'd waited, I'd spend the day picking out paint colors with Mom. Instead, I'm choosing a dress to wear to her funeral." She shook her fist at the sky. "Why did you let this happen?"

Scott pulled her close and stroked her hair. "It was an accident, sweetheart. Let me help you find the strength to let our town heal."

Emily's lifelong yearning for a sister erupted. "Oh yeah, and who's going to help me heal?" She pushed Scott away. "Tell me, who will take her place when I need a mother?"

"Me." He planted his fists on his hips. "Even if I have to put on a skirt, high heels, and mascara and take you on shopping trips to Atlanta."

An image of him wearing a dress, traipsing through the mall, loaded down with shopping bags, eased her tension and gave her the strength to put her shoes on and follow Scott to the car.

On the way to church, a stop sign at the corner of her parents' street forced Scott to brake. Emily squeezed her eyes shut and gripped the armrest.

He touched her arm. "Are you okay?"

"Just keep driving."

He pulled into a reserved spot behind the church, escorted Emily up the back steps, and knocked on the door. Nathan's wife, Mary, answered and led them into the sanctuary. The sweet perfume from a sea of flowers drifted in the air. The choir director played a piano rendition of *I'll Fly Away*. Residents crowded into pews and stood three-deep along the walls.

She and Scott slid in the front row beside Pepper and Mitch. Muffled whispers and a sense that hundreds of eyes stared at her made Emily want to bolt from the building, escape to her home, climb into her bed, and pull the covers over her head. She counted the polka dots on her skirt to keep from springing out of her seat.

Scott leaned close. "The flowers in front of the podium are from my brother. He'd be here if he wasn't stuck with his squad somewhere in Afghanistan. Maybe when his tour ends, he'll settle down in Willow Falls."

"If there's a town to come back to." Emily gazed at the rainbow of colors filling the space between the railing and altar. An impressive array considering the town's financial woes.

Nathan entered from the side door, looking dapper in a navy suit and white shirt with blue collar and cuffs. He straightened his red-and-white striped tie and folded his hands on the podium. "This morning, our community grieves with one heart. Not for Nora and Roger, because we know they rest in our Savior's loving arms. We grieve because a tragedy stole two precious people from our midst. And yet, their footprints will forever remain etched in the fabric of our community. So, we gather together to celebrate their lives and bid them farewell until we meet them again in paradise."

He pointed toward the back. "If you're wondering why their caskets are in the vestibule and not up front, it's to allow us to focus on their lives. I'm also opting not to quote scripture or preach a mini sermon. Instead, I invite everyone who chooses to come forward and talk to us about this beloved couple."

Nathan stepped aside and waited. One by one, friends moved to the front to share their stories—some humorous, some serious, all flattering and heartwarming.

Emily closed her eyes and listened to Patsy sing Nora's praises. Her parents' presence seemed so real, she caught herself glancing over her shoulder to see if they were strolling up the aisle to sit beside her.

Pepper squeezed her hand and brought her back to reality before stepping to the front and turning to the crowd. "I remember when Roger returned to Willow Falls with Nora and baby Emily and moved into the house next door to my family. You may not know this, but he left a lucrative job with a big-city construction firm to raise his daughter in his hometown. Lucky for us, he brought his skills with him. And as a small-town girl, Nora fit right in." She paused and glanced around the room. "Like Mitch and I, some of you live in a home Roger built or repaired."

Images of properties her parents touched tumbled around in Emily's mind. The reno on Nathan's home when a hard freeze led to broken water pipes. The transformation of a palatial home to the town's hospital after a lightning strike burned the original building to the ground. All physical reminders of their impact on the town they chose to call home. She cringed, wondering if their work would comfort her or forever cause her pain and grief.

Pepper sniffed and dabbed at her eyes. "And so, we must honor the Reddings' legacy by building on their efforts to transform our town into a tourist destination."

Reality exploded in Emily's head. The responsibility to open and manage the inn, refurbish the hotel, and save the town fell on her shoulders. The magnitude of the task sent a bolt of fear surging through her. Was it even possible to get the job done or did a drunk driver land a fatal blow on the town she loved? What about her plan to boost her writing skills and finish her novel? Was her dream another innocent victim? She didn't realize Nathan had closed with a prayer until he held his hand out to her.

Emily forced her body upright. She tucked her chin to her chest, held Scott's hand, and followed Nathan down the aisle. When she approached the back of the room, she lifted her head and spotted a woman standing close to the door, wearing a big floppy hat and oversized sunglasses.

In the vestibule, Emily moved toward two white caskets, trimmed in gold, draped with sprays of red roses. She placed a hand on each and whispered. "Thank you for giving me life. I love you both more than you can imagine. How can I … possibly say goodbye?" Her voice caught. She kissed the caskets and willed her feet to move away.

Scott led her from the building to a black limousine. She climbed into the back seat and let her body collapse before covering her face with her hands and sobbing until no tears remained.

Emily stared at the back of the driver's head until the limo turned onto County Road for the short ride to the cemetery. The long stretch of straight pavement leading to miles of treacherous curves lay dead ahead. An image of a mangled car lying upside down at the bottom of a deep ravine exploded in her mind. Her hands clenched as her anger intensified and gripped her soul.

Chapter 10

Emily blew her nose and wiped her eyes with a tissue before adjusting her sunglasses. She let Scott steer her from the gravesite back to the limousine. Friends and neighbors spoke in hushed tones while sidestepping headstones and returning to their cars. Sheriff Mitch fired up his vehicle's blue strobe lights and led the mile-long procession away from the cemetery.

Back in town, drivers scrambled for parking spaces. The limo pulled to the curb across the street from Pepper's Café. Scott held the door open. Emily stepped on the sidewalk bordering the lakeside park, clung to his arm, and took in the view.

Flower arrangements from the church transformed the lakeside park into a Monet-worthy landscape and perfumed the air with a sweet scent. Shimmering fabric draped over buffet tables and dozens of card tables added sparkle and elegance to the scene. Country-pop music—her dad's favorite—created an upbeat atmosphere.

Scott squeezed her hand. "It looks like a reception fit for royalty."

Emily swallowed the lump in her throat. "Except the king and queen aren't here to see how much they're loved, or how much Willow Falls needs them." She pressed her hand to her chest. "How will I ever fill their shoes?"

"I know it seems difficult now, but I know you'll find a way." Scott tilted his head to the right. "Like our good friend who masterminded this event."

Pepper approached carrying a covered casserole dish. "Isn't it amazing how God blessed us with perfect weather?"

Emily's anger clung too tight to connect God with any kind of blessing. "Scott gives you the credit for creating this canvas. How did you manage to help him with the funeral arrangements and get all this done?"

"The reception is Sadie's doing. She has a good eye despite spending years in a drab prison surrounded by barbed wire."

Emily watched neighbors carrying platters, bowls, and casseroles brimming with food move toward a row of tables. "I didn't see her at church."

"Did you notice the woman wearing the floppy white hat and enormous sunglasses?"

"By the back door?"

Pepper nodded. "Sadie in disguise."

Emily scanned the crowd. "I don't see her here either."

"She knew someone would see past the hat and shades camouflage, so she opted to skip the reception."

Mitch nodded. "Truth is, she didn't want to stir up a ruckus."

Emily spotted Mirabelle hustling toward them with a chocolate cake in hand. Before she moved close enough to speak, she veered off the sidewalk and headed to the buffet tables. "I guess our mail lady doesn't want to talk to me. How sad Sadie has to avoid people like her. It's like she's still in jail. When will everyone stop squabbling and accept her back in the fold?"

Mitch shoved his hands in his pockets. "Maybe when the inn and hotel open and out-of-town visitors start spending money."

"Without Mom and Dad to get the job done, that's never going to happen." Emily regretted the comment the moment it tumbled off her tongue. "I don't mean to sound pessimistic."

"Maybe we can cheer you up. We have a table and a pitcher of lemonade reserved for the four of us." Pepper nodded toward the right. "Over there, away from the crowd. Is it okay if Mitch and I bring lunch to you both?"

Emily puffed her cheeks and blew out air. "Better than okay. It's a big relief. I'm nowhere near ready to talk to people."

"That's what we figured."

Scott guided Emily to the park's edge, close to the water. She settled in a chair facing the lake, kicked her shoes off, and let her feet soak up warmth from the freshly mowed grass. She breathed in the scent of a rose arrangement and watched two young sisters dangle their legs over the stone retaining wall. They giggled and splashed water on each other. Did the girls have any inkling how blessed they were to have each other to share happy times and sad? If she had a sister, perhaps losing her parents would be a little less devastating.

Emily shifted her gaze to the long line of neighbors waiting to load up their plates at the buffet. Others settled at tables or on blankets and beach towels. "Will everyone think I'm ungrateful if I don't mingle?"

Scott pushed a lock of hair away from her cheek. "Not a chance. They understand."

"I hope you're right." Sunlight shimmering on the water's surface like thousands of tiny diamonds captured Emily's attention. She held up her left hand and stared at her mother's engagement ring—a one-carat reminder of what she'd lost.

From the corner of her eye, she spotted Mitch and Pepper approaching. "We brought everything except dessert." Pepper placed a plate in front of Emily. "Patsy's coming over in little while with something special she baked for you."

After Mitch blessed their meal, Scott filled glasses with lemonade. Emily picked up a chicken leg and pointed it toward the crowd. "It looks more like a July Fourth or Memorial Day picnic than a funeral reception."

Pepper spread a napkin on her lap. "We know how much your parents loved picnicking in the park. They'd rather have their friends enjoying a good time instead of standing around all sober-faced."

"Scott said no one's upset about me hiding out over here."

"He's right. In fact, you're keeping folks from stumbling over words to tell you how sorry they are."

"Or make some other mundane comment to try and make me feel better." Emily sighed. "Thank you, guys, for all your help. In the past few days I've barely been able to get out of bed, much less make a decision."

"Hey, your friends are looking out for you. Besides, everyone has their own way of grieving. Some people, like me, have to stay busy." Pepper patted Emily's arm. "Others need solitude."

Emily bristled. "What I need is a time machine to take me back to Friday, so I can tell Mom and Dad to stay in Savannah. If I hadn't told them about the twins, maybe they wouldn't have been so eager to get home early." She gasped. "Oh no. I'm the reason they were on County Road when that drunk …" She buried her face in her hands. Her shoulders trembled. Tears erupted.

Scott moved his chair beside hers and stroked her arm.

Emily lifted her head and wiped her eyes with a napkin. "Sorry for the waterworks, but I don't understand why God doesn't keep bad things from happening to good people."

Pepper laid her fork down. "I think you have a misconception of our Creator."

"What do you mean?"

"A couple of months ago, I heard a pastor suggest that God isn't a bodyguard, existing to protect us from every harm this world lays on us. Instead, He's a loving Father who helps us through pain and suffering, and often turns tragedies into blessings."

Emily let the comment resonate. "I suppose that makes sense, but I don't see how my parents' death could possibly turn into anything other than a horrible curse."

"Of course you don't. Because the pain is still too fresh, too raw. Given enough time, something good will happen."

Patsy, wearing a white hat with three peacock feathers, moseyed over and laid a cake on the table. "I baked your favorite. Lemon with buttercream frosting. It's a gift for you and Scott and a peace offering for you, Pepper. I took Emily's suggestion to heart and crossed over from the dark side."

"Are you saying—"

"I'm supporting Sadie no matter what Mirabelle and her cronies have to say."

Pepper popped out of her chair and embraced Patsy. "You're a good woman, my friend. Welcome to the sunny side."

"Speaking of good women, I invited someone to join us." She pointed to a tall woman with stylish, short, white hair gliding in their direction. Her ankle-length, floral skirt, bright-green jacket, and paisley scarf made her look like one more colorful arrangement in the sea of flowers.

Pepper squinted. "Is that Willow Falls' famous artist?"

Patsy nodded. "She came back for the funeral. You know we went to high school together, so we stay in touch."

Scott and Mitch stood and offered the two newcomers their seats. Naomi sat beside Emily and touched her arm. "Your mom and daddy did a great job fixing up the old Liles estate." She pushed her sunglasses up.

"Their influence will touch future generations in ways we can't even imagine."

Patsy cut the cake and gave the first slice to Emily. "Naomi's agent believes her old studio has tourist appeal."

"He wants me move it to Charleston. Believe me, I was tempted until Patsy told me about that old hotel getting a facelift."

Patsy grinned. "She's considering retiring here in Willow Falls and opening an art gallery in her family home."

"Wow," said Pepper. "All we need is a live theater and we'll become the artistic hub of north Georgia."

Emily slid a forkful of cake into her mouth, hoping the sweet, lemon taste would ease her growing anxiety about the hotel's future. "Oh, my gosh." She clutched her belly. "I think one of my babies just kicked me." Her eyes opened wide. "There it is again."

Scott kneeled beside her. She grasped his hand and pressed it to her tummy. "Do you feel it?"

"I wish I could say yes."

Pepper grinned. "Don't feel bad. This early, it's likely only Emily can feel the movement."

"Good to know." Scott stroked his wife's cheek. "I think the kick is telling us that life goes on."

Despite his comment, her babies' first movements, and Naomi's revelation, anger continued to grip her soul like an ugly scab clinging to a deep cut.

Chapter 11

Rachel closed her computer and drilled her fingers on the desk. Other than population statistics and the name of a biweekly newspaper, her internet search didn't provide much information about Willow Falls. So why did Streetman's client choose the remote area to plant a vineyard? "Only one way to find out." She left her office and stopped at her assistant's desk. "I'm going to talk to Brent."

"Oh my." Nancy held her palm against her cheek and whispered. "It must be something important to draw you into the lion's den."

"Let's call it an uncontrollable case of curiosity. If I'm not out in twenty minutes, send in a rescue squad."

Rachel passed a row of cubicles, smiled at associates, and knocked on Brent's open door. His invitation to enter sent a jolt of adrenaline shooting through her. "Here goes." She took a deep breath and stepped inside. "Do you have a minute?"

He dropped his pen on the desk and sprang to his feet. "For you, I have all the time in the world, and then some."

"Relax. This isn't a social call."

"You know, I keep a bottle of Chivas Regal in my bottom drawer—strictly for special occasions. I can close the door, pour us a couple of shots, and turn your visit into a private party."

"Keep a lid on your scotch and your imagination. I want to talk about the Willow Falls real-estate deal."

"You mean old man Bricker's itch to increase Georgia's wine production?"

"Yeah. What's the scoop?"

Brent dropped onto his chair and propped his feet on his desk. "The guy wants to turn his love affair with fine wine into a retirement venture. He spent a year studying the craft before he broached the subject with us."

"Why did he choose the land near Willow Falls?"

"According to Bricker, it has all the characteristics needed for a pro-ductive vineyard. Plus, it's been on the market for years, so the price was ridiculously low. But …"

"There's a problem?"

"Yeah, a big one. A fatal accident a few miles from the property killed three people. In Bricker's mind, it's a bad omen and a valid reason to walk away from the deal."

"What a crazy reaction."

"To you and me maybe, but not to him. For a successful business guy, he has some quirky ideas. Like never exiting an elevator on the thirteenth floor, even if the button says fourteen. And forget about doing business on the thirteenth. He'd prefer to lose a deal than jinx his luck. Can you believe, he even picks up pennies off the ground."

He shook his head. "The guy's rich as Solomon and he picks up pen-nies. He claims it's bad luck to ignore them." Brent lowered his feet to the floor and leaned forward. "Why are you asking?"

"The boss—"

"Your father?"

"Yes. He asked me to search for investment opportunities in north Georgia. But that's beside the point. When I read about the accident, I couldn't stop thinking about the town and the victims' family."

"Victims?"

"The innocent couple killed by the other driver, a drunk who should have been in jail."

"I didn't hear that part of the story."

Rachel fingered the sapphire-and-diamond tennis bracelet she and her father selected for her mother's last birthday, before cancer stole her from them. "My mom's death broke my heart. At least her illness gave me time to prepare. I can't imagine losing a loved one, especially to a senseless accident, without the opportunity to say goodbye."

"I see your point. But what does it have to do with Willow Falls?"

"It's a small town, which means everyone knows everyone—like one great big family."

"You're a city girl. What do you know about life in a small town?"

"I go to plays and read a lot. I presume the residents would welcome some good news, which means you have to convince Bricker to go through with the deal."

"I do, huh?" Brent stared at her for a long moment. "Tell you what. The guy has an eye for pretty women."

"What are you suggesting?"

"I'll set up dinner for the three of us and let you work your magic on him."

Deep down Rachel knew using feminine charm was unprofessional. But then, was it any different than her father and Brent plying clients with eighteen holes of golf and rounds of drinks at an exclusive country club?

"Okay, I'll go along with your idea." She jabbed her finger toward Brent. "But know this. If we show up and he doesn't, I'll rush out of the restaurant so fast it'll make your head spin around and stare at your backside."

Brent leaned back in his chair and crossed his arms. "Talk about deflating a guy's ego."

Heat crept up Rachel's cheeks. Had she crossed the line? "Sorry for the drama. The thing is, I don't want any misunderstandings between us. I want to convince Bricker to close a good deal, nothing more."

"Except your weird connection to a town you've never seen."

"And unless there's a big-time development opportunity there, most likely never will. But I still want to do everything possible to guarantee the sale goes through."

"I can't wait to see if you manage to overcome the old guy's insane superstitions." Brent cocked his head and grinned. "Do you want to make the task interesting?"

Rachel's brow furrowed. "Interesting, how?"

"With a friendly wager?"

"Are you serious?"

"You better believe it. It'll help take the sting out of your rejection."

"Point taken. What do you suggest?"

"If you get Bricker to sign, I'll buy you a case of Georgia wine."

"And if he doesn't?"

Brent leaned forward and grinned. "You let me treat you to dinner. Strictly business, of course."

"Hmmm. I guess I'd better brush up on my charm."

"I'll take your comment as dedication to Bricker and Streetman Enterprise and not another put-down."

"Wise decision." Rachel stood and pivoted toward the door. "Let me know when you schedule the dinner meeting."

"Got it."

Rachel returned to her office and searched the internet for more news about the crash. Nothing surfaced. She reached into her memory for the name of the north Georgia artist her father mentioned. Naomi Jasper. A Google search took her to the woman's bio. It turned out Willow Falls was her hometown. An interesting coincidence but not a valid reason for Bricker to plant a vineyard.

Eager to win the bet with Brent and come through for Willow Falls, she carried her laptop to the couch and propped her feet on the coffee table. She spent the remainder of the afternoon researching everything she could find about winemaking.

Chapter 12

Emily strolled to the water's edge behind the vacant hotel, lifted her hair, and let the warm breeze kiss the back of her neck. She spotted a tabby cat curled up on the steps leading to the building's porch and gripped Cody's leash tighter. He barked once but didn't budge. "What's the matter, fella? Do you miss Mom and Dad too much to chase the kitty?" She responded to Cody's whimper. "Yeah, me too."

She sat on the ground, ran her fingers over a patch of weeds, and nodded toward the porch. "Mom envisioned guests relaxing in comfy rocking chairs, chatting with each other while drinking in the view. And on the other side, folks sitting at white-linen-covered tables, dining on a leisurely dinner."

She stroked her dog's back. "We have to make her vision a reality. If we get the money and if I find someone to manage the project and do the work. Two mighty big ifs, huh, Cody?"

Before she left home, Emily pulled up her parents' business bank account and discovered no activity for more than a month. Worse, she couldn't remember the name of her dad's friend. Somehow, she gathered the courage to reach for her father's cell phone—the one item not destroyed in the accident—and scrolled through his contact list. One name from Savannah popped up. Ben Crawford.

"I've waited long enough. I have to make the call." She crossed her fingers, dialed the number, and talked to the man's assistant. When the call ended, she pocketed her phone. Her back stiffened as she massaged her temples. "Is there no end to the bad news? Our investor left town on a family emergency and won't return until next week. If he backs out of the deal, we're dead in the water."

Emily pulled her knees up to her chest, wrapped her arms around her shins, and closed her eyes. Chirping birds and rustling leaves summoned childhood images of Sunday picnics in the park with her parents and dozens of other families, their blankets spread out on the grass like a colorful checkerboard.

The happiest days were those when Mr. and Mrs. Hayes showed up with Scott and his brother in tow. While the children played, their moms laid out banquets of delicious goodies. The memory of cinnamon and vanilla scents wafting from her mother's picnic basket made her mouth water and her heart ache. "Dad loved those oatmeal raisin cookies almost as much as he loved Mom's kisses. I have to find her recipe and give it to Patsy."

Emily opened her eyes, stood, and ambled through the gravel parking lot beside the hotel. At the sidewalk, she pivoted toward the Willow Inn and noticed a woman sitting on the porch railing facing away from the street. Her gray ponytail hinted at her identity. Emily shuffled her feet. She wanted to talk to Sadie and learn more about her experiences. At the same time, she feared saying something to upset and further alienate her.

Sadie turned her head to the side. "Well, are you gonna come up and talk to me or keep staring at me like I'm a monkey in a zoo?"

This should be interesting. Emily climbed the steps and moved toward Sadie. "Do you know who cleaned up all the paraphernalia left from the funeral?"

"I hear Jacob and his brother ditched the flowers and stashed all the other stuff in Nathan's garage."

"No kidding. I guess I owe the Dixon brothers a great big thank you. Are you taking a break from work?"

"There's not much going on at the café. Most likely because a lot of folks around here don't think an ex-con serving food is such a good idea."

"Don't blame yourself. The fact is, business was slow long before you showed up."

"I know, but me being here isn't making things better." She shoved her hands in her pockets and stared straight ahead.

Emily reached down and unleashed Cody. He sprawled out, yawned, and plopped his head on his paws. Her reporter instinct kicked in and compelled her to mentally tick through a long list of questions. One floated to the top. Anxious to end the awkward silence, she leaned on the railing three feet from Sadie. "I'm curious."

"Good quality for a journalist."

She cleared her throat. "Why did you come back to Willow Falls? You could have started fresh someplace where people don't know about your past?"

"I reckon everyone else in town is wondering the same thing." Sadie paused for a long moment. "I spent more than half my life behind bars. After Mama died—her name's Carlie—no one except Pepper, and later Mitch, came to visit me."

"No one from your family?"

"I don't have any brothers or sisters. My grandma and pop lived too far away. Besides, they passed on while I was in the slammer."

"What about aunts or uncles?"

"The last time I saw my mother's crazy brother I was five. I have no idea where he ended up. I don't even remember what he looks like." She shuffled her feet. "The simple answer is, I had no place else to go."

"I suppose that makes sense."

Sadie pivoted and pointed to the two-story, southern-style building across the street. "When we lived here, that was a private home, not the local hospital."

"I know. Ten years ago, the town's hospital caught fire and burned to the ground. Luckily, no one was hurt. Anyway, that house had been vacant for a few years following the owner's passing. It was cheaper to buy it and add an extension than it was to rebuild."

"At least it's convenient if one of your guests has a heart attack or some other medical emergency." Sadie turned, moseyed to the bay window, and peered inside. "Do you know what I missed most when they locked me up?"

"Living in luxury?"

"Nope. The total loss of privacy. Every hour of every day I was trapped in a cramped space with my cellmate or in the dining hall, yard, or a work room with dozens, or hundreds of women. Lots of them angry. Some dangerous."

"How'd you deal with it?"

"Prisoners have to stay on guard and watch their backs, so I learned to daydream with my eyes wide open. Out in the yard, I pretended I was sitting on a beach. The noises around me became seagulls, waves, and wind. The passing cars were great big yachts appearing and disappearing on the horizon. I made up stories in my head about the people on board. Movie stars, rich politicians, even some smart criminal types."

Her shoulders slumped. "At night in my bunk, I closed my eyes and imagined walking into empty rooms in mansions and decorating them with fancy furniture, paintings, and pretty things."

Sadie tapped her temple. "I stored lots of swanky rooms up here before my nightly imaginings changed. But that's another story." She spun around and pointed at Emily. "I have a question for you."

"Turn around's fair play. What do you want to know?"

"Why, after all these years, did your parents decide to turn this house into an inn?"

Emily remembered the night they invited her and Scott to dinner and shared their plan. "After ... you know."

"I shot my stepfather?"

Emily nodded. "No one dared step a foot inside, except Mom. For years she dreamed about turning it into an inn but couldn't afford to until her father passed away. He left her enough money to buy the property and refurbish it. When she expanded her vision to include the hotel, Dad began looking for an investor." Emily crossed her arms. "Now I'm thinking what's the point of finishing her work here? Six guest rooms won't bring in enough visitors to make a smidgen of difference."

"You're right, but sixty rooms next door will do the trick."

Emily frowned. "So far, the money hasn't come through. Even if it does, I don't have anyone to do the work or manage the property."

"No matter what happens with the hotel, you have to finish the inn. It's part of your mama and daddy's legacy."

"If they'd never started the project in the first place they'd still be alive, and I wouldn't be an orphan."

Sadie squatted and stroked Cody's head, triggering a tail wag. "I like your dog."

"He belonged to Mom and Dad. He misses them almost as much as I do."

"Lots of things happen we don't understand." She glanced up at Emily. "You have to find a way to move on with your life."

"Bringing two babies into this world without any grandparents isn't my idea of moving on."

"You've got Pepper and a town full of friends to love on them."

"It's not the same."

"I know. But at least it's something." Sadie stood and glanced at her watch. "I have to get back to work in time for lunch. Someone might decide to show up. It was nice talking to a lady not wearing state-issued prison garb. Maybe we can do it again sometime."

"I'd like that." Emily walked Sadie to the stairs. She sat on the top step and watched her trek down the sidewalk, past the hotel, and across Main Street.

Cody stood and stretched. He rested his head in her lap, inviting a head stroking. "She's right about moving on, but I don't know if I can."

Chapter 13

As Rachel strolled into Cut's Steakhouse, the scent of wood-grilled steaks made her mouth water and her stomach grumble. She spotted Brent and slid into the booth across from him. "Have you been waiting long?"

"Nope. You look especially gorgeous tonight."

His grin conjured up an image of a love-struck school boy. "Stop with the compliments already." She drummed her fingers on the table. "Where's Bricker?"

"You sure are quick to jump to conclusions. I got a text from him." He tapped his cell phone. "He's ten minutes away, stuck in traffic. Which gives us time to talk strategy."

Rachel leaned back and eyed her opponent. "What do you mean? We agreed to a friendly competition."

"I know. The thing is, I want this deal to go through."

"Are you admitting defeat?"

"Nope. I'm kowtowing to your dad."

Like a lot of other people.

"He wants to get it done, so I'm upping the ante. Two cases of wine if you succeed."

"I'm game. What kind of wild and crazy strategy is knocking around in your head?"

He pocketed his phone and locked eyes with Rachel. "Besides charming the pants off the guy, play into his two biggest superstitions. Rainbows and itchy hands."

"What in the heck are you talking about?"

"Bricker believes rainbows are good luck and itchy hands are a sign of financial windfall. Figure out how to work those tidbits into the conversation and you'll have him hooked before he polishes off his first glass of wine."

Rachel crossed her arms. "What do you think I am, some shady snake-oil salesman?"

"Don't get all high and mighty on me. This guy's a hard nut to crack when he gets an idea in his head. I'm just suggesting some tactics that might work."

"How about an honest conversation about the property's suitability?"

"Good luck with that approach."

"Look, I hear what you're saying. But using the man's superstitions to manipulate him doesn't sit right with me. So my answer to your suggestion is a flat-out no. And I'd appreciate it if you'd get on the same page with me."

"In my opinion, you're wasting a good opportunity. But I'll go along if it gives me more time to spend with the boss's daughter."

"Don't get used to the idea. This is a one-time thing."

"Unless the boss hears about our successful collaboration."

Rachel's eyes narrowed. "Are you and my father colluding?"

He brushed her question aside with a flip of his hand and nodded toward the door. "Our victim has arrived."

Rachel reined in her irritation as she imagined preparing for the opening scene in a Broadway play. She pictured stage curtains parting. *Ladies and Gentlemen, presenting Ms. Rachel Streetman, playing the part of enchantress to a wealthy eccentric and hero to a town full of strangers.* She stood to greet Streetman's client. "It's a pleasure to meet you, sir."

Bricker bowed and kissed her extended hand. A grin deepened the lines around his eyes and the creases in his cheeks. "The pleasure's all mine, Ms. Streetman. Please, call me Brick."

"Only if you ditch the formality and call me Rachel."

He slid his wiry frame into the booth beside her. "Done." He tilted his head toward Brent. "How's it going, young man?"

"Couldn't be better. What would you like to drink?"

"How about a robust cabernet sauvignon, if Rachel approves?"

She nodded. "Perfect choice to compliment a big juicy steak."

Brent signaled the waiter, reviewed the options, and made a selection.

Brick massaged his white goatee and eyed Rachel. "Are you a wine enthusiast, my dear?"

What happened to him calling me Rachel? "I especially enjoy a good cab or red blend."

"Hearty reds are my favorite. But don't underestimate a crisp white on a hot summer day."

"I know what you mean."

The server returned with the bottle, filled three glasses, and took their dinner orders.

Brick swirled the wine in his glass and breathed in the scent before taking a sip. "Excellent choice. Big and bold with a hint of pepper." He tipped his glass to Brent's, then Rachel's. "Here's to life filled with four-leaf clovers."

Brent nodded. "And skies filled with rainbows."

Rachel glared at him, hoping he had enough sense to notice her displeasure. She smiled at Brick. "I hope your future is filled with hundreds of cases of exquisite wine."

He smiled, took another sip, and patted Rachel's hand. "You don't look anything like your old man. Are you sure you're his daughter?"

"That question seems to come up a lot. The fact is, I favor my mom, hair color and all. My creativity also comes from her. The business skills are Dad's influence. But enough about me. Tell me what motivated you to transition from successful business owner to an up-and-coming vintner."

Brick tapped the rim of his glass. "Appreciation for good wine and apprehension about retirement. Last year I turned my company over to my oldest son. He did such a great job, I knew if I kept hanging around I'd become a nuisance. So, I let him throw me a big retirement party and I hit the road. It didn't take long to get bored out of my mind. Besides, idle hands are the devil's workshop."

Rachel nodded. "So I've heard."

"I spent three months in France, visiting all the wine regions." He ran his fingers through his thinning white hair. "The trip inspired me to create a first-class vineyard and winery right here in my home state. When I came home, I spent a year learning everything about winemaking."

Rachel leaned forward. "And you searched for the best possible site with the right climate and gentle-sloping terrain higher than the surrounding land."

Brick raised an eyebrow. "You know about winemaking?"

"I also did some research. Brent gave me details about the property outside Willow Falls. It sounds perfect for your needs."

"The best I've seen. Unfortunately, a fatal accident a few miles from town is a bad omen."

Before Rachel could respond, Brent scratched the back of his hand vigorously and jumped into the conversation. "I know exactly what you mean. When I heard about the accident, I figured the town was jinxed."

What is he doing? "I don't think—"

"Hold on, Rachel. I'm not finished." He continued scratching.

She gripped her knee to keep from kicking him in the shins.

"Until I found three shiny pennies on the sidewalk outside our office. That's when I knew you were the town's good-luck charm. So, how about it? Are you ready to get that contract signed?"

"Nice try, Brent. But I want to hear from someone who isn't trying to pull a fast one on me."

She watched Brent's eyes narrow as he yanked his hands off the table. She almost felt sorry for the guy.

Brick turned to Rachel. "I want to know what you think."

"Well, sir, everything I read tells me you selected a great piece of property. I envision grapevines stretching across the land and first-class wines— reds and whites. And a beautiful Italian-style winery with charming tasting rooms."

"And a restaurant with a deck looking out over the vineyard."

"Exactly. And there's something else. I understand your hesitation, but if you move forward with your plan, you'll give Willow Falls' residents hope when they most need it."

"Thank you for treating me with respect." He nodded toward Brent. "You can learn a thing or two from this smart young woman."

"I didn't mean to—"

"Oh yes, you did."

Brent shifted in his seat. "Sir—"

"Don't wet your pants, son, I'll chalk it up to your misguided ideas about persuasion. Go ahead and contact the seller and let him know I'm ready to move forward with the deal."

"My priority first thing tomorrow morning."

"Good answer." Brick took another sip of wine. "We need to get the word out. Do either of you know if Willow Falls has a newspaper?"

Rachel nodded. "A biweekly."

"I want you to put a publicity package together and pitch a story to the editor."

"I'll have our marketing department take care of it for you."

He shook his head. "I want you to handle it."

"I'm not sure I'm your best option. I know very little about pitching to the media."

"I suspect you're smarter than any of your marketing experts. Despite our friend's lame attempt to exploit my idiosyncrasies, you, my dear, are my good-luck rainbow."

The guy's brilliant. "Do you have a name for your new venture?"

Brick's eyes gleamed. "Willow Oak Vineyard and Winery."

"It has a nice ring." She extended her hand. "You've got a deal."

Chapter 14

Emily spread blueberry jam on a piece of toast and carried it, along with a cup of decaf, to the kitchen table. Her phone pinged with an incoming text.

"Pepper wants to meet me at the inn at nine to talk about something important." She glanced at the microwave clock. "Thirty minutes from now. What do you suppose is up?"

Scott shrugged and stirred sugar into his coffee. "I suggest you go meet her and find out."

Emily texted okay, picked up her toast, then dropped it. She gripped the table edge and willed the wave of nausea to pass.

"Nerves or morning sickness?"

"Maybe both. I think I'll ride in with you and walk to the inn. Fresh air and exercise might ease my queasy tummy. Besides, I need to get back to work, so once I talk to Pepper I'll head over to the newspaper office." She pushed up from the kitchen table and shoved her toast down the garbage disposal. "I'll be ready in ten minutes."

During the short ride to the store, Emily's mind drifted back to her conversation with Sadie. She couldn't imagine living far away from friends and family under the watchful eye of guards and people intent on doing her harm.

Scott pulled into his reserved parking spot behind the store. "You seem deep in thought."

"I'm wondering how much prison changed Sadie. After all, she was still a teenager when they locked her up."

"I imagine a lot." He stepped out, dashed to the passenger side, and opened the door. "You can pick this up following your meeting with Pepper." He slung Emily's computer bag over his shoulder.

"And give you the scoop?"

"Of course." He wrapped a fleece scarf around her neck. "It's a little nippy this morning. This will help keep you warm."

"What would I do without you to take care of me?"

"Sweep another good-looking guy off his feet."

She kissed his cheek. "But he wouldn't be near as much fun." She strolled from the store, passed through the park, and stopped at the hotel. The faded, glass-inlaid doors reminded her of stories kids made up about ghosts lurking in the vacant space. Despite not believing in apparitions, she'd kept her distance. One of these days, she'd find the nerve to peek inside the lobby.

A car drove past, honked, and stopped in front of the inn. Pepper hopped out carrying a thermos and two cups. "I thought you might need some warm ginger tea. It's good for morning sickness."

Emily clutched her tummy. "How did you know?"

"Lucky guess. There's a surprise waiting for you on the porch." Pepper led her up the stairs to a pair of rocking chairs with floral cushions. A marble topped, wrought-iron table sat between them. "Patsy took up a collection during the reception in the park. Read the plaque on the table."

"In memory of Nora and Roger Redding." Tears welled up in Emily's eyes. "You've gotta love this crazy little town." She settled in a rocker. "Is this the something important you wanted to talk about?"

"No." Pepper sat beside her, poured two cups of tea, and handed one to Emily. "Have you made any progress with the inn since the funeral?"

Emily shook her head and swiped her fingers beneath her eyes. "I bought a truckload of furniture the day before … the crash."

"I know. Nathan told me it's still at the store."

She sipped her tea and watched a chickadee alight on the railing she helped her mother paint a week before the accident. "I picked out the pieces, but Mom had the eye to put it all together and make every room look like a million dollars. I can't imagine decorating it without her expert guidance."

Pepper stared straight ahead. "I remember back in the day whenever I buried my head in *Seventeen*, Sadie poured through her mother's pile of decorating magazines. They fascinated her. She even made her room look like a spread right out of *House Beautiful*."

"Which explains why she decorated mansions in her head."

"Yeah, at night in her cell. You know she blames herself for our town's troubles."

"It did start with the murder."

"I know, and she wants to make amends."

"Which she's doing by working at the café."

"Not exactly." Pepper set her rocker in motion. "With people like Mirabelle continuing to give her a hard time, her guilt is escalating. She needs to sink her teeth into something meaningful. Something to make a real difference."

Emily's brow furrowed. "What are you suggesting?"

"Let her help you decorate Willow Inn."

"Did she put you up to this?"

"She doesn't know anything about it. I'm thinking you can make the offer. You know, it could be a blessing for both of you."

The thought of collaborating with someone other than her mom churned Emily's stomach. "Even if I did get all the stuff from Nathan's sent over here, there's no one to manage the inn. So, what's the point? Besides, what makes you think Sadie would want anything to do with this place?"

Pepper refreshed her tea. "Did you know she comes over here and sits on the porch every afternoon?"

"Does she ever go inside?"

"I don't think so."

"Well, there you go." Emily stood and laid her cup on the table. "Thanks for the tea, I think it helped. Right now, I'm going back to work for the first time since the funeral."

"Will you at least entertain my idea?"

"I'll think about it and text you my answer later today."

Pepper hopped up and embraced Emily. "I'll wait to hear from you. Can I give you a lift to the office?"

"No thanks. I have to stop by the store and pick up my computer on the way."

Pepper collected the thermos and cups, carried them to her car, and placed them in the trunk. She hesitated before opening the driver's door. "If you want to talk some more before making a decision, feel free to call me."

Emily nodded and headed back down Main. As she passed the park, she remembered how Sadie turned the space into a work of art for the reception following the funeral. She had to admit the woman had an eye for decorating.

She moved on to the store and stepped inside. Scott waved her over. "What's Pepper's big news?"

"You're not going to believe this. She wants Sadie to help me finish the inn."

"I bet you didn't see that coming." He lifted a box off the counter and stashed it underneath. "You know, it's not such a crazy idea. You need help and Sadie could use another friend around here."

"It sounds like you and Pepper are ganging up on me."

"I'm thinking of you. Maybe her idea will help you finish the inn and give you more time to spend on your book."

"I suppose that makes sense."

"Then I suggest you give it serious consideration."

Emily reached in a candy jar for a lemon drop. She popped it in her mouth and savored the sugary, sour taste. "I will, but don't give me a hard time if I don't go along with it."

"I promise I won't. But I might cut you off from dipping into my candy jars without paying."

Chapter 15

A sneezing fit triggered gut-wrenching coughs. Rachel dabbed her eyes, blew her nose, and dug in her purse for a cough drop. Because her father complained about employees using colds as excuses to miss work, she refused to stay home.

Brent charged into her office and plopped on a chair facing her desk. "Got a minute?"

She sneezed again.

"Allergies or a cold?"

"The latter. I'm up to my neck in work. What do you want?"

"Did you contact the Willow Falls paper?"

"Not yet. But I plan to."

"Today?"

She dropped her tissue in the trash can under her desk. "Why the big rush?"

"Old man Bricker hired a company to clear the land. They start work soon."

"And he wants residents to hear about the vineyard and winery before they show up and churn up rumors."

"You've got it."

"I promise to call, even though my nose is so stuffed up I sound like I'm talking through a mile-long pipe."

"You sound mysterious, maybe even a little sexy."

"You have a strange idea about what sexy sounds like."

He unbuttoned his cuffs and pushed his sleeves up. "It's hotter than blazes in here. Did you turn the thermostat to eighty?"

"I'm trying to keep my chills under control."

"Maybe you need something cold to drink. Which reminds me, I have two cases of wine for you. Payment for you winning our bet. They're mostly from Georgia, with a couple bottles of expensive French Bordeaux in the mix. I'll deliver them to your home later tonight."

"Nice try, but not a chance."

"What's with the attitude?"

"I'm just saying there's no need to go out of your way when you can bring them to my office. Or better yet, before I head home, I'll let you load them into my car."

"The boxes are heavy. How will you get them into your house?"

"Believe me, I can handle the weight."

Brent plunked his left ankle on his right knee. "Too bad I didn't bet something too heavy for you to move by yourself."

"I'd still reject your offer for home delivery."

He joggled his foot. "It seems there's no end to your rejection."

Rachel pulled another tissue out and blew her nose again, wondering why he didn't get the hint and stop pushing.

"Here's the thing. Getting Bricker to close the deal impressed the heck out of your father. He wants us to work together on more projects."

"He does, huh? Funny he hasn't said a word to me. Does he know our agreement included a hefty wager?"

"Not unless you told him."

"I haven't talked to him since we met with Brick, which means any information he has came from you, not me."

"In which case he doesn't know about the bet." Brent grasped the phone clipped to his belt. "Text from a client. I have to go." He took a step toward the door and spun back around. "I'll bring the wine tomorrow. If I'm lucky, you'll let me open a bottle and toast our success. It's the least you can do to soothe my wounded ego."

"I'll consider a toast if we invite Nancy to join us."

"A chaperone?"

"Nope, a fan."

"What?"

"Nothing." She flipped her hand toward the door. "Go. Your client awaits."

"Until tomorrow."

Rachel reached for her phone, pushed her earbuds in place, and pressed the iTunes app. She hummed along to an instrumental medley of Broadway show tunes while reviewing her notes until her father strolled in and lowered into the chair vacated by Brent. She yanked the earbuds out and dropped them in her desk drawer.

"How's your cold?"

"Not much better, but I'll survive. What's on your mind, boss?"

"You and Brent hit a home run convincing Bricker to get off the fence and make a decision. You shaved months off the process, maybe even saved the whole transaction."

"It wasn't a big deal. We simply appealed to his practical side and helped him understand what a good thing he had going."

Greer pressed his palms together and tapped his fingertips. "It worked because you and Brent make a darn good team."

"In whose opinion, yours or his?"

"Both. I have a new client coming in tomorrow morning, potentially worth millions. I want the two of you to meet with him. Strength in numbers."

Rachel's eyes narrowed. "Your idea seems an unnecessary waste of time and energy. You know Brent's capable of handling new clients without me interfering."

"I don't consider two of Streetman's brightest stars collaborating interference. It's good business." He leaned forward and propped his elbows on his knees. "What do you say, Strawberry Girl?"

Rachel swiveled her chair toward the window and eyed storm clouds moving in from the west. The desire to say no clashed with memories of her father taking care of her following her mother's death. He could have sent her away to boarding school or hired a full-time nanny. Instead, he sacrificed for her. She owed him. "Okay. Unless I lose my voice or get too sick to come in."

He stood. "I knew you'd see things my way."

Watching him smirk and swagger from the office countered her sense of obligation and strengthened her resolve to stand up to him.

Chapter 16

Emily kissed Scott, shouldered her computer bag, and strolled to the newspaper office. She found Jacob hunched over his desk, reading a document. Before her parent's accident, he held two part-time jobs—newspaper editor and laborer for her dad. Now he was one more innocent victim of a town in decline and a drunk driver with a suspended license. "Are you engrossed in something important?"

Jacob dropped his pen and spun around. "Hey, welcome back."

"I figured it's time I got back to work. Anything going on I need to know about?"

"Same old same old. Except for the uproar over Sadie. I'm thinking you should write an editorial about her return. Something to rouse sympathy instead of anger."

She opened her bag and placed her computer on the table she used as a desk. "I suppose it couldn't hurt. I'll give it a whirl."

"Any word about the money for the hotel?"

She shook her head. "I'm beginning to think the entire deal is a bust. Even if it does come through, with Dad gone, I don't have anyone to manage the project or do the work."

Jacob strolled to the table and sat across from Emily. "I've been toying with the idea of pulling a crew together to pick up where your dad left off."

Emily stared at him.

"From the look on your face, I suspect you're wondering how I can possibly fill his shoes."

Could anyone?

"The thing is, he taught me everything about the business. He even wanted to hire me full time but never made enough money to pay me for more than part-time work."

Emily broke eye contact and opened her computer. "With more people moving out of town every year, their business took a huge hit."

Jacob shifted in his seat. "I know I just tossed you a curve ball. Is it okay if I put a proposal together?"

"What about the newspaper?"

"Something else I've been thinking about. You could take over. It's obvious you write circles around me,"

"You do know I'm pregnant with twins and I started writing my novel?"

"The job's not hard. Besides, you could bring in a couple of high-school wannabe reporters as apprentices."

"I don't know."

"About the paper or my proposal?"

Emily leaned back and glanced around the office. She and Scott could use the extra money until she managed to finish her book, find a publisher, and collect royalties. "How long will it take for you to put a proposal together?"

"A couple of days."

"Okay then. I'll take a look at it and talk to Scott."

"I appreciate it and I promise not to disappoint you. Since you're here, I have errands to run before I grab lunch at Pepper's. Can I bring you something?"

"Thanks for asking. Maybe an egg-salad sandwich, if it's on the menu."

"Got it. I'll be back around one."

Emily strolled to the window and noticed Nathan and his wife planting pansies in a flower bed across the street beside the church steps. A stab of guilt tightened her chest. She hadn't ventured back inside since the funeral. The pain was still too raw.

Sadie's plight and residents' anger filtered through her grief. Could an editorial possibly sway their points of view? Or would she do nothing more than add to the controversy? It was a toss-up but worth the risk.

Ideas floated in her mind and began to take form. Her pulse quickened. With renewed energy, she returned to her computer and let her fingers dance across the keyboard. When she finished, she leaned back and read her work. "Not bad for your first day back."

The office door swung open, letting cool air waft in and nip the back of her neck. Jacob laid a bag on the table. "Pepper made an egg salad sandwich especially for you. She called it a subtle bribe. I have no idea what she meant."

"It doesn't matter. I know. I finished the editorial."

"Why am I not surprised?"

She turned her computer toward him. "Let me know what you think."

Jacob sat down and read out loud. "The Homecoming. A Journalist's Perspective. Who among us would have the courage to return to the scene of our crime, knowing we'd face wrath from people holding us responsible for our town's plight? I can say with near certainty, I would not. But then, I'm not Sadie Liles. Like everyone else in town, I questioned why she chose to come back instead of escaping to a place where no one knew about her past. The truth is, the only family she has lives among us, and so she came home.

"The question now is, how will our town respond? We've already proven our ability to ridicule and condemn her. Is that who we are at the core? Or are we fair-minded people with the capacity to welcome, with open arms, a woman who paid for her crime. The way I see it, Willow Falls' soul is on trial. Will we continue to reject Sadie, or will we dig deep and find it in our hearts to forgive and let her move on with her life? The decision and our town's future rests on our shoulders."

Jacob massaged the bridge of his nose. "It's powerful writing, not at all what I expected."

"Are you rejecting or approving?"

"The real question is, are you prepared to deal with the fallout when Mirabelle and her ilk take offense?"

Emily ran her fingers through her hair. "What's the point of an editorial if it doesn't rouse emotions?"

"We're sure to get some opposing letters, which we're obliged to print."

"I know, and I admit my words could make some people a whole lot madder."

"One thing's for sure, we'll find out how many when the paper hits the streets." Jacob tapped the computer screen. "Double check your punctuation, but don't change a word. In the meantime, I've got some paperwork to finish." He strolled to his desk and pulled a folder from the drawer.

As Emily read back through her work, Pepper's suggestion bubbled up and tugged at her conscience. How could she expect friends and neighbors to accept Sadie if she didn't first reach out? Asking her to help decorate the inn would prove her editorial was more than empty words devised to evoke emotions.

The office phone jangled.

Jacob peered over his shoulder. "Do you mind answering?"

"Glad to." She lifted the handset. "Willow Post. Emily Hayes speaking."

The caller coughed. "Sorry, I've come down with a nasty cold. My name is Rachel Streetman. I work for Streetman Enterprise, a real-estate-development firm."

Emily's ears perked up. "In Savannah? Are you calling for Ben Crawford?"

"No, to both questions. I'm in Atlanta."

"Sorry, I didn't mean to jump to conclusions." *Get a grip, Emily. You sound like a nut job.* "How can I help you?"

"I'd like to talk to someone about a new business venture coming to your town."

"Are you kidding me? What I mean is, I'm a reporter. You can talk to me."

"Perfect. If you will, indulge me for a moment and picture lush grapevines stretching across the hillsides on a large swath of land close to your town."

Emily sat up straight. "Are you describing a vineyard?"

Jacob swiveled his chair around and stared at her.

"You catch on fast," said Rachel. "How about a winery producing world-class wines under the label of Willow Oak?"

Is she pulling my leg? Maybe she's mistaken. Why would anyone want to start a business in a town struggling to survive? "Are you sure you called the right number?"

"You're in Willow Falls, right?"

"I am."

"Then yes, I'm positive. It's the retirement vision of a wealthy client. Mr. Bricker wants residents to know about it before land clearing begins. I emailed you the details. Are you willing to write an article for your paper?"

Emily motioned to Jacob, pulled up the email, and scrolled to the message.

He looked over her shoulder, gave her a thumbs-up, and returned to his desk.

"Of course, and your timing is perfect. We go to press tomorrow."

"I hope residents welcome the good news, especially following the fatal accident. I read about it in the Atlanta paper. It's criminal the judge didn't lock the guy up and throw away the key. Did you know the couple who died?"

Emily squeezed her eyes shut. "They were ..." Her voice quivered. "My mom and dad."

A gasp resonated through the phone. "Oh, my gosh. I'm so sorry."

"It's okay. You had no way of knowing."

"I lost my mom years ago, following a long illness. At least I had time to say goodbye. I can't imagine the pain you're going through."

Tears trickled down Emily's cheeks. "It's beyond difficult. My parents were working to make a difference in our little community, so the whole town is suffering from their loss."

"I've always lived in a city full of strangers. In a small town, I suspect everyone knows everyone."

"In many ways, we're like one big, crazy family with tons of good qualities." The town's reaction to Sadie exploded in Emily's head. "And way more than our share of prejudices and flaws." She cringed, shocked she'd verbalized her thoughts to a stranger. "I'm sorry for the inappropriate comment."

"No need to apologize." Rachel sneezed. "People say time heals the pain from losing a loved one, and it does get easier. But the truth is, you'll never stop missing your parents. There are moments when I still yearn to have my mother by my side."

Rachel's words cut deep, yet somehow provided a dab of salve for Emily's aching heart. "Thank you for your honesty. It means a lot."

"You're welcome. Even though we're strangers, we're connected by the loss of our mothers. So, if you ever need someone to talk to, please don't hesitate to call me."

Emily pressed her hand to her chest, thinking perhaps they wouldn't remain strangers for long. "About the winery, I'll get to work on the story right away."

"I look forward to reading it."

After replacing the handset, Emily wiped the tears from her cheeks.

Jacob looked up from his work. "Are you okay?"

"Yeah." She sniffed and tamped down her emotions. "Who'd have guessed someone wants to plant a vineyard in our back yard?"

"The news will surprise the heck out of everyone. Go ahead and write the article. Maybe it will help neutralize your editorial."

"Or stir up a heap more controversy." By the time she finished writing, the tug on her heart compelled her to reach for her phone and send a text to Pepper. *My answer is yes. Tell Sadie to meet me at the inn today at three.*

Chapter 17

Emily left the newspaper office, scurried around the corner, and collided with Mitch, knocking her purse off her shoulder.

"Whoa. Who knew walking out of a bank could be hazardous to your health?"

"I'm sorry. I should've kept to the right."

He grinned and straightened his badge. "Maybe the county should put up a pedestrian yield sign. Where are you headed in such a hurry?"

"To meet with Sadie."

"Oh yeah, the big offer. Pepper told me about it. I hope everything goes the way you want."

"Thanks, I think." She shouldered her purse, slowed her pace, and continued up Main. When she reached Pepper's Café, she glanced inside. The sight of Sadie clearing a table bombarded her with a string of questions and filled her with angst. How would she react to her offer? Would she consider the request for help an act of charity? Would Sadie turn her down? What if she accepted? Could they work together?

She crossed Falls Street and quickened her pace until she reached the white-columned hospital. Three doors farther up Main Street stood Naomi Jasper's family home and, behind it, her studio. The artist's comment about retiring in Willow Falls and opening an art gallery tugged on Emily's heartstrings. One more reason the money for the hotel had to come through.

She sighed, crossed the street, and climbed the inn's porch steps. After settling on a rocker, she fingered the plaque adorning the table between the two chairs. She choked back tears as images of working with her mom floated up from her memory. Discussions about paint colors and tile choices for the renovated bathrooms. What about updating the kitchen? Should they keep the original wallpaper or replace it?

The sound of wood creaking dashed her thoughts. Emily caught sight of Sadie sauntering over and leaning her back against the railing. Her white, button-down shirt contrasted with her black slacks and matched the painted wood. A breeze rustled the leaves on the willow tree standing proudly in the front yard.

Emily moved to the railing and breathed in a faint, floral scent wafting around Sadie. "You smell nice."

"First time I've worn perfume in thirty years. I hope it's not too strong."

"It's perfect. How'd lunch go?"

Sadie shrugged. "Nothing much happened. Pepper said you want to talk to me about something important."

Emily cleared her throat and mentally searched for an opening statement. "I've been thinking …" She grimaced at the lame comment.

"Is this a newsflash or is thinking a habit?"

Sadie's teasing tone relaxed Emily's tense shoulders. "It's something I do every now and then."

"Yeah, me too."

"The last time we talked, you encouraged me to finish the inn. You called it my parents' legacy."

"Let me guess. You decided I'm right."

"The thing is, I need help. Preferably from someone who cares about this old house as much as Mom did."

Sadie moved to the window and pressed her palm against the glass. "There are lots of memories lingering in those rooms. Some of them good."

Emily moved to her side and gazed at the empty parlor. "I purchased a truckload of furniture and accessories." She rubbed a smudge of dirt off the window. "No one knows other than Nathan and me, but most of it is from Robert Liles' estate."

Sadie's mouth gaped. "Are you pulling my leg? How? Why?"

"It seems an investor bought everything left in the house. When he died, he willed it back to Willow Falls."

"Robert's killer and his possessions return to the scene of the crime."

"I know. Ironic, isn't it?"

Sadie ran a fingernail along a crack in the window sill. "Did he return a painting of a silver-footed compote filled with pears, apples, and grapes?"

"Sitting on a marble table with a rose, a white lace napkin, and a fancy paring knife?"

"Yeah."

Emily nodded. "It's in the mix."

"Mama loved that painting. It hung over the fireplace. She'd sit on a chocolate colored settee—"

"The one with gold inlaid wood trim?"

"You bought it too?"

"I did."

"Well, I declare. Anyway, it reminded her of God's bounty in our lives. Sometimes, when I sat with her, she'd tell me stories about her childhood and her crazy brother, before he landed in a heap of trouble." The hint of a smile crinkled the skin around Sadie's eyes. "Did you also get hold of a watercolor of an old village street scene?"

"With a horse-drawn carriage?"

"That's the one. It was my favorite. You know it's a Naomi Jasper original?"

"I do."

"It decorated every room I created in my head at night in my cell. Sometimes, I'd wake up and expect to find it hanging on the wall."

"I suppose both pictures were meant to find their way back home." Emily touched Sadie's arm. She flinched but didn't pull away. "I want you to help me find a place for everything."

She hesitated for a long moment. "Is this your idea or Pepper's?"

"Originally Pepper's, but the more I think about it, the more it makes sense."

Sadie spun around and leaned her back against the window. "You know it's my fault the hotel never opened."

"It's possible Robert's financial troubles would have caught up with him even if you hadn't ... you know."

"Pulled the trigger?"

Emily nodded.

"You might be right. If you do get the money to bring it back to life, you have to pick a name to honor your parents. Maybe the Redding Arms or Hotel Redding."

"Instead of the man who built it in the first place?"

Sadie's eyes narrowed. "Robert Liles doesn't deserve to have a doghouse named after him, much less a hotel where women and children will lay their heads."

Emily squelched the impulse to probe, fearing she'd upset Sadie. "What do you say about helping me?"

"I don't know yet. What did your parents do with the space over the garage out back?"

"They turned it into an apartment—complete with a little kitchen— for guests who want to stay awhile."

"I spent a lot of time up there before ..." She pushed away from the window. "I've gotta go help Pepper. Meet me here at two tomorrow and I'll give you my answer." Sadie pivoted and headed down the porch steps.

As Emily watched her walk back down Main Street, she waffled between needing to hear a yes and hoping she'd hear a no.

Chapter 18

Emily forced her eyes open, grabbed her vibrating phone from the nightstand, and checked the ID. Jacob. Seven thirty. "Hey, what's going on?"

"I suggest you skip coming to the office today."

"Why?"

"Protestors are marching and waving signs out front. Reaction to your editorial and the winery story."

She swung her legs over the side of the bed. "How is that possible? The paper's only been out for a couple of hours."

"You know news around here travels faster than a brush fire in a hay field."

So much for Mr. Bricker's good news easing the impact of the Sadie editorial. "Look, I appreciate your suggestion, but I won't shy away from the controversy I stirred up. As soon as I pull myself together, I'll come in and bring Cody as my bodyguard."

The dog wagged his tail and barked twice, inviting a head pat. "You'll take care of me, won't you?"

Emily tossed her phone on the bed, slipped into a jogging suit, and dashed to the kitchen.

Scott kissed her cheek. "I thought you were going to sleep in this morning."

"I was, until Jacob called. It seems my editorial stirred up a giant hornet's nest."

"I'm not surprised." He poured a glass of orange juice and handed it to her. "What are you going to do?"

"Confront the troublemakers."

He popped two pieces of bread in the toaster. "My wife, the activist. At least the protestors are relatively tame. Do you want me to scramble you some eggs?"

"I don't have time to sit and eat." Emily drank her juice and grabbed a banana.

"Let me know what happens."

"I will."

Ten minutes later, she pulled into a parking spot and glared at the commotion outside the Willow Post headquarters. When she stepped out of the car, the smell of exhaust from a passing school bus made her nose crinkle and triggered another wave of nausea. She leaned against the doorframe until it passed.

"Okay, fella, here we go." She grasped Cody's leash and marched toward the protestors.

Mirabelle shook a rolled-up newspaper at Emily. "Sadie Liles obviously did a number on your brain. The real story is that Willow Falls' soul took a beating the day Pepper brought her back here, and your little editorial won't keep us from pushing to get her to leave."

Cody tucked his tail and growled at the woman.

"And keep your dog away from me."

Emily gripped the leash tighter. "I'm surprised, in your profession, you aren't an expert at dealing with ticked-off canines."

Mirabelle huffed.

"You know, you're welcome to write an opposing view and submit it for our next issue."

"And have you and Jacob toss it in the trash? I don't think so."

"If you write it, I'll do my best to convince Jacob to publish it."

"No matter what I have to say?"

She nodded. "As long as you don't use profanity."

An elderly woman approached Emily. She waved a homemade cardboard sign with red letters reading *Keep Our Town Sober.* "I don't want to cause trouble, but I'm afraid making wine in our town would doom us."

Mirabelle glared at the woman. "Doom us to what, moral corruption or economic disaster? Sadie did both the day she shot Robert Liles. The vineyard is the only good thing we've got going on around here."

Emily planted her fists on her hips. "Hold on a minute. Are you forgetting about the work Mom and Dad did on the inn and their efforts to refurbish the hotel?"

"Did you get the money?"

"Not yet."

"Of course not. I bet the investor found out about a killer living here and bailed out of the deal."

The comment cut deep and planted a seed of doubt in Emily's mind. Maybe the accident did spook the guy. Rachel read about it in the Atlanta paper. Was it possible Ben Crawford read the same story and changed his mind? Emily forced the idea aside and touched Mirabelle's arm. "I'll look for your letter to the editor. In the meantime, don't you have mail to deliver?"

"I'll get to it when I'm good and ready."

"I hope residents aren't anxiously waiting for their checks and letters." Emily turned her back on the protestors and headed into the office.

Jacob patted the dog's head. "You were serious about bringing protection."

"Cody's normally as gentle as a newborn kitten. I'm surprised he growled at Mirabelle."

"You know dogs have a sixth sense about people."

"It's obvious he doesn't much like her." She unleashed Cody. "I think most of the protestors are Sadie fanatics and not winery worriers."

A loud thud prompted another growl from Cody and made Emily jump. "What the heck?" She jerked her head around and spotted a spattering of juice, seeds, and tomato skin cascading down the window.

"It looks like the protesting is about to get out of hand." Jacob rushed to the door, swung it open, and confronted the crowd. "I demand to know who threw that."

Mirabelle tilted her head to the right. "Some kid riding by on a bike."

"You people are lined up two-deep. Do you expect me to believe a child managed to get a tomato through to the window?"

"Maybe he's a good shot."

"Look, you have the right to voice your opinion, but not to damage property."

"Don't get your britches in a wad, Jacob. It's just a tomato."

"What's going to hit us next, a dozen eggs or a brick? If another object smashes into the window, I'll get Mitch involved and press charges against everybody out here. Do you people understand?"

Mirabelle shrugged and spun away.

"In the meantime, who's going to clean up the mess?"

The vineyard protestor lowered her sign. "I will."

"Thank you, Miss Gertie. You're a good woman."

Jacob headed back inside and brushed his hand through his hair. "You'd think thirty years is enough time for that woman to forget the past and move on. Instead, she's holding on to her grudge tighter than a penny-pinching millionaire holds onto his money."

"Great simile." Emily noticed Mirabelle shaking her finger at three protestors as they tossed their signs on the sidewalk and walked away. "Maybe there's more going on than meets the eye. Do you know how long she's been married?"

"A long time, I think. Why?"

"Maybe she had a thing for Robert Liles and he up and married an out-of-towner."

"A bit far-fetched, don't you think?"

The idea nudged Emily's conscience and wouldn't let go. "Do you mind if I take a break now instead of lunchtime?"

"Are you hungry?"

"No, I want to go talk to Patsy. She might shed some light on Mirabelle's past."

"It sounds like you've got an itch you can't scratch."

"Call it creative curiosity."

Jacob laughed. "I suspect you're writing a killer novel. Say hi to Patsy for me."

"Is it okay to leave Cody with you?"

He stroked the dog's back. "We'll keep each other company."

Emily made her way through the remaining protestors and strolled around the corner. When she reached Patsy's Pastries and Pretties, she opened the door and was welcomed by mouth-watering cinnamon, chocolate, and vanilla scents.

The upbeat atmosphere created by oldies music, a life-size peacock sculpture, and artfully displayed gift items made her smile. She took a seat at one of the three ice-cream-parlor tables in front of a glass case and eyed the array of pastries and decadent desserts.

Pearl stood at the counter and carried on about the latest styles while Patsy boxed a cake. Dressed in a short, black-leather skirt and red sweater, the woman looked more like an entertainer than the owner of Pearl's Hair and Nail Salon—or, as Pepper called it, Willow Falls' gabfest and gossip parlor.

"Tell your husband happy birthday for me," said Patsy as she handed over the box.

"I will." She stopped beside Emily. "What you wrote about Miss Sadie is causing a great big stir. Personally, I think everyone should settle down and leave the poor woman alone."

"I'm glad we're on the same page."

She tapped Emily's left hand. "Love the ring but, girl, you can use a manicure. Call me sometime and set up an appointment. See you later, ladies." She waved over her shoulder and headed out the door.

Patsy grinned and settled in a chair beside Emily. "Everybody's talking about your editorial."

"What'd you think?"

"I loved it. In fact, if I hadn't already crossed over from the dark side, your words would have convinced me to make the move. I can't imagine anyone continuing to hold a grudge against Sadie, except Mirabelle Paine and her cronies."

"She's a hard nut to crack and the reason I'm here."

Patsy repositioned her straw, peacock-feathered hat. "You want to know why she can't let the Sadie thing go, don't you?"

"How'd you know?"

"Lucky guess. How about I close up shop and give you a dose of local history."

"I knew you'd have the inside scoop."

Patsy stepped to the door and flipped the open sign to closed. Then she moved behind the counter and returned with two pieces of lemon cake. "You have to promise the story I'm about to tell you won't show up in your book."

"Cross my heart."

"Okay then. To begin, Mirabelle's family was a troubled bunch. The father worked part-time as a handyman. When a neighbor accused him of stealing money, he hightailed it out of town faster than a bank robber with a sheriff on his tail. He left Mirabelle and her older brother alone with their unemployed, alcoholic mother."

Emily swallowed a bite of cake. "What a bummer."

"Worse, the day her brother turned eighteen, he enlisted in the Army and left his fifteen-year-old sister to fend for herself. When my Tommy died, I needed help running the store, so I hired Mirabelle the day she graduated from high school. Back then she was slim, attractive, and naïve as a newborn baby. It didn't take long for her to trust me enough to share her dream about marrying a rich man and living in a big house. When Robert Liles' second wife left—"

"Hold on, are you saying he was married three times?"

Patsy nodded and took a bite of cake. "Number two was another pretty out-of-towner with a young daughter. Two years after Robert married her, mother and daughter left town and never came back. There were lots of rumors, but none were ever proven."

Emily remembered Sadie's comment about her stepfather not deserving his name on a doghouse. "It seems there's something odd about Robert."

"Maybe more grim than odd. Anyway, Mirabelle practically threw herself at the man. I tried to tell her he was too old for her, but she didn't listen. Would you believe he hired her as his full-time housekeeper? I can't say for certain, but I suspect he wanted her close to exploit her infatuation, if you know what I mean?"

"He took advantage of her?"

"Precisely."

"How did Mirabelle respond?"

"She was crazy in love with him and believed he'd make her the third Mrs. Liles. Until he fired her for no apparent reason. A couple of weeks later, he shows up with a beautiful new wife and a teenage daughter."

"Sadie and her mom. I suspect Mirabelle was furious with Robert."

Patsy rapped her fork on her plate. "You'd think, but that's not what happened. She told me Carlie seduced Robert. Mirabelle convinced herself he'd eventually come to his senses, dump the new wife, and marry her. Until Sadie shot him."

Emily's brow scrunched. "But it turned out Robert was drowning in debt."

"Again, Mirabelle blamed Carlie for spending all his money. Years later, she married Frank, a nice guy and a good mechanic. But I suspect deep down she believes Sadie stole her chance to become a rich woman."

"Well, that explains a lot. How many people know the real story?"

"As far as I know, just me and now you."

"Do you suppose Mirabelle will ever let go of the past?"

"She's lived in a fantasy world for so many years, it would take a miracle."

Emily swallowed the last bite of cake. "I stopped believing in miracles the day the drunk driver slammed into my parents' car."

Patsy reached across the table and patted her hand. "One of these days, something will happen to renew your faith."

"I'm curious. You lost your husband decades ago. Why didn't you marry again?"

A smile lit Patsy's face. "Tommy was my perfect soulmate. No one else could ever take his place."

"Is he the reason you still live in the apartment upstairs?"

"I suppose it seems odd to a lot of people, but when I walk into those rooms, I'm surrounded by things we shared and comforted by his memory. He's also the reason I wear my peacock hats. The day he left to fight in Vietnam, I vowed to wear one every day until he returned. My favorite is a ball cap with one peacock feather stitched to the side. I wore it the day he arrived home on a bus."

"It sounds like you had a wonderful relationship."

"One in a million."

"How did he die?"

Her smile disappeared. "Brain aneurysm. Although I cherish the short time we spent together, it pales in comparison to the eternity I'll spend with him when it's my time to go home."

A knot formed in the pit of Emily's stomach. Why did God allow accidents and illness to snuff out the lives of good people?

Patsy pointed to an elderly neighbor pushing the shop door open. "So much for my closed sign."

Emily leaned close and whispered. "Thank you for trusting me to keep Mirabelle's past a secret. At least now, I better understand her anger." She spoke to the intruder and sauntered back to the newspaper office, relieved to see the front window clean and the sidewalk clear of protestors. Cody stretched and greeted her with a soft bark and a tail wag.

Jacob lifted his fingers off his keyboard and yawned. "What'd you learn about our pesky protestor?"

Careful not to divulge any secrets, she relayed snippets of the conversation.

"So much for your theory about a connection with Robert Liles."

"You know how theories are, not worth their weight in cotton. Thanks for dog sitting."

"He's good company. You're welcome to bring him in anytime."

"Any responses to the editorial, other than the tomato throwing incident?"

Jacob thumped his computer screen. "A half-dozen supportive emails. I expect we'll get some letters to the editor in the next couple of days."

"Mirabelle mentioned she might write one."

"I hope it's G-rated."

Emily plopped down in a chair. "Whatever it is, I promised her I'd convince you to print it."

"Maybe the controversy will boost sales."

"We could sure use the extra revenue. Anything else happen while I was gone?"

"Nope. In fact, there's no need for you to hang around. I'll let you know when I have my proposal ready for your review."

"Thanks. I'm meeting Sadie at two. I think I'll visit Scott before I head over." She trudged out the door and headed to the store. Maybe her husband would ease her unyielding uncertainty about wanting to hear an acceptance or a denial from Willow Falls' ex-con.

Chapter 19

Rachel sat facing her father's antique desk. She dabbed a tissue at her puffy eyes and coughed. "There's no way I'm up to meeting with a new client today—not feeling this lousy and looking like I've been on a three-day drinking binge."

"Okay, but I'm not letting you off the hook in the future. Bricker's youngest son Charlie is coming in to thank you for getting his old man to make a decision. Can you handle five minutes with him?"

"I'll try not to sneeze on the guy and make him sick. At least it'll give me a chance to tell him about the article in the Willow Post."

"How did people react?"

"I don't know yet. I'll call Emily Hayes later today. In the meantime, I'll try to get some work done." She schlepped from the office and stopped at Nancy's desk.

Her assistant stopped typing. "In my opinion, you need to go home, eat some chicken soup, and spend the rest of the day in bed."

"Do I look that bad?"

"Just sick."

"I can't leave now. Mr. Bricker's son is coming by to talk to me. Don't let anyone bother me until he shows up."

"If Brent comes over, I'll wrestle him to the floor and hogtie him like a calf."

Rachel laughed. "If you do, I'll have to start calling you rodeo Nancy."

"You go get some rest."

Rachel stepped into her office and closed the door behind her. She plopped in her executive chair, crossed her arms on her desk, and cradled her head in the crook of her elbow. In minutes, she drifted into a fitful dream about her father charging into her office, clutching a Broadway Play-bill, and accusing her of abandoning him to chase a foolish fantasy. She cowered. He snarled and shouted, *You can't leave. You belong to me.* In one rapid move, he whipped chains from behind his back and shackled Rachel's ankles to her desk. Then he ripped the Playbill to shreds, tossed the pieces in the air, and roared with laughter as they fluttered to the floor and turned to dust.

An audible gasp startled Rachel awake. She pushed her chair away from her desk, checked her ankle for shackles, and pressed her hand to her forehead. "At least you're not raving mad from a fever."

She opened her computer but couldn't shake the nightmare. Truth seeped into the deepest recesses of her conscious. Invisible shackles constricted her as much as physical chains. She reached for a pitcher on the corner of her desk, poured a glass of ice water, and gulped it. Desperate to cool down, she closed her eyes and held the icy-cold glass against the back of her neck.

Her cell phone buzzed, forcing her eyes to pop open. She hesitated before checking caller ID. "Good morning, Emily."

"Are you feeling any better today?"

"I can't say I am."

"Colds are tough to shake. Did you have a chance to read the article I wrote about the winery?"

"I did and I loved it. Is it too soon to get a read on the town's reaction?"

"Around here, five minutes isn't too soon. Other than a few naysayers, folks consider the vineyard good news."

Rachel succumbed to a coughing fit. "Thanks for getting the story out on such short notice. I'm sure our client will be pleased."

Nancy opened her door and slipped inside. "He's here."

Rachel held one finger in the air.

"I apologize, Emily, but I have a meeting with Mr. Bricker's son."

"I understand. I hope you and I have an opportunity to meet sometime."

"As do I." Rachel ended the call and motioned Nancy over. "Is Brent hogtied behind your desk?"

"Nope. Lucky for him, he didn't show up."

"Too bad. Anyway, I need a minute to pull myself together. I'll buzz you when I'm ready."

Rachel dug in her purse for a mirror, touched up her lipstick, and dabbed her watery eyes. A sneeze prompted her to pull a bottle of hand sanitizer from her desk drawer. She checked her image again, buzzed Nancy, and stood to greet her guest.

A medium-height, muscular man with brown hair and hazel eyes moved toward her. "I'm Charlie Bricker. It's a pleasure to meet you."

Rachel reached across the desk and held her hand out to him. "I sanitized, so it's germ free." His grin and touch sparked an electrifying quiver in her limbs and sent heat creeping across her cheeks. "You don't look anything like your father."

"And I'm not superstitious, but I do have his gift for managing projects. Which is why he put me in charge of getting the vineyard and winery up and running." He released Rachel's hand. "I want to personally thank you for convincing my old man to make a decision."

She pointed to the chair. "Please, have a seat."

"Are you sure? Nancy said you're not feeling up to snuff."

She nodded before pulling a tissue from her pocket, turning her head, and sneezing. "I feel better than I look."

He dropped onto the chair and crossed a leg over his knee. "Then you must feel terrific, because you look like a million bucks."

"You're a gentleman and maybe more than a little nearsighted." Rachel settled in her chair, leaned back, and folded her hands in her lap. "So, Brick put you in charge of his retirement venture."

"Yep. Good thing I thrive on challenges. Initially, it's a two-year commitment, but if I adjust to life in a small town, it could become my new career."

"I take it you're a big-city guy."

"Born and bred Atlanta native."

"Me too."

Charlie grinned. "Something else we have in common."

"What do you mean?"

"We both work for our dads."

Rachel fingered her tennis bracelet, wondering if his involvement in his father's business was voluntary or forced servitude. "Have you been to Willow Falls?"

He shook his head. "I'll head up there next week to supervise the land clearing. As soon as the rootstock is planted, I'll look for a construction company to start building the winery."

"From what I hear, Willow Falls' residents are taking the news well."

"I hope they realize it will be a while before we bring in any business."

"I suspect they do. Have you found a place to stay?"

"Not yet."

Rachel's door swung open. Brent swaggered across the space. "I see you've met my partner." He winked at Rachel. "She and I have a special relationship."

Rachel cringed and struggled to keep her tone neutral. "He means a working relationship, nothing more."

"You know what they say about office relationships." Brent clasped Charlie's shoulder. "I have some papers for you to take to your dad."

Charlie stood and extended his hand to Rachel. "It's been a pleasure, Ms. Streetman. If it's okay with you, I'll call you tomorrow to give you an update."

Oh, it's way more than okay. "Please, do. And call me Rachel."

Brent's eyes narrowed as he punched Charlie's arm. "I hear you plan to spend a lot of time up there at the winery site."

Rachel watched the two men stroll from her office. One she considered irritating. The other she found interesting. She sauntered to the window and let her eyes follow a plane moving across the horizon. Random coincidences seemed to have flown into her world. Nancy's comment about her dreams. Meeting Alicia. The tragedy in Willow Falls, Bricker's retirement gig, and now meeting Charlie.

Nancy popped back into her office. "Your father wants to talk to you."

"No way I'm up to another meeting." Rachel dashed to her desk and snatched her purse. "Tell him I headed home to nurse a nasty cold." She brushed past Nancy, rushed to the elevator bank, and tapped her foot until the doors opened. The moment she felt a jolt and the descent, she sighed and imagined a hairline crack developing in the invisible shackle chaining her to Streetman Enterprise.

Chapter 20

Sadie stood on the concrete pad, gripped the hand rail, and stared at the landing at the top of the staircase. She'd last fled to the space above the garage two days before the sheriff cuffed her and drove her to the county jail. Now, with a decision hanging in the balance, she forced her feet to climb. Her breath quickened as she turned the doorknob and crossed the threshold. The once wide-open space with warped wood floors, exposed rafters, and unfinished walls had been transformed into a beautiful two-room apartment. A miniature kitchen anchored one end of the living room.

She breathed in the scent of fresh paint as she moved to a dormer window—the same spot where she'd spent untold hours daydreaming about a life far different than the one she'd been forced to endure. She sat on the floor, pulled her knees up, and wrapped her arms around her shins.

Memories of Pepper accompanying her to the space danced in her head. They'd talk for hours about topics important to teenage girls—boys, homework, prom dresses, would their high school football team beat their rivals? Happy moments when she could pretend all was well. Pepper and Mitch were the sister and brother she never had. Somehow, she had to find a way to stay in Willow Falls.

She glanced at her watch. One hour to go before Emily expected an answer. Helping decorate the rooms in the Liles mansion both intrigued and terrified Sadie. Although she'd learned about forgiveness during a two-year Bible study in prison, bitterness remained etched in her heart. She didn't know if she could muster the courage to walk into those rooms and touch her stepfather's possessions.

A spider weaving its web outside the window distracted her. She'd learned to deal with all sorts of bugs crawling around and making their homes within the prison walls. At least spiders served a useful purpose.

Sadie moved away from the window and moseyed into the bedroom, twice the size of her cell. She twirled in a circle, picturing the room decorated with elegant furniture and pretty pictures. She imagined country music filling the air.

In the bathroom, she ran her fingers over the white porcelain sink and caught her image in the mirror. Real glass. A banned item behind bars. She stepped in the sparkling-clean, stone-tiled shower and envisioned hot water washing over her for as long she chose—without prying eyes sending shivers up her spine.

One last space beckoned to her. She opened the closet door and pressed her hand to her chest. Her mother's favorite suitcase—the one that belonged to her grandmother—sat in the corner. Sadie dropped to her knees, unbuckled the leather straps, and lifted the top.

Inside, she found memorabilia from her childhood. Her grandma's tattered copy of *The Boxcar Children*. She'd read the book dozens of times, pretending she was one of the characters.

She removed a bundle of pictures tied with a pink ribbon. Photos of Christmas at her grandma and pop's house. Pictures of her best friend the day before she left Thomasville forever. Sitting with her mother on the front porch following their move to Willow Falls. She and Pepper posing in their prom dresses. So many happy memories.

Something odd struck her. She searched back through the photos. There wasn't a single picture of her stepfather. She remembered a dinner guest taking pictures of her and her mother posing with Robert. And her mom snapping shots on Christmas morning. Maybe there weren't any photos because her mother knew. No, that wasn't possible.

* * *

Emily sauntered through the park to the yard behind the abandoned hotel. A mother duck, trailed by four ducklings, waddled along the water's edge, coaxing a bark from Cody and a leash tug from Emily. "No duck chasing today." She pivoted toward the porch. "Do I have enough courage to peek inside this old building?"

A spider web covering half the landing at the top of the stairs caught her attention. Although she found spiders fascinating, she always kept her distance. Curiosity overcame the ghost stories planted deep in her mind. She climbed the steps and ducked under the web.

The stale odor of mold and wet dirt made her nose pucker. She peered through a jagged hole in a grime-crusted window. The sight of dense cobwebs hanging from the ceiling and layers of dirt, debris, and rotting canvas cloths covering abandoned building materials made her shiver. "Maybe my childhood friends were right. The lobby looks like a scene from an old black-and-white horror movie."

The mental image shook her to the core. "Mirabelle's right about one thing, a curse infects this dilapidated old building." She gripped Cody's leash, dashed down the stairs, and scurried to the inn's front yard. At the porch stairs, she paused to catch her breath.

"It looks like Cody took you for a run."

Emily swiveled and stared at Sadie peering over the railing. "Sorry we're late." She climbed the stairs and disconnected Cody's leash before settling in a rocking chair. "I looked inside the hotel for the first time in years. It spooked the dickens out of me."

Sadie sat beside her and set her rocker in motion. "The day Robert broke ground, it seemed the whole town turned out to cheer for him. Did you know people elected him as mayor?"

"I'd heard."

"Everyone thought they knew the man."

Emily struggled to keep from probing. "Maybe we should bulldoze the hotel and expand the park."

"That doesn't make sense. How would more empty land help the town's economy?"

"It wouldn't."

"Then don't be so quick to fly off the handle." Sadie swatted a fly away from her face. "I found the suitcase." She thrust her thumb over her shoulder. "That one, with all the pictures."

"Oh yeah. Mom discovered it under an old blanket in the space over the garage."

"I'm glad she didn't throw it away. It's all I have left of Mama's." She sniffed and wiped her nose. "I've been thinking about your offer."

The moment of truth. "And?"

"We're two motherless women in a town looking for a reason to carry on."

Emily gazed into Sadie's eyes and noticed they looked different than she remembered—more blue-green, like the eye on one of Patsy's peacock feathers. "What are you trying to say?"

She stopped rocking. "I need to make up for all the trouble I've caused. So, I'll work around Pepper's schedule tomorrow and help you get this place ready for guests."

"I'll ask Nathan to deliver everything."

"Do you mind if I take a look at all the stuff you bought? To get a head start on planning?"

"That's a good idea."

Sadie stood and stretched. "I'll head on over now. Do you want to come with me?"

She hesitated. If she said yes, Sadie might think she didn't trust her judgement? "No thanks, I'll leave the details to you."

"Okay, then. I'll see you tomorrow."

Emily watched her stroll down the stairs, thinking a short-term partnership might work out after all.

Chapter 21

Morning sunshine streaming through the bedroom window roused Rachel. She stretched and waited for her eyes to focus before reaching for her phone. Ten fifteen. Three missed calls. Two from her father. One from an unknown caller.

She pushed her feet into slippers, put on a robe, and trudged to the kitchen. Chicken soup, green tea, and twelve hours of sleep made it possible for her to breathe without setting off a gut-wrenching coughing fit. She pocketed her phone, poured a glass of juice and carried it to the deck. It seemed odd, yet liberating, to watch a squirrel scamper along the ground and scoot up a tree trunk on a weekday morning. "What should I do, little furry friend? Go to work or pretend it's Sunday and play hooky all day?" She took a sip of juice, tipped her glass toward the squirrel, and nodded. "Yeah, you're right. I need to stick with the second choice."

Rachel settled on the chaise lounge and closed her eyes. She let the sun kiss her cheeks and the breeze tousle her hair as an image of Charlie sitting across from her desk crept into her mind. What was it about him that stirred her emotions? He was good looking but not male-model handsome. He seemed charming, even flirtatious. And he was related to a client, which technically put him in the hands-off category.

Her phone vibrated, prompting one eye to open—the unknown number. She assumed it was a telemarketer asking for donations or repeating a rehearsed sales pitch. Or maybe it was a business call. Curiosity won out.

"Hello."

"Hey, good morning. It's Charlie Bricker. I hope I'm not disturbing you."

She pulled her knees up to her chest. "Not at all."

"I called your office. Nancy told me you're trying to shake your cold. Are you feeling better?"

"It's amazing what a good night's sleep can do. What's up?"

He cleared his throat. "We didn't get much time to talk yesterday."

Thanks to Brent charging in.

"I'd like to treat you to dinner Saturday night so we can talk about plans for the winery."

Is he asking me for a date? "I, uh—"

"I'll understand if you don't think it's a good idea."

Should she defy her father and ignore his "don't date clients" policy? "No, I mean yeah, why not?" Rachel clenched her lower lip between her teeth, thinking she sounded like a silly school girl.

"How about the Sun Dial?"

The rotating restaurant was visible from her office window. On the seventy-second floor of the round Westin Peachtree Plaza Hotel, it often conjured up memories. "My mom took me and my friends to the Sun Dial to celebrate every birthday from my seventh to my tenth. I love the panoramic view from up there."

"Yeah, so do I. Should I pick you up, or do you want to meet me at the restaurant?"

It seems he's a gentleman. "I'll text you my address."

"Good. I'll see you at seven. In the meantime, you take care of your cold."

"Thanks, I will." Out of nowhere, the prospect of inscribing Charlie's name on her non-existent list of suitors piqued her interest. "Don't get ahead of yourself, Rachel. It's one business dinner with a client's son."

Her phone vibrated again. Her father. Should she answer or let it go to voicemail? Guilt forced her finger to slide the bar.

"I've been trying to reach you all morning. I heard you left the office yesterday following your meeting with Bricker's son."

"Yeah, I couldn't stop coughing and sneezing."

"If you're sick enough to miss two days of work, you need to go see a doctor."

His unsympathetic tone made her cringe. She sensed the hairline crack in the invisible chain closing. "This isn't a medical emergency. All I need is rest. Besides, you don't want me spreading germs to your entire staff, do you?"

"Good point. How did the meeting with Charlie Bricker go?"

"I suppose fine."

"Brent called the guy a thirty-five-year-old playboy."

Rachel's body tensed. "What are you trying to say?"

"Don't let him hit on you. I don't want old-man Bricker getting wind of his favorite Streetman VP rejecting his son."

The comment unleashed a flood of anger. Rachel bolted from the chaise lounge, gripped her glass, and charged into the kitchen. "Look, I appreciate your concern, but you don't have to worry about me. I won't let my personal life interfere with your company's success."

"That's my girl. I knew I could count on you. Hold on a minute. Brent just walked in. He wants to talk to you."

"No—"

"It sounds like Bricker's kid made you sicker." Brent's smug voice was more irritating than fingernails scraping down a chalkboard. "Too bad, because Greer and I need you here."

"I'm confident you two will carry on splendidly without me." Lingering anger strengthened Rachel's resolve. "You tell the boss I'll come back to work when this cold runs its course."

Brent relayed the message. "He has some paperwork you need to review. I can bring it to you."

"Not a chance. If it can't wait, he can email me the files. Right now, I have to hang up before a sneezing fit hits me." She punched the red icon and tossed the phone on the counter. To ease her anger, she refilled her glass with juice and returned to the deck.

The resident hawk swooped down and settled on a limb. She tipped her glass toward the bird. "Hello there. Are you looking for lunch or enjoying the view? Me, I'm hiding from my father and his exasperating crony. And no matter what either of them thinks about Charlie, I'm going out with the guy. Who knows, maybe a playboy is exactly what I need to spice up my mundane life."

Chapter 22

Startled to see the inn's etched-glass-inlaid, double front doors standing wide open, Emily held her breath and crossed the threshold. She found Sadie sitting on the bottom step of the curved grand staircase hugging a pillow to her chest. Relieved, she let the air escape, strolled over, and settled beside her. "I hope you like the carpet we picked for the stairs. It's the closest pattern we could find to the original."

"You did good." Sadie lowered the pillow, revealing an intricate floral design. "I found this at Nathan's."

"It's beautiful. I don't remember seeing it."

"My grandma made it and sent it to us a month after we moved here." She held it to her nose and breathed in. "It still has a faint floral scent. Mama's favorite."

"Chanel Number 5 was my mother's signature fragrance. She wore it on special occasions and every Sunday." Emily eyed the elaborate crystal chandelier spilling multiple splinters of light on the marble foyer floor. "I'm curious. What attracted your mother to Robert?"

Sadie fingered a pink rose on the pillow. "After he met her at the antique mall—it's where Mama worked—he came back to town every week to take us out to dinner. He was like prince charming swooping down to sweep a pretty lady off her feet with expensive gifts. The truth is, Mama was flat worn out from scrimping by, so marrying an older, rich man she'd met three months earlier was her dream come true."

"Sort of like a Cinderella story."

"Except it turned out the handsome prince wasn't so charming."

The roar of a truck engine followed by the squeal of brakes forced Emily to refocus. "I think our delivery has arrived." She moved to the porch.

The driver trudged up the steps and tipped his hat. "Afternoon, Miss Emily."

"Hey, Jimmy, how's the family?"

"Fair to middling." He shifted toward the truck. "We had specific instructions about how to load up."

"From Nathan?"

"From me." Sadie strolled from the foyer to the porch steps. "The furniture's loaded by room. It'll make things go faster."

Emily stared at her.

"Don't look so shocked. Besides a long list of criminal tactics, I learned some good stuff in prison. Like how to organize work when the warden assigned me to manage the kitchen."

A real school of hard knocks. "I get it. So, what's coming in first?"

"The dining room furniture. Mr. Jimmy, you can start with the buffet, then bring in the table and chairs. We'll show you where to put everything." Sadie walked back inside.

Surprised by her take-charge approach, Emily followed her into the dining room and found her looking up at the antique brass chandelier with etched glass globes.

"Robert expected Mama to be a proper southern lady and help him entertain important town folks with lots of fancy dinners. She spent hours in the local library reading books and magazines to learn how to set a formal table and fix delicious meals."

"Your mom sounds like an extraordinary woman."

"She was eager to please … no matter what happened."

Jimmy's voice echoed through the empty room. "Where do you want this piece?"

Sadie pointed to the wall opposite the front window. "Over there, right in the center."

"The moment I saw that piece, I knew it had to come back here." Emily moved close to the massive, carved mahogany buffet with lion claw feet. "I imagined a gentleman dressed in a tuxedo, wearing white gloves, arranging serving bowls on it."

"Mama always polished Robert's silver bowls before dinner parties. She looked real pretty when she smiled and served her guests."

Emily remembered Patsy's story about Robert hiring Mirabelle. "Didn't she have someone to help her? Maybe a maid?"

"We heard he'd fired his housekeeper shortly before we moved in. I guess he figured a young wife didn't need any help."

For the next hour, Sadie directed furniture placement for the dining room, parlor, library, and first-floor bedroom suite. Paintings and boxes filled with accessories were pushed up against the foyer wall. She stood at the bottom of the staircase with her hand on the intricately carved newel post.

The two men carried an antique dresser into the foyer. "Where to, boss?"

"Everything else goes upstairs." Sadie took a deep breath, motioned for the guys to follow, and lumbered up the stairs.

Emily waited for the movers to reach the top before following.

"It goes in there." Sadie stood in the common area pointing to a front bedroom.

"When we were painting these five bedrooms, Mom and I assumed a lot of overnight guests visited Robert."

"Not one the whole time I lived here."

Emily's brows lifted. "Are you kidding me?"

"Nope. You know his daddy built this house."

"I'd heard."

"Robert was an only child, so when his old man passed on, he inherited everything, including a heap of money."

Emily shook her head. "He must have spent it all, because he left a mountain of debt."

"And a house full of antiques that got sold for peanuts."

"It's funny how things turned out."

The men hauled a tall dresser up the stairs and set it on the floor. Jimmy rubbed the back of his neck. "That's one heavy piece. Miss Sadie, it has your name written on the back."

"You can take it to the room in the left, rear corner."

"The one with vintage tan and white damask wallpaper," Emily said. "Was that where you slept?"

"The bedroom on the other corner was mine."

A question popped up from Emily's mental list. "I hope I'm not meddling, but I'm wondering if Robert adopted you. After all, you have his last name."

Sadie strolled to her old room and leaned on the doorframe. "Sometimes, when he was out of town, Pepper spent the night. One time, we snuck out at midnight for a secret party with friends in the park. I got sick as a dog guzzling cups of spiked punch."

She eyed Emily. "I'm glad you changed the color in here. Pale yellow brightens it up a heap. About my name, Mama had it legally changed a week after she and Robert got married. I never knew my real daddy. He was some hot-to-trot college guy who got her pregnant when she was a high-school senior and skedaddled out of town faster than a jackrabbit hopped up on speed. Mama believed changing my name to Sadie Clair Liles would make me respectable."

Relieved she hadn't upset Sadie, Emily forced a smile. "Sadie Clair has a definite Southern flair. Right up there with Daisy Mae and Dixie Rose."

"When Mama called me by both names, I knew I was in a heap of trouble."

"Same thing my mom said about her mother calling her Nora Jane."

"And there's one big reason why parents tag their kids with two names. What about you? Are you giving your babies middle names?"

"We haven't thought that far ahead yet."

"You have lots of time." Sadie shuffled her feet and cleared her throat. "I'm putting the set of twin beds and hand-painted dresser you bought in here."

"They aren't from the estate."

"I know. We don't have enough pieces to fill all these rooms." She returned to the center of the common area. "And nothing for this big open space. I'm thinking you should make it a cozy little living room. A place for visitors to hang out and visit."

Emily stared at the ten-foot-high ceiling with an ornate gold medallion surrounding a crystal chandelier. She pictured guests gathering in the area to relax before heading out to see the town. "If I don't find a manager, there'll be lots of empty rooms at the inn."

"Did you put the word out you're looking for someone?"

"Not yet."

Sadie propped her hands on her hips. "Well, get on with it, girl."

"You're right. I'll post some notices, maybe put an ad in the paper."

Another hour passed before all the furniture was moved from the truck. Sadie took one last look around upstairs. "Monday afternoon, I can meet you here to help hang pictures and find a place for the accessories you bought. We'll need a ladder, a hammer, and some picture hanging hooks."

"I'll get Scott to bring them over."

Sadie glanced at her watch. "It's time to head back to the café and help Pepper get ready for dinner in case anyone bothers to show up." She moved to the top of the stairs, gasped, and dropped to her knees.

Her hand trembled as she reached out and touched a stain in the oak floor.

Emily knelt beside her. "Is that—"

"Robert's blood." She snatched her hand away. "I didn't see it on the way up."

"At least it faded over time. It looks more like a flaw in the wood than a bloodstain."

"I guess it was too much to expect Mama to clean it. I learned about her illness after they locked me up." Sadie's voice quivered. "If I'd known before I pulled the trigger, maybe I might not have ..." She bolted to her feet "No, it wouldn't have mattered."

"Do you want to talk about it?"

Sadie gripped the handrailing. "There's nothing to talk about. I shot the man. He's dead. Mama's gone. I'm guilty. I paid for my crime." She ran down the stairs and rushed out of the inn.

Emily shuddered as she pictured the door leading to the truth about Robert Lile's death slamming shut forever.

Chapter 23

Rachel peered at a full-length mirror, assessing her fourth change of clothes—a sleeveless, teal sheath, silver dangle earrings, and white sandals with four-inch heels. "Enough already. You're acting goofier than a star-struck teenager waiting for her first date to show up."

The doorbell chime echoed through her townhouse. She sneaked one more glance before rushing to the first floor and opening the door. "You're right on time."

Charlie held out a bouquet of spring flowers. "A get well or glad you're all better gift, whichever best fits."

She breathed in the sweet scent. "They're beautiful, and both sentiments work. Come on in to the kitchen." She pulled a crystal vase from the cabinet, filled it with water, and arranged the blooms.

"Nice townhouse." He tapped his knuckles on the glass doors. "And a great deck. A perfect spot to spend a lazy Saturday afternoon."

"Most Saturdays I'm too busy with work."

He moved close to her. "Because you're a workaholic or is Greer Streetman a hard-nosed slave driver?"

Tread carefully. You don't know anything about this guy. "How about a third option? I'm a loyal daughter." She placed the last flower in the vase and carried it to the table. "You missed the deck assessment by one day. It's my refuge every Sunday morning, weather permitting. I read the paper and have interesting one-way conversations with the neighborhood hawk. He's a good listener."

"I suspect he's mesmerized by your brains and beauty."

The glint in his eyes prompted her to consider Brent's comment about the man being a player.

Charlie cleared his throat. "The sky's clear as glass. Perfect weather for dinner seventy-plus stories above the city." He touched her shoulder. "Are you ready to go?"

She dismissed the tingle his touch sparked. "Ready and eager to enjoy the view."

"And, I hope, the company." He led her down the front steps to his Ford F150 truck, held the door open, and grasped her elbow to help her step in.

His choice of vehicles surprised her. She'd expected an exotic sports car, fitting for a wealthy playboy.

He climbed into the driver's seat and backed out of her driveway. "How do you like living in Buckhead?"

"It's nice enough, I suppose. Close to downtown so it limits my commute time."

Idle chatter about the weather and Atlanta traffic kept the atmosphere casual during the short ride. At the Peachtree Plaza hotel, Charlie turned his truck over for valet parking and escorted her through the lobby to the queue waiting to ride to the hotel's top floor. When they moved to the head of the line, they stepped into the glass elevator hugging the outside of the tube-shaped building. With the rapid ascent, Rachel closed her eyes and clutched Charlie's arm.

He clasped his hand over hers. "I take it you're not crazy about heights."

"It's this glass cylinder that makes me nervous. One thing's for sure, I'll never strap a parachute to my back and jump out of a plane."

"Or base-jump off a bridge."

"Are you the daredevil type?"

"Evil Knievel wild, no. Adventuresome, yes." Charlie kept his hand on hers until the hostess escorted them to the restaurant's revolving surface. The woman seated them at a table beside the floor-to-ceiling windows, curved to conform to the building's tube shape.

The restaurant's neutral, gray-and-tan color palette served as a perfect backdrop to the spectacular view of Atlanta's skyline. Rachel gazed down, past the Skyview Ferris Wheel to Centennial Olympic Park. Red brick sidewalks outlined large square swaths of green grass. "Tickets were hard to come by, but my parents and I attended the 1996 Olympic diving finals and opening ceremony."

"Dad managed to get us into the field and track competition and closing ceremony." He nodded toward the window. "My name is etched on one of those centennial bricks."

"Maybe it's close to mine. Although I don't remember the location."

"One of these days we'll hunt them down together."

She imagined strolling arm in arm through the park with Charlie, until the waiter arrived with menus and asked for drink orders.

"When I'm driving, I limit myself to one glass of wine."

Rachel mentally started a list of Charlie's attributes. He was responsible. "That's plenty for me."

Charlie made a selection and pointed to the menu. "What suits your fancy?"

"I'm thinking rack of lamb."

"Perfect choice." He pushed the menu aside and smiled at her. "So far, I know you work a lot of hours, talk to birds, and prefer to keep your feet planted on the ground. What else makes you fascinating?"

"I don't have any brothers or sisters. In my father's opinion, it's best to mold and perfect one child. He claims it worked for him, so why not continue the pattern?"

"From what I can tell, he succeeded with high honors."

Her mental list expanded. He was charming. Or was he a shameless flirt?

"What about your mom? Did she have the same opinion?"

"I doubt it. She loved having my friends around." Rachel caressed her mother's tennis bracelet. "She died before I turned twelve—cancer."

He broke eye contact and spread a linen napkin on his lap. "At least she didn't run off with another man and break your father's heart."

"I take it your parents are divorced."

He nodded.

"Does your mother stay in touch?"

"She did for a couple of years. But, enough about our parents. Where did you go to college?"

Grateful for the change of subject, Rachel smiled. "I graduated from the University of Georgia."

"Aha. The first rift in our relationship. I'm a rambling wreck from Georgia Tech. I'll chalk up your choice for higher education to a youthful lapse in judgment."

"Not mine, my dad's."

"And your choice?"

"Julliard's in New York City. I'm a big fan of live theater."

"Does your school preference mean you wanted to be on the stage, not in the audience?"

"An unrealized childhood fantasy."

He rested his forearms on the table. "How many famous showbiz people have you rubbed shoulders with?"

"None, unless you call Alicia Adams famous."

"The local reporter?"

"I sat next to her at a play. I didn't ask for an autograph, but I have her business card." She relayed the information about her blog and invitation to join her improv group.

"Sounds interesting. Are you going to accept her offer?"

"Most likely not, with my busy work schedule."

"Maybe you should take more time to relax and have fun."

The waiter arrived with the wine, took their dinner order, and stepped away. Charlie touched his glass to Rachel's. "To a bright future where all your choices are your own."

Rachel nodded, fearing the floodgates would burst open if she let the slightest bit of vulnerability guide her response. "You know my favorite form of entertainment, but I don't know yours."

"In addition to sports, watching thrillers and action movies are my gig. But I did see *Jersey Boys* at the Fox. I took my Dad for his sixty-first birthday. He loves good old rock and roll."

Rachel tilted her head. "You seem close to your father. How long have you worked for him?"

"Nine years. I wanted to sign on the day I graduated from Tech, but he insisted I get my feet wet with another company. He did the same with my brother. Ends up it was a smart move, because we both joined the family business by choice."

Rachel glanced out the window and caught sight of the building housing Streetman Enterprise. So far, Charlie seemed like a nice guy, yet her brain continued to caution her to play it safe and keep the conversation neutral. "I'm curious. You grew up in Atlanta and spent your college years smack dab in the middle of the city."

"And your point is?"

"How will you handle spending a couple of years in a town the size of Willow Falls?"

"I'm counting on the challenge of creating a first-class winery to get me through the culture shock. Who knows, I might discover I'm a country boy at heart. At least I've got a head start in the tune category."

"I take it you're into country music."

"I'm partial to Brad Paisley and Carrie Underwood. Maybe I'll learn to pluck a guitar and shout yeehaw when our grapes produce the first batch of drinkable wine."

Rachel laughed. "And raise your own cows and chickens?"

"I'm a vintner, not a farmer. So I'll settle for a couple of well-trained dogs to sniff out diseases and pests and keep the deer from eating my vines."

The waiter arrived with their entrees. She cut a piece of lamb and savored the taste. "You're right, this is delicious."

Charlie's charm and sense of humor intrigued Rachel and made her wonder why, at thirty-five, he was still unattached. Maybe he wasn't the settling-down type. Or did he have a dark side? *Stop with the crazy mental questions. After all, you're still single. So relax and enjoy his company.*

Following dinner, they moved to the lounge for a cup of cappuccino and conversation about their college days, city versus country life, and the difference between acting on stage and in film.

Shortly past midnight, he drove her home and walked her to the door. "If you can tolerate another date with a guy who drives a truck and likes country music, how about dinner and a play next weekend? I'm tied up Saturday, but Sunday's free."

"I'm game."

"Good." He smiled and kissed her hand. "Until Sunday."

She stepped inside, closed the door, and convinced herself it was way too soon to put Charlie's name on her otherwise empty list of prospects.

Chapter 24

Emily thrashed, kicked off the covers, and cried out. Cody jumped on the bed and licked her face.

Scott's voice forced her awake. "Were you abducted by aliens or running from a grizzly bear?"

"What are you talking about?" She pushed Cody away.

"Your dream."

Emily wiped beads of sweat from her forehead as snippets of the nightmare broke through the fog in her head and quickly disappeared. She squeezed her eyes closed and massaged her temples. "What time is it?"

"Three fifteen."

"In the morning?"

Scott smiled. "Yeah."

"Sorry I woke you. Go back to sleep. I'm going to get something to drink." She kissed his cheek, slipped out of bed, and strolled to the kitchen. Cody padded behind her.

"What's the matter, fella, did you have a bad dream too?" She poured a glass of milk and tossed a dog biscuit to him. "Since I'm awake, I might as well do something productive."

She settled at the kitchen table, booted her computer, and scrolled through the Willow Post emails. One subject line caught her attention. She opened the message, downloaded the attachment, and read Mirabelle's letter to the editor.

The Unwelcome Return. A Resident's Perspective.

Thirty years ago, Sadie Liles killed the town hero, destroyed Willow Fall's potential, and sent people like me to a prison without bars. She deserved her sentence. We didn't deserve ours. To all the residents rushing to forgive her, I ask what about your neighbors whose futures Sadie Liles stole? Where is your compassion for us? What about our souls?

Her return opens too many old wounds to forgive and move on. Turning Robert's house into an inn doesn't help, because it was meant to be a private home for him and the love of his life. A place to entertain town folk, not cater to strangers. And so, if Sadie chooses to stay, she'll continue to face resistance until she understands how much we've lost and how hard it is to forget.

Mirabelle's invisible pain bristled between the lines and tugged at Emily's heartstrings. Maybe she was right about the inn. Pepper's hint at the truth about Robert Lile's murder, Patsy's story about Mirabelle's infatuation—not to mention Sadie's reaction to the bloodstain—weighed heavy on Emily.

Cody rested his head on her lap, his eyes begging for attention. She scratched behind his ears. "One thing about her letter surprises me—her writing is good."

Scott wandered into the kitchen, opened the fridge, and pulled out a bottle of water.

"Was I talking too loud?"

"Nope. I couldn't fall back asleep without you beside me." He plopped down and rubbed his eyes. "Are you working?"

"Not exactly." She turned the computer toward him. "Take a look at this and tell me what you think."

After reading the letter, he sat back and stretched out his legs. "I think the woman's delusional."

Emily chewed on her fingernail and wrestled with her conscience. She'd promised Patsy she wouldn't share the story about Mirabelle's infatuation with Robert with anyone. But Scott was her soulmate, her other half. She didn't want to keep secrets from him. "I have something to tell you." She lowered her voice and leaned close. "But you have to promise to never repeat it."

He snickered. "Uh oh. It sounds like you're about to fess up to something big. Like smashing the bumper on your car or your secret desire to rob a bank."

"Talk about a wild imagination. No, silly, it's about Mirabelle." She relayed the story, leaving out the detail about Robert Liles taking advantage of her.

"Now I know she's delusional, but at least it explains her actions."

"I wonder what her husband thinks about her infatuation."

"Dollars to donuts he doesn't know anything about it, unless she told him. Do you suppose Jacob will print her letter in the paper?"

"I don't know why he wouldn't."

"How about you? Are you itching to write a response?"

"Unless Jacob insists, I'm leaving this alone. I've already stirred up enough trouble."

"And you're so good at it."

"I'm not sure that's an attribute."

Scott stretched his arms over his head and yawned. "Are you going to the office in the morning?"

"For a little while, before I meet Sadie."

"I don't know about you, but I could use a few more hours of sleep." He winked and stroked her hand. "After a little recreation."

"Are you making me an offer I can't refuse?"

"I sure hope so." Scott pulled Emily to her feet, encircled her waist, and steered her toward the hall. At the bedroom door, he leaned down and scratched Cody's nuzzle. "Sorry, fella, you're not invited to this party."

Chapter 25

Eager to get Jacob's take on Mirabelle's editorial, Emily rushed into the Willow Post headquarters and laid her bag on the table.

Before she could utter a word, Jacob swiveled around. "Have you heard Mirabelle's latest rant?"

"You mean in addition to her letter to the editor?"

"Oh, yeah."

Emily pulled her computer from the bag and opened it. "What's she saying now?"

"She can't find her credit card and claims Sadie stole it."

"Where'd she come up with that theory."

"It seems she left her purse on Pepper's counter when she went to the ladies' room. When she came back and pulled out her wallet to pay for breakfast, she discovered the card was gone."

"I suspect Pepper was furious."

"The way I heard it, she told Mirabelle to stay away from the café until she came to her senses. Mirabelle insisted she was going to get Mitch to investigate."

"I've a good mind to delete her editorial and write one about false accusations. Unless …"

"Unless what?"

The comment Sadie made about learning criminal tactics exploded in Emily's mind. "What if Sadie's guilty? I mean she did spend thirty years living with all kinds of felons."

Jacob glared at Emily. "I can't believe you're siding with Mirabelle."

"I'm just saying it's possible."

"The word is also out on the street about you needing a manager for the inn." Jacob reached across his desk for a manila envelope and handed it to Emily.

"Is this an application for the job?"

"It's my proposal to refurbish the hotel, if the money ever comes through and if you aren't afraid I'll rob you blind."

Emily huffed. "Look, Sadie told me she learned a lot of bad stuff in prison."

"And I read espionage and military thrillers. It doesn't mean I plan to spy on my neighbors or blow up buildings."

"That analogy doesn't make any sense."

"Neither does believing Sadie's a thief."

"Okay, I get your point, so can we move on?"

Jacob nodded and pointed to her computer screen. "I want you to write a follow-up story about the winery for next week's paper. Research the positive impact of Georgia wineries and interview Willow Oak's owner."

"The guy's phone number is in Rachel Streetman's press release." Emily pulled up the email, found the number, and dialed R. Bricker. The call went to voicemail, forcing her to leave a message. She stuffed her computer in her bag. "I'm going out to the property to snap some photos. Any idea how I can find it?"

"Look for a wooden for-sale sign nailed to a tree on the left."

"I know the spot. By the way, I'm meeting Sadie at the inn this afternoon to finish decorating."

"Be sure to hide your credit cards."

"Good grief, can't you let it go?"

He grinned. "It's too much fun to watch you get your dander up."

"You'll have to wait until tomorrow to keep picking on me." She shouldered her bag.

"Say hi to Scott."

"I will." She hiked to her car and drove home to pick up Cody.

A mile outside of town, she found the faded, peeling sign. She pulled off the road and opened the door. Cody bounded over the front seat and out the driver's door to sniff out and claim the unfamiliar location.

While snapping photos, Emily's mind drifted back to her high-school homecoming. Half the senior class hiked to a clearing on the property for an overnight camp-out. She smiled as she remembered the gang gorging on s'mores and struggling to stay awake until dawn. The majority of those classmates no longer lived in Willow Falls. If her father-in-law was still alive, neither would she and Scott. She tried to imagine what life would be like if they lived close to a big city.

Her phone buzzed. "Hello?"

"Ms. Hayes, Brick Bricker, here. I'm returning your call."

"Thank you, sir. I'm not at my desk to take notes. Do you mind if I record our conversation?"

"I promise not to say anything incriminating."

Following a discussion about winemaking, Emily paused to compose another question. "I'm curious. Why did you choose a site away from any big towns?"

"It started the day I walked the land and discovered it had all the characteristics needed to produce a quality crop of grapes. A good sign. So, I headed in to town and stopped for a late lunch in a little restaurant across from a park."

"Pepper's Café."

"That's the place. Anyway, there were a handful of people hanging around. I wanted to keep a lid on my plans—didn't want the property owner to jack the price up—so I explained I liked to take long drives out in the country."

"What was your first impression of Willow Falls?"

"Quaint, with plenty of potential, until I learned the nearest place for visitors to stay was twenty-five miles away. That threw up a big red flag until I learned about an inn some folks were getting ready to open and plans to finish a sixty-room hotel. It's crazy what a stranger can find out with a couple of open-ended questions."

One mystery solved.

"So, I moved forward with my idea until I heard about a big accident not far from the property."

Emily clasped her hand over her mouth to stifle a gasp.

"I was ready to bail until Rachel Streetman convinced me to close the deal. By the way, how's progress on the inn and hotel coming along?"

Her mouth went dry. Should she give him all the ugly details or fudge the facts? If he knew the truth, would he abandon his plans? She cleared her throat and forced an upbeat tone. "Funny you should ask. As soon as I hang up, I'm heading over to the inn to help finish decorating. We'll have everything up and running long before you harvest your first grapes." She held her breath and crossed her fingers, hoping he wouldn't ask more questions.

"That's good to know. I'll head back to town and take another look around one day soon."

Emily exhaled. "I look forward to meeting you." She ended the call and pocketed her phone.

Cody romped to her side, panting, his tongue hanging from his mouth. Emily stroked his head. "I made a promise, now I have to find a way to keep it. Come on, fella, we've got a lot of work to do."

Back in town, she pulled into the inn's driveway, stepped out of the car, and opened the back door.

Moments later, Sadie walked past the hotel and turned onto the sidewalk leading to the front steps. Cody jumped out and greeted her with an exuberant tail wag. She patted his head. "If I'd known you were coming, I would've brought you a chew bone."

Emily closed the car doors. "Last-minute decision."

The trio climbed the stairs and walked into the foyer.

Sadie nodded toward the parlor. "Did Scott bring the ladder?"

"It's in there, along with a hammer, picture-hanging hooks, and a tape measure." Emily clamped her jaw to resist questioning her about Mirabelle's missing credit card.

"Good place to start." Sadie carried her mother's favorite landscape into the parlor, set it down by the hearth, and put the ladder in place. "People are talking about you needing a manager to run the inn."

"I need someone to do more than talk."

"The right person is bound to step up."

"All I can say is it'd better happen fast."

Sadie climbed up and stretched the tape measure across the space. She found the center, marked it with a piece of chalk, and pulled a picture-hanging hook from her pocket. "I'm ready for the hammer."

Emily handed it to her.

She nailed the hook in place, hoisted the painting up, and straightened it. Then she climbed down and stepped back. "What do you think?"

"It's perfect."

"Just like it was when Mama lived here." She sniffed. "Come on. We've got lots more pictures to hang and pretty things to put out."

Two hours later, accessories and wall décor adorned the downstairs rooms. Additional pieces were stacked on the first four steps of the grand staircase.

"I could use a break before we head upstairs." Emily moseyed into the parlor. Sadie followed.

"You sure are a hard worker."

"I learned to stay busy in jail. It helped make time go faster."

A knock on the door, followed by a cheery hello, announced Pepper's arrival. "I brought you ladies some refreshments." She carried a picnic basket into the parlor and set it on an antique sideboard between two tall, etched-glassed windows. "Wow, it looks like professional decorators did a number to this room. You two are doing a great job."

Emily dropped into a wingback chair and massaged the back of her neck. "The credit goes to my partner. She made all the decisions."

Sadie settled on the settee, kicked her shoes off, and propped her feet on the smoke-glass top of the vintage neoclassical coffee table. "The upstairs rooms don't have enough furniture. We should go to Nathan's store and buy more."

"That's not gonna happen." Emily crossed a leg over her knee and pumped her foot. "I need to save the little bit of money left in Mom and Dad's business account to keep the lights on and pay an innkeeper until this place generates revenue."

Pepper carried a tray of lemonade, finger sandwiches, and cookies to the coffee table. "What about Nora and Roger's house?"

Emily's foot stopped. "What are you suggesting?"

"You could finish the rooms with your parents' furniture. Unless you and Scott are planning to take everything."

Shocked by the suggestion, she uncrossed her legs and moved to the bay window facing the front porch. Cody followed and sat beside her. She dropped to her knees, wrapped an arm around his neck, and let tears flow as the weight of Bricker's expectations and the prospect of going through her parents' belongings pressed down on her.

Pepper hastened across the room and knelt beside her. "I'm sorry for being so abrupt."

"I know you're just trying to help, and I suppose it makes sense to bring their things here. It's just … I haven't been to their home since they've been gone."

"Maybe it's best not to put it off any longer."

She let the comment linger. "I suppose you're right. I'd need help deciding what to put where."

"How about I close the café Wednesday when my last breakfast customers leave and help you?"

Sadie moved behind Emily and touched her shoulder. "You can count me in as well."

Grateful she and Scott chose to live in Willow Falls, Emily wiped her eyes with her sleeve and thanked God for her old—and new—friend.

Chapter 26

Rachel exited the elevator with a spring in her step and stopped at Nancy's desk. "Did anything exciting happen while I was gone?"

Her assistant stared at her. "You must have found a miracle cure for your cold, because you look like a New York newbie who landed a starring role on Broadway. "

"A few days off and chicken soup did the trick." Rachel strolled into her office, closed the door, and stood in front of the window. "Hello, adoring fans. I present Rachel Streetman, playing the role of a woman confused by a guy who drives a truck and listens to country music. Act One, the first date."

She paused and pulled her ringing phone from her purse. "Good morning."

"It's getting better every second." Charlie's voice oozed charm. "Any chance you can get away and join me for lunch?"

Rachel hesitated. She rarely left the office at lunchtime unless she had a meeting with a client. But Charlie was a client, or at least related to one.

"Or are you too busy?"

"I'll make time. How about noon at the café in the Peachtree Plaza? I'll meet you there."

"It's a date."

She dropped her phone in her purse. "Act Two, lunch." She headed to her desk, booted her computer, and continued researching north Georgia. Memories from Saturday night kept creeping into her thoughts. "Stop it, Rachel, you're acting like a silly schoolgirl again. It's one date with a guy you've known for a handful of days." She poured a glass of water and forced her mind to focus on work.

A half-hour later, Brent swung her door open. "I heard you were back."

She glared at him. "Did you forget how to knock? Or doesn't a closed door mean anything to you."

147

He trudged to the chair in front of her desk. "Now I know what the term fiery redhead means."

"Why'd you storm in here like a hungry bear attacking a campsite?"

"To find out how you're doing. I called you a couple of times when you were home, but you didn't answer."

I can't believe he doesn't get the hint. "I was too sick to talk."

"You must have recovered fast, because you look fine." Brent laced his fingers and tapped his thumbs. "How about going to lunch with me to make up for rejecting my calls?"

Rachel closed her computer. "Look, you're a smart guy and you have a great future with Streetman Enterprise. But you have to understand I'm not interested in anything other than a professional relationship. So, please, do us both a favor and stop pushing."

His eyes narrowed. "You're seeing someone, aren't you?"

"With all due respect, my personal life doesn't concern you."

"Did playboy Charlie cast his spell on you?"

She clenched her hands. "Like I told you, what I do away from the office is none of your business."

"I don't know what's going on with you, but if Greer finds out, he's not going to take your attitude lying down."

"This is between you and me. It has nothing to do with my father."

"If I wasn't a gentleman … but I am, so I'll wait for you to come to your senses before I come back." Brent stood and headed to the door.

Fearing Brent would run tell her father as if he were a grade-school tattletale once again summoned images of shackles inching toward her ankles like slithering snakes. A knot formed in the pit of her stomach. She couldn't bear another scene before lunch. She grabbed her purse and dashed from her office.

Nancy looked up from her desk. "I'm sorry about Brent barging in on you. I didn't have a rope to lasso him to the ground."

Rachel touched her arm. "It's hard to stop a raging bully. I'm going out. If anyone asks, I'm running errands and you don't know when I'll return."

"I've got you covered."

On the way to the elevator, Rachel silenced her phone and checked her watch—forty minutes to kill before meeting Charlie. Outside, she dug her sunglasses from her purse and made her way to Centennial Park where a breeze ruffled cherry trees, sending blossoms floating to the ground like fat snowflakes. The splash of water cascading from the Olympic ring fountain drowned out the roar of traffic. She remembered running through the fountain with friends while her mother laughed and took pictures.

She found a seat, tucked her purse under her arm, and engaged in a new activity—people watching. A senior couple eased onto the adjacent bench and held hands. As snippets of their conversation drifted toward her, Rachel tried to imagine where she'd be in forty years.

A ball, chased by a young boy, rolled in her direction and landed at her feet. She picked it up and tossed it to him. "Here you go, young man."

"When I grow up, I'm gonna be a soccer player."

"Do you play on a team now?"

"Uh huh. I'm the goalie."

"You hold on to your dream, and practice real hard."

An elderly woman caught up with him. "This boy's going to be the death of me yet."

He tucked the ball under his arm. "You run too slow, Grammy."

The woman gripped his hand. "And you run too fast. Come on, slugger, I'll buy us a couple of hot fudge sundaes."

Just what he needs, thought Emily, *a big dose of sugar*. As she watched grandmother and grandson walk toward the CNN building, she wished she'd found the courage to follow her own dreams before it became too late.

The elderly couple helped each other off the bench and stepped over to her. The woman smiled at Rachel. "I heard what you said to that little boy. You looked so sad when he walked away, like you let something or someone you loved get away. I hope you don't think I'm an old busybody, but I want to tell you it's never too late to get back what you lost."

Rachel's jaw dropped as she watched the couple link arms and stroll out of the park. Why would a stranger make such an outrageous comment? Or was it? She'd lived with the belief her dream was shattered for so long, her mind couldn't fathom another option.

A satellite truck from a local television station pulled to the curb. The same station where the woman she met at the theater worked. The blogger. The amateur actor. She reached in her purse for Alicia's business card. Should she call? She glanced at her watch. "Oh, no, I'm late."

Rachel pocketed the card, rushed to the Peachtree Plaza, and found Charlie waiting at the café entrance.

"I was about to think I'd been stood up."

"Sorry, I lost track of time."

"A busy executive's occupational hazard." His arm slipped around her shoulders. "For the next couple of hours, you're off duty. So no talk about business. Are you hungry?"

She breathed in his scent—clean and masculine. "I'm starving."

They found a seat, ordered, and continued conversations from Saturday night. During lunch, Charlie's lighthearted banter warmed her heart. When her fork dug into their shared dessert and touched his fork, a tingling sensation traveled from her fingertips to her heart and sparked an image of his name scrolled on her otherwise empty list of suitors.

Long after paying the bill, Charlie glanced at his phone. "I'd like to spend the rest of the afternoon with you, but I've got a three-thirty call with the guy I hired to plant my vineyard."

"I need to get back to work as well."

He moved to her side of the table and pulled her chair out. On the sidewalk in front of the hotel, he kissed her hand. "Until Sunday."

Rachel's mood and smile remained until she strolled into the office and saw Nancy's face. "Uh oh. Something's wrong."

"Your dad's been calling for hours. I can't tell if he's angry or worried sick. I told him you had errands to run and most likely stopped for lunch."

"Thanks for covering for me." Rachel pulled her phone from her purse. Five missed calls. Three from Greer. Two from Brent. She resisted the urge to flee, sauntered to her father's office, and spoke to his assistant. "I hear Mr. Streetman is looking for me."

The woman buzzed her boss and nodded. "Go on in."

Rachel opened the door and moved to a chair facing his desk. "Sorry I missed your calls."

"Where have you been?"

"I took a walk and ate some lunch. After suffering from a nasty cold, I needed a big dose of sunshine and exercise to get my strength back."

He glared at her. "Brent thinks you met Charlie Bricker. I told you to steer clear of the guy."

In her absence, it appeared her father's rising star had taken on the role of watch dog in charge of keeping the boss updated on his little girl's personal life. Heat flushed through Rachel's body. "Where I go and who I go with doesn't concern him. And what I do outside this office is on my personal time."

Anger overpowered her sense of duty and loyalty. "In here, I'm your employee, but when I leave this building, I'm your daughter. So, please treat me with some fatherly respect."

The vein in Greer's neck pulsed. "Don't get all bent out of shape." His tone was unsympathetic. "It's my job to make sure nothing or no one keeps you from the role you were born to fill—the future leader of my company." He pointed his finger at her. "And you know my policy about staff mingling romantically with clients."

His father's a client, not Charlie. Rachel dug deep to find another reservoir of courage. *Tell him he's wrong about your destiny. Now's your chance. Don't let it pass.* The words formed on the tip of her tongue.

Greer's assistant knocked on the door. "Your three-thirty appointment is here, sir."

"Show him in." He stood to greet his guest. "Hank, I want you to meet my daughter."

Rachel swallowed hard, forced a smile, and extended her hand. "Pleasure to meet you, sir. I have work to do, so I'll leave you two alone."

She fled to her office to find refuge and sort through conflicting emotions. Satisfaction for standing up to her father, regret for missing the chance to tell him the truth, and resolve to continue seeing Charlie.

She dropped on her office chair, reached for her mother's photo, and held it to her chest. "You have no idea how much I miss you." A new sensation shot through her—fierce determination to take control of her life. She pulled Alicia's card from her pocket, dialed the number, and left a message.

Chapter 27

Rachel closed her laptop and glanced at her watch. Because her father expected his executives to continue working long after their support staff headed home, she rarely left the office before seven. "Not today." She reached for her purse and hurried out the door.

Nancy looked up from clearing her desk. "I didn't know you had a client meeting."

"I don't."

"You mean you're leaving at five with the minions?"

"Nope, I'm leaving with the backbone of this company. And if the mood strikes me, I'll come in late tomorrow."

"Wow, you're turning over a new leaf."

"Maybe I am, thanks to your suggestion."

After engaging support staff in light-hearted conversation on the elevator, Rachel exited at the parking garage and aimed her key fob at her car. She climbed in and tossed her purse on the passenger seat.

Her phone buzzed. She smiled, hoping to hear Charlie's voice. A quick glance vanished the possibility. She considered ignoring the call until she recognized the number.

"Alicia?"

"Hi, sorry I didn't return your call earlier. I was in the middle of an interview."

"I understand."

"What's up?"

Rachel pushed her key into the ignition. "I've been thinking about our conversation and ... I want to hear more about your improv group."

"I had a feeling I'd hear from you. Where are you?"

"Getting ready to leave downtown."

"Perfect. We're meeting tonight at a church near Lennox Square. If you don't have any plans, why don't you come on over and join us?"

Rachel stared through the windshield at the gray cement wall. *What if ... no, it doesn't matter what my father or anyone else thinks.* "Good idea."

She entered the address in her navigational system, pressed a button to play a Broadway CD, and drove out of the garage. To ease the tension created by maneuvering through heavy traffic, she sang along with the music until she arrived at her destination.

When she pulled into the parking lot, reality struck. With the exception of a couple of weddings, she hadn't stepped inside a church since her mother died. Staring at the massive, white columns adorning the front entrance prompted a question. Did God know or even care? She dismissed the thought as an illogical stab of guilt, stepped out her car, and headed toward the activity building.

As she neared the room Alicia had described, second thoughts gave her pause. A man with pale skin and a Greek-theater-mask tattoo on his forearm approached. "Are you looking for the improv group?"

She nodded.

"Come with me."

Rachel followed him into a large space painted pale-blue, smelling of vanilla, with chairs arranged in a semi-circle.

Alicia popped up. "Hey, everyone, I want you to meet my new friend, Rachel Streetman." When she finished introducing everyone, the group formed a circle and joined hands. Alicia closed her eyes and launched into a fervent prayer.

Rachel's muscles tensed. Had she been snookered into meeting a group of fanatics tasked with attracting newcomers to their strange cult? Should she escape now while she had a chance? At the sound of Alicia's amen, she clutched her purse to her side, ready to flee. Until her new friend announced the acting assignment.

"Okay, fellow players, tonight our task is to portray a drunk who finds a church envelope full of cash and struggles with a moral dilemma."

Rachel's shoulders relaxed. She selected a seat, settled down, placed her purse on the floor, and watched the first player step to the middle of the circle.

During the interpretations, Rachel's mind drifted back to her college days. Every time she auditioned for a play, she landed a lead role. The hours she spent rehearsing and performing compensated for the mundane classes she endured to satisfy her father's plan for her life.

Despite her loyalty to his wishes, she had held on to a tiny hope of breaking free and following her own path. Until he managed to attend one performance, the last night of *42nd Street*. He presented her with a bouquet of roses and said, *Nice job, Strawberry Girl, but it's time to grow up and take your place in the real world*. Tonight, for the first time since he uttered those gut-wrenching words, she was in the presence of like-minded people.

The tattooed man pointed to Alicia. "You're up last."

"I'm ready." Her comedic interpretation of a tipsy woman in a conversation with an angel on one shoulder and the devil on the other elicited laughter and handclaps. When she finished, she approached Rachel and whispered. "I don't want to put you on the spot, but you're welcome to take a turn."

"Thanks, but no thanks. Especially following your brilliant performance. Your acting is amazing. Why aren't you a professional?"

"The demands of parenthood." Alicia sat beside her. "It takes my husband's salary—he's a police officer—and mine to raise and educate our three sons. Don't get me wrong, I'm not complaining. I enjoy my job and I adore my family." A smile lit her face. "But this experience and my blog nourish my love for performing. Not to mention keeping my skills honed. When our sons are grown and on their own, and I can afford to retire, I might pursue a second career as a pro."

"What about the rest of the group?"

"All amateurs, although the two guys and Tammy have performed in small, regional theaters. We meet right here, every other week. You're welcome to join us."

"Do you six make up the entire group?"

Alicia shook her head. "We're ten strong, but seldom does everyone show up at the same time. We all have busy lives."

The opportunity to perform in front of a small group of flesh and blood people instead of a phantom audience appealed to Rachel. Not to mention the prospect of defying her father. "I'll think about it."

"Okay. For now, I've got to get home to my boys, but I'd love to do lunch sometime."

"I'd like that." Rachel pulled a business card from her wallet. "Give me a call when you get a chance."

"Will do." Alicia stood, took a step toward the door, and paused. "By the way, I invite my followers to comment on my blog posts. I don't know how you feel about writing, but your comments about the comedy at Alliance were insightful."

"Are you asking me to contribute?"

"If you want to and if you have time."

"I suppose I can come up with something."

On the way back to her car, Rachel stopped to gaze at the elaborate steeple stretching high above the church. The stark-white color stood out as a beacon in the sunset-filled sky. Why did Alicia's prayer unleash so much cynicism? Maybe she shouldn't wait for a wedding invitation to venture inside a church.

Another thought floated in her mind. Was it possible meeting Charlie and Alicia and connecting with Emily were more than random coincidences?

She dismissed both questions as absurd.

Chapter 28

Rachel punched the remote to close her garage door and climbed the stairs to the main level of her townhouse. Energized by her secret visit to the improv group, she poured a glass of Chardonnay, sat at the kitchen table, and opened her computer.

She'd never written a post for a blog or, for that matter, ever read one. To get an idea about the process, she found Alicia's blog page and read her entries. It looked simple enough. She positioned her hands on the keyboard and mentally returned to the Alliance theater to assess the plot, the pacing, and the dialogue, which still made her laugh. Within moments, her impressions flowed from her head to her fingertips.

Twenty minutes later, she read her analysis and tapped her glass to the computer screen. "Good work, considering it's your first post." She emailed a copy to Alicia, along with a thank you for inviting her to improv.

Too stimulated to sleep, she strolled into her living room—decorated in a tasteful blend of contemporary and traditional style. With a heightened sense of awareness, she ran her fingers along the back of her diamond-patterned couch. The soft, velvety fabric invoked memories of her favorite stuffed animal. A life-size, brown-and-white puppy—a gift from her mother on her seventh birthday when her father refused to grant her wish for a real dog. She'd slept with Brownie all through elementary and middle school. Was he still packed in a box in her father's attic? One of these days she'd muster the courage to ask him.

She plopped down on the couch, aimed the remote at the television, flipped through channels, and landed on an old episode of *The Andy Griffith Show*. Barnie's antics reminded her of a character in the play she critiqued. Did interesting people like him and Andy and Aunt Bee live in Willow Falls? Maybe she should make the trip to north Georgia and find out.

Her phone rang. She muted the TV. "Hi, Charlie."

"I hope it's not too late to call."

"Any time before ten is fine."

"I take it you're not a night owl."

"I need my eight hours and I'm up before six, so not usually. What about you?"

"It depends on what I've got going on, but I'm mostly a morning guy." He paused. "During lunch this afternoon I didn't answer your question about past relationships."

She had regretted asking the moment he took a bite of his sandwich and changed the subject. "Not a problem. The truth is, we haven't known each other long enough for me to pry into your personal life."

"You had every right to ask. And I want us to be honest with each other from the get-go."

Rachel pulled her knees up to her chest and wrapped one arm around her shins. *Uh oh.*

"Here's the thing. Six years ago, I was engaged."

I guess he's not opposed to marriage.

"She was a tall, drop-dead-gorgeous blonde."

I wonder how he'd describe me? Short and cute?

"We met at a party and hit it off like gangbusters." He cleared his throat. "In less than a week, our relationship ... let's just say it got real serious, real fast."

Rachel winced. "You don't have to continue."

"Yeah, I do. She loved to flirt and have a good time—any place the booze flowed and her wild circle of friends showed up. At first, it was fun, and I for darn sure didn't want her to get away. So, two months later, I gave her a diamond ring."

I don't like where this is going.

"Dad tried to tell me I was moving too fast. I didn't listen. Instead, I pushed her to set a wedding date. She resisted, claiming marriage was too confining for anyone younger than thirty. The truth is, she wanted to keep her options open. Six months after she accepted my ring, she ditched me for some hot-shot, professional football player."

"I'm so sorry."

"Don't be. Like a fool, I jumped into the relationship with blinders on."

Rachel bit her lower lip. "I guess it all worked out for the best."

"Yeah, I learned my lesson. All my relationships since have been short and casual. That's all I've got say about the matter." He paused for a long moment. "It's strange, I haven't shared the story with anyone except you."

She watched Barnie accidently lock himself in Mayberry's jail cell. What compelled Charlie to confess? Guilt? Respect?

"How about you?"

Or a clever ploy to pry into her past?

"Any regrets in your love life?"

What love life? Other than a two-year, high-school crush, she hadn't seriously dated anyone. She pictured her empty list of suitors. "I've been too consumed with work to have much of a social life."

"That's one way to avoid mistakes."

"I suppose."

"Anyway, are we still on for Sunday?"

She lowered her feet to the floor and shifted her phone to her other ear. If she backed out now, he'd think she didn't value honesty. "Of course."

"Good. Can I pick you up at six? That will give us enough time to eat before the play."

"Sounds good."

Rachel waited to find out what happened to Barney before clicking the remote and heading upstairs. She changed into her pajamas, climbed into bed, and reached for the novel on her nightstand—a modern take on *Romeo and Juliet.* The love story roused a thought and warmed her heart. Maybe Charlie shared his story because he envisioned a future with her. She drifted off to sleep with visions of him dancing in her head.

Chapter 29

Startled by Cody's bark, Emily gripped the arm rest in Scott's Chevy. He pulled into her parents' driveway and turned off the engine.

"Why didn't I remember to grab the garage door remote?" She released her grip and wiped moisture off the inside of the windshield. "We're going to get soaked to the bone."

Cody pressed his nose against the side window, while his tail slapped against the back of the driver's seat. Fat raindrops pelted the car and drowned out his panting.

Scott leaned across the back of the seat and scratched the dog's back. "No need to get all worked up, they're not in the house."

Emily clutched her purse in her lap. "Maybe we should back out and go home."

"No way we're gonna let a little storm scare us off. Besides, Pepper and Sadie are due to show up in three hours. We need to decide what's going to our house and pack it all up before they get here."

He cracked the door open and pushed an umbrella up. "Here goes." The second he stepped out of the car, Cody jumped over the front seat and leapt past him. "Crazy dog darn near knocked me down."

"It's a good thing you're bigger than Cody, otherwise you'd be flat on your backside in a puddle of water." Emily scooted across the console. She huddled under the umbrella with Scott and dashed to the front door.

He shook water from the umbrella. She wiped her feet on the doormat and fished a key from her purse. "I don't know if I can do this." She hesitated before pressing it in the lock.

"It's okay, honey, you're not alone." He placed his hand over hers and turned the doorknob.

Cody squeezed past them and raced through the living room into the kitchen. The sound of his paws clicking on the wood floors echoed through the downstairs. He rounded the corner in the dining room and sped up the stairs. Moments later, he padded down with his tail tucked. He looked up at Emily and whimpered.

She dropped to her knees and stroked his neck. "He doesn't understand that Mom and Dad are gone. They're never coming back here."

Cody licked her face, then dropped to his belly and laid his jaw on his front paws.

Scott knelt beside Emily. "Don't worry about Cody. He'll adjust."

"I know, but the question is, will I?" She pressed her hand to her tummy. "Another kick from one of our babies."

"Perfect timing." He helped her to her feet. "Where do you want to start?"

"I think in the living room." She took a deep breath and moved to the fireplace mantel. "Do you know what Mom told me before the photographer snapped this?" She picked up a photo of her posing with her parents before she walked down the aisle to marry Scott.

"You were about to make the biggest mistake of your life?"

"Not a chance. She said, next to her, I'd landed the best catch east of the Mississippi."

"I guess it's good you didn't spend any time west of the mighty river."

Emily thumped his arm. "Yeah, who knows what hunk of a guy I might've found." She winked, returned the photo to the mantel, then gazed around the room. She pointed to a matching pair of throw pillows embellishing the blue-and-white striped couch. "Those date back twenty-nine years—welcome-to-town gifts from Patsy."

"No kidding? I'm surprised they aren't covered with peacock feathers."

"If they were hats they would be." She reached for one and hugged it to her chest. "These are going to our house."

Scott retrieved a flattened box from a stack in the foyer, assembled it, and carried it to her. "Good start. What goes in next?"

She picked up a throw blanket draped over the back of a recliner. "For the nursery. Oh, and all the pictures on the mantel."

"What about the furniture?"

"It's all going to the inn, except for a few bedroom pieces." She took one more look around. "I think I'm finished in here."

Emily crossed through the foyer and entered the dining room. An overwhelming sense of loss sent a tremble through her. She gripped the back of a chair to keep her balance.

Scott stepped behind her and wrapped his arms around her waist. "We enjoyed a lot of family dinners in this room."

"What if I forget?" Her voice faltered. "What if time erases all those memories?"

"Not a chance."

"I have to make sure." She released her grip on the chair, slipped away from Scott, and opened the china cabinet's upper glass doors. "I'm taking all of Mom's formal dishes. When our daughters are old enough to sit at our table, I'll fix some of her favorite recipes and tell them how their four amazing grandparents are up in heaven watching over their grandbabies."

She opened the bottom doors and pulled out a dinner plate. "I also want all her holiday china. Mom loved Christmas. It took her two weeks to decorate. Dad teased her about boosting the electric company's profit with all the lights."

"Yeah, Willow Falls' holiday season didn't officially begin until Nora opened her house for a tour."

"She had a tree in every room, each one with a different theme. For years, Dad drove her to Atlanta the day after Christmas so she could take advantage of big discounts on decorations."

"What do you want to do with all of it?"

"I don't know yet. We can keep everything in the attic until I decide what to do with their house."

"Good idea." Scott assembled another box, grabbed a stack of newspaper, and began packing dishes. "I'll pack all this up while you decide what else you want from downstairs."

She strolled into the paneled den and dropped on her dad's recliner. She and Scott watched nearly every Super Bowl since their high-school days in this room. She'd never forget her dad's expression when the Atlanta Falcons lost in overtime.

Cody moseyed in, clenched a pair of her dad's slippers in his teeth, and dropped them at Emily's feet. She laughed and choked back tears. "I have to teach you to do that for Scott."

He barked and wagged his tail.

An hour later, she stood at the foot of the stairs and studied the array of family photos embellishing the stairwell wall. "We're definitely taking all these pictures."

Scott stepped beside her. "I'll take care of them last."

They climbed the stairs and turned toward her old bedroom—long ago transformed into a guest room. Emily leaned against the door frame and hugged her arms to her chest. "Do you remember back in our high-school days when we sat in here on the floor doing homework?"

"Yeah, and every fifteen minutes, your father checked to make sure the door was open. It was hard to steal a kiss with the warden watching over us."

"How do you suppose you'll respond when our baby girls become teenagers and think they're head-over-heels in love?"

"Are you kidding? Boys will have to sit through an hour-long Q and A session under my eagle eye before they come within ten feet of my daughters."

Emily wrapped her arms around him. "Daddy warden in action?"

He stroked her back. "You bet, mama bear. So, what do you want me to pack up from this room?"

She glanced over her shoulder. "The antique, silver mirror over there on the dresser. It belonged to my grandmother. Everything else goes to the inn." She released Scott, picked up the mirror, and ambled down the hall.

Inside the home office, Emily pulled a chair away from her grandfather's antique cherry desk. "The stories this could tell."

"Didn't one of his clients give it to him to pay for legal work?"

"Uh huh. Back then, country lawyers didn't make much money. He used to say the cost of doing a will was fifty dollars or a chicken and a bushel of tomatoes."

"If business doesn't pick up soon, I might resort to trading merchandise for food."

Emily grinned. "Make sure the chickens come from the grocery store and not someone's back yard."

"Hey, what kind of country girl are you if you aren't willing to pluck feathers before frying up a bird?"

"A smart one." She dropped to her knees, opened the bottom drawer, and pulled out file folders filled with financial papers, deeds, and business contracts. Overwhelming sadness filled her chest as she read her parent's birth certificates and marriage license. "I want to find Mom's wedding dress before I leave. I think it's in her closet."

She removed the last file and rifled through the papers. "I don't believe it. I hit the jackpot."

"Let me guess. Documents signed by a Civil War general, worth a fortune?"

"I wish. They're details about the hotel renovation. Everything Jacob needs to get the job done."

"It sounds like you're taking my advice and getting on board with his offer."

"I promised Mr. Bricker the hotel would open, and Jacob's proposal was spot on, so yeah, I'm accepting it."

"Does he know?"

"Not yet." She tossed the file on top of the desk with the other documents, gripped the edge of the desk, and pulled up.

"Hold on, there's something else in the drawer." Scott reached to the back. He retrieved a manila envelope with a thick layer of tape sealing the flap. "It's marked personal. What do you suppose this is?" He handed it to Emily.

"I bet these are the letters."

"From a famous general?"

"No, silly. The love letters my parents wrote to each other when Dad worked on a construction crew out of the country for six months, before I was born. Mom told me one day when she and Dad were way up in years they'd bring her comfort." Her voice lowered to a whisper. "When our daughters are older, I'll open the envelope and read the letters to them."

"Sadie and I are here. Are you guys upstairs?" Cody's ears perked up from the sound of Pepper's voice drifting up from below.

Scott stepped to the door. "Yeah, come on up."

Emily dropped the envelope in a box with the other files and stretched her arms over her head.

"From the looks of the boxes in the foyer, I'd say you two got a lot done," said Pepper as she stepped into the office.

Scott closed the box flap and hoisted it to his shoulder. "I suspect you three ladies don't need a guy getting in your way. Pepper, if you'll drive my wife to the store when you finish here, I'll go open shop. Someone might decide to come in today and trade a chicken for a bag of kitchen tools."

Pepper laughed. "Is livestock your new currency of choice?"

"Nope, the chickens have to be cleaned and ready to cook." He kissed Emily's cheek. "I'll see you later."

"Thanks for your help, honey. Oh, don't forget the stairwell photos."

"I've got it covered."

Sadie moved to the built-in bookcases lining one wall and pulled a Francine Rivers novel off the shelf. "There was a broom-closet-sized library in prison. Filled mostly with tattered, old books nobody wanted. I think I read every one in there at least once."

"I'm taking some of Mom's favorites with me." Emily smiled. "She loved books about the South, especially Eugenia Price's novels. And, of course, *Gone with the Wind*. I'll send the rest to Willow Inn. Dad built the bookcases in the little library nook between the parlor and downstairs suite for our guests to relax and read."

Sadie flipped the book over and tapped the back cover. "Is it okay if I borrow this one?"

"Better yet," Emily said, "I'll give you this and nine more as gifts for helping me."

"You don't have to."

She touched Sadie's hand. "I know, but I want to."

Her eyes moistened. "Thank you."

"You're welcome."

"Which nine?"

"You decide. But first, tell me where you think we should put the desk."

Sadie clutched the book to her chest and tapped a brass drawer pull. "I bet this piece is older than me."

"It dates back two generations to my grandfather." Emily shared the trade-for-work story.

"With that history, it definitely belongs in the foyer as the check-in desk."

Emily sighed and mumbled, "If someone steps up as innkeeper."

Pepper tapped her shoulder. "And if your guests don't rely on the barter system to book a room."

She laughed. "It depends on what they bring to trade. What about the rest of this furniture?"

Sadie laid the book on the desk and removed a notepad and a pencil from her jeans pocket. "Maybe the sofa, end tables, and lamps can go to an upstairs bedroom?" Sadie tapped a pencil to her chin. "The one in the front over the dining room. What do you think?"

"I like it."

"And the series of architectural prints—"

"Dad's favorites."

"The middle bedroom is more masculine. How about hanging them in there?"

Emily nodded. "That takes care of the office." She stepped to the door and stared across the hall.

Pepper stood beside her. "The last room to tackle?"

"I can't put it off any longer." She willed her legs to carry her into her parents' bedroom. Cody plodded past her, laid his head on the four-poster bed, and whimpered.

Emily choked back tears. Her dad's favorite baseball cap hung on a closet door knob. Her mom's Bible lay open on the nightstand. She picked up a dark-red pillow embellishing the gold bedspread and held it to her nose. The faint scent of Chanel Number 5 clinging to the fabric evoked a mountain of memories. Baking cookies with her mother for the church bazaar. Shopping trips to Atlanta. Nora's gleam when she first learned she was a grandmother.

Pepper traced the pattern on an intricately carved bedpost. "It's beautiful."

"A wedding gift from Grandma and Grandpa Redding."

"You and Scott should take it."

Emily sat on the edge of the bed and stroked Cody's head. She couldn't imagine making love to her husband in her parents' bed. "No, it has to go to the inn. One upstairs guest suite still needs a bed."

"That room is too small." Sadie tapped her pencil on a chest of drawers. "You know, there's enough furniture in here to fill the garage apartment behind the inn."

"Mom's favorite suite." Tears trickled down Emily's cheek. "She wanted to spend a romantic weekend there with Dad … before the inn opened."

Pepper pulled a tissue from a box on the bedside table and handed it to Emily. "One day, you'll take your daughters up there and tell them stories about their amazing grandparents."

Emily wiped her cheeks and pointed her thumb over her shoulder. "Everything goes to the apartment. Except the dresser. I'm taking it for the nursery."

She sniffed and tapped Pepper's arm. "You and Mom are about the same size. Will you come back another day and pick out the clothes you want?"

"Of course, but you have to take all her jewelry."

"I know." Emily held up her left hand, splayed her fingers, and stared at her mother's engagement ring. "First, I have to find her wedding dress." She ambled to the closet and pointed to a cedar-lined box on the top shelf. "That's it. Pepper, you're taller than me. Can you reach it?"

"I think I can." She retrieved the box and carried it to the bed.

Emily stepped back and noticed a cardboard box on the floor marked *Emily's Treasures*. She picked it up and laid it on top of dresser. "One of these days I'll find out what Mom kept."

She moved to the bed, lifted the cover off the wedding-dress box, and peeled back a layer of white tissue paper. She touched the delicate white lace and imagined her mother strolling down the aisle to become one with her father. "After all these years, they were still madly in love." She closed the box and held it close. "They had so many good years left, with so much to offer."

She tamped down her anger and lumbered to the door. "Sadie, decide where to put the guest room furniture while I get us some bottles of water from the kitchen."

At the top of the stairwell, Emily gawked at a dozen empty picture-hanging hooks. Another stark reminder of her loss. Needing to hear Scott's reassuring voice, she found her purse, dug for her phone, and discovered a missed call from Savannah. She crossed her fingers and punched in the number.

The momentary hope for good news vanished in an instant. Ben Craw-ford had left his office ten minutes earlier—another emergency trip. His assistant didn't know how long he'd be gone. Why couldn't he call her from someplace other than his office?

Reality gripped her. Maybe he changed his mind about the money. Emily pressed her fingers to her temples. She envisioned her parents' plan to refurbish the hotel disappearing into oblivion like ashes from a dying bonfire drifting away in a cold night sky.

Chapter 30

Rachel crossed her arms and leaned back in the chair facing her father's desk. *Why didn't I find an excuse to avoid this useless meeting?*

She tuned out the conversation between her father and Brent and eyed the original Remington horse-and-rider statue holding center stage on his credenza. A beautiful piece, which stood in stark contrast to the Picasso-like painting—by some hot, up-and-coming young artist—hanging on the wall above. Two photographs completed the arrangement. One of her posing with her father at a ceremony honoring him with a lifetime achievement award, the other of him shaking hands with Georgia's governor. His choice of office ornamentation was consistent with his need to surround himself with expensive items and status symbols.

Brent's outrageous boast about motivating Bricker to sign a contract for the winery property caught her attention and roused her indignation. The man had no shame. She wanted to set the record straight but didn't want to deal with the two-to-one odds against her.

Greer propped his forearms on his desk. "You two make a darn-good team." He nodded toward Rachel. "Can you clear your schedule tomorrow night and join Brent for another client dinner?" His tone was more demand than question.

Brent's smug expression churned her stomach. She vowed to have it out with him in private.

Her phone vibrated. She glanced at the screen and cleared her throat. "I need to return a client's call. I'll get back to you about tomorrow night." Before either man could respond, she rushed out of the office.

Back in her own space, Rachel closed the door and pressed Charlie's number. "Sorry I missed your call. I had to escape a meeting with the king of the hill and his number one knight."

"Your father and Brent?"

"Bingo, you win the prize for best guess. So, what's up?"

"I have a request and a business proposition. What do you want to hear first?"

At least he wasn't calling with another confession about his past girlfriends. Rachel strolled across her office, settled on her desk chair, and rested her head against the back. "I think the latter."

"Before I meet with the vineyard land-clearing crew, I'd welcome a second pair of eyes to help me make some decisions."

"You want me to go to Willow Falls with you?"

"I'm thinking a Saturday. Strictly business, at least for a few hours."

Her spine stiffened. "What do you mean?"

"The next day we can play tourist and hike up to the waterfall the town's named after. Which is where the request comes in. Can you call your reporter friend and find us a place to stay the night? Two rooms, of course."

Charlie's revelation about the drop-dead-gorgeous blonde exploded in her head. Was he expecting their relationship—as he put it—to get real serious, real fast? Had she given him any indication he could make such a move?

Curiosity about the town and Charlie's intentions collided with angst over an inappropriate trip with a guy she barely knew. *He hasn't even kissed me, so maybe it is safe to say yes. But, then again, am I foolish to trust him?* Besides, how could she leave town without her father finding out?

"Your silence speaks volumes."

She closed her eyes and pressed fingertips against her temple. "Sorry, I'm a bit distracted. Which Saturday are you talking about?"

"The one after next."

She tried to remember snippets of the conversation between Brent and Greer when she let her mind wander. Something about a weekend get-together with a new client. But which weekend? "I need a couple of hours to think about it."

"At least you didn't say no. By the way, I got us tickets to a comedy at the Alliance Theater for Sunday."

She didn't have the heart to tell him she'd already seen the play. Besides, watching it a second time might give her new insight for a blog post follow-up. "How fun. I hear it's a hoot and a half."

Brent popped into her office, forcing her to shift gears. "Thank you for calling, sir. I promise to check my schedule and let you know."

Charlie snickered. "Uh oh, the king or the knight must've invaded your space."

"That's right. I'll be back in touch soon." Rachel laid her phone on the desk and eyed Brent. "I tuned out for a couple of minutes when you and my father were talking. What's the deal about a Saturday meeting?"

"An outing Greer and I plan to attend in Boca Raton. A potential client is looking to build a golf resort somewhere in the South. We're pitching Georgia."

"When?"

"Weekend after next. If we close the deal, you and I will work on the project together."

"Not a chance. And about you and I entertaining a client over dinner tomorrow night, no way I'm going."

"Your father's likely to reject your rejection."

She tapped her foot and glared at him. "He'll get over it. You know that little story you told him about our meeting with Bricker was a total fabrication."

"Maybe I see things differently than you. Besides, why do you care, as long as we got the job done?"

"Because I have integrity and the truth matters. Why'd you come in here, anyway?"

He laced his fingers and tapped his thumbs. "Did you know Charlie Bricker was arrested for drunk driving a few years back?"

That explains his one-glass-of-wine rule. "And you're telling me this why?"

"Because you need to know."

"Well, now I do, so if you don't mind, I have a ton of work to do." She dismissed him with a wave of her hand and opened her computer.

Brent shook his head and moved toward the door. "Don't say I didn't warn you."

The news about Charlie's arrest sent up another red flag. How many revelations were yet to come? And would they make a difference? Feeling like a pawn in a high-stakes chess game, she needed to clear the fog clouding her perspective. The lure of fresh air and sunshine provoked her to grab her purse, scribble a note to Nancy, and scurry to the elevators.

On the sidewalk in front of the building, she donned her sunglasses, turned toward Centennial Park, and mentally calculated Charlie's invitation. Despite his comment about honorable intentions, an overnight trip this early in their relationship seemed more appropriate for a playboy's ploy than an innocent outing. However, he did say two rooms. Was he hoping for adjoining rooms?

Rachel stopped beside the Peachtree Plaza hotel, shielded her eyes, and let her gaze wander to the top of the elevator tube hugging the outside of the building. She remembered feeling secure while she held on to Charlie's arm during their ride to the Sun Dial Restaurant.

Dizziness set in and threatened to throw her off balance, much like Charlie's proposal. She leaned against a lamp post to steady herself. When the sensation passed, she resumed her walk and turned the corner.

A block past the hotel, she noticed a man dressed in tattered clothes crouching on the sidewalk. A dirty baseball cap served as his collection plate. A mongrel dog, it's tongue hanging from its mouth, sprawled beside him. What was his story? Too many drunk-driving arrests? Out of the blue, an overwhelming feeling of compassion tugged on her heart, forcing her to move closer. "You look like you could use a good meal."

She dug her wallet from her purse, pulled out a fifty-dollar bill, and dropped it in the cap.

The man stared at the money before stashing it in his pocket. He pushed up, focused his blood-shot eyes on Rachel, and popped the cap on his head. "God bless you, lady."

"You too, sir." She moved past, wondering if she'd made a mistake by giving an alcoholic or a drug addict enough money for a week's worth of fixes. She glanced back over her shoulder, discovered the man and his dog were gone, and questioned what madness made her throw away good money.

She turned another corner and caught sight of the Skyview Ferris Wheel. Sun glinting on glass-enclosed gondolas beckoned to her. All these years, she'd stared down at the massive structure, wondering what it felt like to ride.

"It's about time I find out." She hastened her step, crossed Luckie Street, and bought a ticket. While waiting in line to board, reality cut through the haze in her head. Here she stood, in the middle of a busy workday, abandoning her responsibilities to ride on a giant wheel. And only one day after secretly meeting Charlie for lunch and attending Alicia's improv session. A delicious sense of guilty pleasure unleashed an adrenaline rush.

She turned to the woman and two young girls standing behind her. "Is this your first time to ride?'

The youngest child hugged her mother's leg and stared at Rachel. "This one's a bit shy, but my oldest daughter will talk a blue streak."

The girl pointed toward the top of the wheel. "I hope we get to stop when we're way up there."

Rachel smiled. "Me too."

"Today's my birthday. I'm seven."

"What a fun way to celebrate. I was your age when my mother and I came downtown to watch the Olympic opening ceremony."

"After we ride, we're going to the Aquarium. Have you been there?"

"No, but I hear it's the best place to spend a special day."

The younger daughter released her mother's leg. "I have two goldfish."

Rachel smiled. "I also had pet fish when I was a little girl. I named them Belle and Pocahontas."

The wheel stopped.

"It looks like it's my turn to climb aboard. You're next." She stepped forward, paused, and glanced over her shoulder. "Oh, and happy birthday."

She climbed aboard and watched the family hurry to the next gondola. As the ride rose to the pinnacle, a new awareness formed and filled her with courage. She wasn't a pawn on a giant chess board but a grown woman, capable of controlling her own moves and making her own decisions. Besides, if she did go to Willow Falls with Charlie, she had enough sense to keep everything above board. And he did ask her to find a place to stay, so the choice of rooms was her responsibility.

Before the big wheel made one full revolution, she pulled her phone from her purse and pressed a number.

Chapter 31

Emily sat at her kitchen table staring at the document from her critique partner. The red and strike-throughs screamed incompetence. Maybe she should abandon her ridiculous book idea. It had been years since her college writing courses, and reporting for a small-town newspaper didn't enhance her novel-writing skills. Besides, she had enough on her plate with the inn and hotel, not to mention preparing to care for two tiny babies.

Cody padded across the room and pawed the sliding glass doors.

"Okay, fella." She slid it open and followed him outside. The azaleas, in full bloom, created a crimson and green palette against the cedar fence enclosing the back yard. She tilted her head back, let the sun caress her cheeks, and caught sight of a hawk soaring through the crystal-clear, blue sky.

Why had so many dark clouds accumulated in her world? A comment she'd heard about God not giving a person more than they could handle drifted up from her memory. How much more did He think she could shoulder without falling apart?

Cody sidled over, wagged his tail, and dropped a tennis ball at her feet.

"I bet there aren't any thunderstorms brewing in your brain."

He barked and wagged his tail.

"I get it. You want to play catch."

He spun around, ready to spring into action.

She retrieved the ball and pitched it high.

He raced across the yard, caught it mid-air, and bounded back for more.

"Good catch. You're definitely going to have a role in my book." She reached down and paused. "Did I just say my book?"

Cody barked.

She threw the ball again.

He caught it and dropped it to chase a squirrel.

Grateful for the distraction, she stepped back into the kitchen and peeled a banana. Her computer beckoned to her. Pushing her anxiety aside, she returned to the table and read every new-comment bubble twice. "Now what are you going to do, Emily? Follow through on what you told Scott and accept this feedback like a big girl? Or let your babies think their mother is afraid to take some honest criticism?"

Cody pawed the glass doors. She let him in. He lapped water and stretched out under the table.

Emily admitted her critique partner was right. She'd made a whole string of novice mistakes. She found a notepad and pen in a drawer and sat back down. While making a list of needed corrections, lessons from her college writing course came roaring back. "How is it possible I forgot so much?"

If she hadn't joined the critique group she'd have ended up with a first draft loaded to the gills with amateur mistakes. With new perspective, she buckled down and got to work. Following two hours of intense concentration, she needed a break and someone to talk to who could carry on a two-way conversation. Besides, she was curious about Sadie's progress.

She let Cody back out and drove to the café. Inside, she found Pepper clearing a table.

"Where's Sadie?"

"Taking some time off." She carried a stack of dirty dishes to the kitchen.

Emily climbed on a stool at the counter and waited.

Pepper returned. "Mirabelle's credit card accusation stirred up all kinds of controversy." She opened the cash register and dropped a twenty in the drawer. "Sadie's afraid waiting tables will keep a lot of customers from coming in."

"Too many things in this town aren't working out the way we expected."

"You can say that again. What's happening with your book?"

"I've rewritten chapter one."

"Already?"

"Yeah, the first draft pegged me as a genuine newbie."

"I imagine writing is an ongoing process." Pepper straightened a stack of menus. "Sort of like cooking. It gets better with practice."

"I hope you're right."

"I hear your parents' furniture is scheduled for delivery to the inn tomorrow."

"A lot of good it will do. I haven't received one response to my request for an innkeeper."

Pepper stepped around the counter and settled beside Emily. "I've been thinking about that—"

"Hold your thought, I've got a call coming in." Emily pulled her phone from her pocket. "Hey, Rachel, I'm with a friend. Do you mind if I put you on speaker?"

"Not at all."

She pressed the icon and laid the phone on the counter. "I talked to Mr. Bricker—"

"Charlie?"

"No, his dad. I'm writing a follow-up article about the winery."

"I imagine he's pleased."

"He is. What can I do for you?"

"I need some advice. Charlie invited me to go to Willow Falls with him a week from Saturday to look at the land. Can you recommend a place for us to stay one night? We'll need two private rooms.

"I, uh … the thing is …"

"Good afternoon, Rachel. I'm the friend in the room. My name is Pepper Cushman and I own the best café in Willow Falls."

Emily stared at her. *Is she kidding? It's the only café in town.*

"I'd consider it an honor to treat you and Charlie, along with Emily and her husband, to dinner at my place. We'll introduce you to amazing small-town hospitality. We're right on Main Street—Pepper's Café —you can't miss it."

"Thank you. It sounds lovely."

"Folks like to eat early around here. Will five work for you?"

"I'm sure it will."

"About overnight accommodations. An exquisite new inn, with six private suites, is ready to open." Pepper continued before Emily could get a word in. "We'd be delighted to welcome you as our inaugural guests."

"I'm honored. Unless something unexpected comes up, we'll see you Saturday."

Emily ended the call and glared at Pepper. "What on earth were you thinking?"

"You were hemming and hawing around like a confused adolescent. Would you prefer they drive twenty-five miles to sleep in a sleazy, run-down motel?"

"No, but—"

"Okay, then." Pepper slid off the stool, stepped behind the counter, and cut two pieces of cherry pie. "Like I started to say before Rachel called, I have an idea to run by you."

Emily picked up a fork and pointed it at Pepper. "And you're bribing me with sugar?"

"I prefer to call it sweet enticement."

"I don't suppose I can get out of hearing whatever crazy notion is knocking around in your head."

"Actually, it's not so crazy." She tapped her fork on her plate. "You need someone to manage the inn, right?"

"And ..."

"How about offering the job to Sadie?"

Emily's forkful of pie froze halfway to her mouth. "Are you serious? She's been in prison for thirty years. What makes you think she's capable, even if she agreed, which I doubt she would?"

"Nowadays, you can learn anything online. Besides, I can teach her the basics about managing a small business."

"You know it would likely cause a bigger uproar than her working here." Emily swallowed a mouthful of pie.

"Not if we convince Mirabelle and the other naysayers it's in the town's best interest."

"Fat chance of that happening."

"We're two smart ladies. I think we can come up with a plan. Will you at least consider the idea?"

"I suppose it won't hurt to talk it over with Scott."

"Excellent. If he agrees, you can offer the job to Sadie tomorrow as soon as you two finish decorating."

"You don't waste any time, do you?"

Pepper patted Emily's arm. "Your first guests arrive in a week and a half, my dear. We don't have time to dilly-dally around."

"I see your point." Emily swallowed her last bite of pie and slipped off the stool. "Thanks for the—what did you call it—sweet enticement?"

"Did it do the trick?"

"I'll let you know." She left the café, crossed Main Street, and headed to Hayes General Store. She couldn't decide if she wanted Scott to get on board with Pepper's plan or dismiss it as out of the question. Either way, she'd value his opinion.

When she entered the store, she overheard Miss Gertie giving Scott an earful. "Mirabelle is telling everyone that Sadie's starting a credit-card theft ring right here in our little town."

Scott emptied a scoop of candy into a white paper bag. "Come on now, you don't really believe she stole Mirabelle's card, do you?"

"I don't know who else would've taken it."

Emily shook her head. "It's possible Mirabelle lost or misplaced it."

"I suppose, but I'm for sure going to keep an eye on my purse when Sadie's around." Gertie scooped her bag of candy off the counter. "I best be on my way and leave you two lovebirds alone."

Scott grinned at the elderly woman. "Come on in any time, Miss Gertie."

Emily waited for the bell to announce her departure. "What if she's right?"

"About the credit card?"

"Yeah."

"And what if aliens from Mars invade Willow Falls or some kid digs up a dinosaur egg and hatches it."

"I'm just saying, no one knows what happened." She plopped her purse on the counter and climbed onto a stool. "I got a call from Rachel Streetman."

"Oh yeah, what's up?"

She relayed the conversation. "Can you believe Pepper?"

"She must have found someone to manage the inn."

"Yeah, Sadie."

Scott's brows raised. "That's a bold idea."

"Based on the rumors, I'm not convinced it's a good one."

"Why not? I mean, you need an innkeeper and Sadie needs someone besides Pepper to believe in her."

"Are you saying you approve?"

Scott moved from behind the counter and sat beside her. "I'm suggesting you run the idea by her and see where it lands."

Emily scooped a handful of jelly beans from a jar. She picked out a green bean and popped it in her mouth. "Considering I don't have any other options, I guess it won't hurt."

"In the meantime, we can pray Mirabelle finds her credit card and puts an end to this theft ring nonsense."

Chapter 32

Rachel stepped out of the Ferris Wheel gondola and waited for the mother-and-daughter trio to hop off behind her. "I loved my ride. What did you two young ladies think?"

The birthday girl's grin spoke volumes. "It was awesome. I could see all the way to my house." She pulled her mother's hand. "Hurry up, Mommy. I want to go see the pretty, white whales." She waved at Rachel. "Bye, lady."

"Goodbye, it was nice talking to you." As she watched the little family walk away, memories of birthday celebrations with her mother warmed her heart. She strolled across the street to Centennial Park and settled on a bench. Curiosity about Pepper's comments compelled her to search the internet for inns in Willow Falls. Nothing surfaced. How could a new inn expect to attract guests without a website? Maybe it wasn't so exquisite. It didn't matter, she'd accepted Pepper's offer. But she hadn't responded to Charlie's invitation.

She could call him now. No, she told him a couple of hours. If she appeared too eager, he might get the wrong idea.

Her phone buzzed. Brent.

The idea of facing another confrontation at the office didn't sit well with her. A new sense of freedom flowed to her fingertips. She turned her phone to vibrate, dropped it in her purse, and mentally patted herself on the back for taking a stand.

She peeled out of her jacket and let the sun warm her bare arms as she ambled along a path paved with centennial bricks. One day soon, she and Charlie had to search for their contributions to the walkway.

The scent of sizzling beef and French fries drifted in her direction. She licked her lips and moseyed up to the hamburger stand. Not in the mood for a heavy meal, she settled for a vanilla shake and resumed her walk. Smiling and saying hello to people she passed created a sense of community. *Is this what it's like to live in a small town?*

A young woman sitting on a bench tugged on a leash in an attempt to rein in her black lab puppy. Rachel sauntered over, set her shake down, and stooped to pat his head. "Hey there, fella." The dog's tail wag set its hindquarter in motion. He licked her hand.

"He's a beautiful pup, but I bet he's a handful. What's his name?"

The owner grinned. "Onyx, and yeah, he's full of mischief."

"How old is he?"

"Six months. Do you have a dog?"

"No, but one of these days I'll take the leap."

She retrieved her shake and strolled past a statue with pillars and five interlinked rings honoring the founder of the modern Olympics. In the distance, a building—it's metal-and-glass exterior rising, reminiscent of a massive ship breaking through a giant wave—came into view. The Georgia Aquarium.

Other than her goldfish, Belle and Pocahontas, she hadn't much fancied underwater creatures. Yet, she'd heard people in the office rave about the venue. Maybe it was time she found out what all the hullabaloo was about. She sipped the last drop of shake, tossed her empty cup in a trash can, and hastened her step. Five minutes later, she tucked her purse under her arm and stepped in line to purchase a ticket.

A vibration tickled her ribs and elicited a stab of guilt. Was Brent calling her again? Maybe a client was trying to reach her. What would people think if they knew she was shirking her responsibilities? She pulled her phone out. An unknown number. *Maybe I should go back to work.* She hesitated. *Hold on. You haven't taken time off in ages. One afternoon won't hurt anyone.* She pocketed her phone and stepped up to the ticket booth.

Inside the immense building, she passed the gift shop and halted, wondering where to begin. The tropical diver venue on her right beckoned her. She wandered through the exhibit, delighted by the sense she was visiting a gallery of living art. When she reached the large room in the center, her mouth fell open. She gawked in amazement at an enclosed tropical coral reef. Thousands of rainbow-colored fish swarmed and darted about in a free-form ballet of beauty. Children's squeals of delight mingling with adult's oohs and aahs added an atmosphere of joy to the spectacular view.

"There's Nemo, Daddy," a young girl sitting on her father's shoulders shouted.

Rachel smiled, moved close to the glass, and watched a wave crash overhead on the water's surface. She pulled her phone from her purse, ignored the messages, and snapped dozens of photos. When finished, she sat on a bench to admire her work. Halfway through her review, the phone buzzed.

"Hey, Charlie, you'll never guess where I am."

"In Brent's office giving him a pink slip?"

"Better yet, I'm sitting in the tropical diver gallery at the Aquarium."

"Uh oh. Did you get fired?"

She laughed. "No, I'm playing hooky."

"I promise not to tell or send a truant officer after you."

"Funny. This place is amazing. It's like I'm watching an underwater theatrical performance. I had no idea so many different kinds of fish existed."

"God's handiwork is spectacular."

His comment caught her by surprise. They hadn't talked about spiritual matters. Did he go to church or was his response nothing more than an offhand remark? Did it even matter?

"I'm guessing this is your first visit to the attraction."

"Believe it or not, it is."

"Have you seen the Beluga whales?"

She stood and moved toward the exit. "Not yet."

"Save them for last. I suggest you check out Ocean Voyager next."

"I'm heading over there now."

She walked through a hallway and stepped onto a moving sidewalk in a clear, tube-shaped tunnel surrounded by a saltwater world of wonder. "Wow, I feel like Ariel."

"Who?"

"I don't suppose *The Little Mermaid* was one of your favorites."

"*Batman* was more my speed."

"Wow, a huge stingray just swam over my head."

Charlie cleared his throat. "During your covert adventure, have you had time to think about our trip to Willow Falls?"

Rachel spotted a green sea turtle. "I called Emily Hayes and talked to Pepper."

"Who's Pepper?"

"The owner of a café." She toplined the conversation.

"Are you accepting my invitation?"

Choose your word wisely. "After helping close the deal with your dad, I'm interested in seeing the vineyard site. Besides, Willow Falls could present an opportunity for some real estate development."

"I'll take your roundabout answer as a yes."

"I couldn't find any information about the inn on the internet, so I hope the place is satisfactory."

"Hey, pretty lady, as long as you're in a room close by, it won't matter what the place is like."

Similar to a stealth predator searching for unexpected prey, a giant shark swam above Rachel's head. Was it a coincidence or a warning to tread lightly? She made a mental note to call Emily and request a room as far away from Charlie's as possible.

Chapter 33

Emily paced the inn's foyer, waiting for Sadie and her parents' furniture to arrive. She had to find the right time to propose Pepper's suggestion. Deep down, she feared Sadie would reject the idea and dash her only option. Then again, what if she accepted and Mirabelle's credit card accusation had merit?

She pressed her fingers to her temples to ease the tension headache developing behind her eyes.

"You look nervous as a cat caught up a tree." Sadie's voice cut through the silence. "Are you sure you're up to this?"

Emily pivoted and lowered her hands to her side. "I don't know." A shrill squeal sent a shiver up her spine and made her cringe. "Why doesn't Jimmy get those blasted brakes fixed?"

"Maybe he doesn't have enough business to justify the cost."

"Like everyone else around here."

"I'll get him to pull the truck around back so they can unload furniture for the garage apartment first. Do you want to come with me?"

"I think I'll wait here and nurse this nasty headache."

"Do you need help?"

"What do you mean?"

She pulled a bottle of Excedrin from her purse and tapped two tablets into Emily's hand. "These little beauties do wonders for me. I'll see you when we're all done."

"Thanks." Emily headed toward the kitchen then halted. She opened her hand. What if these weren't what Sadie claimed? She looked close and mentally kicked herself when she noted an E etched on each oblong pill. "Get a grip, girl. Do you honestly think our ex-con is dealing drugs and running a theft ring?"

After swallowing Sadie's offering, Emily sauntered to a rocking chair on the front porch and let her mind drift back to the last moments she and her mom spent together—the day before her parents left for Savannah. They had wandered through the inn, chatting about a bright future when guests would sing Willow Falls' praises.

Nora's irresistible charm and outgoing personality made her the perfect innkeeper. How could Sadie—whose smile rarely showed up, and when it did, lasted seconds—possibly fill her shoes? The question intensified her headache. She closed her eyes and set the rocker in motion, hoping the movement would soothe her nerves and bring her clarity.

By the time Sadie finished with the garage apartment, the pain in Emily's head had subsided but ambiguity about popping the question remained.

"Are you ready to finish upstairs?"

Emily opened her eyes. "How does the garage apartment look?"

"Your parents' bed, night stands, and chest of drawers look real nice in the bedroom. The little love seat is in the living room. Add a couple more pieces and you'll have it ready for guests."

"Thanks for taking care of everything. By the way, the Excedrin worked."

"I knew it would."

Jimmy repositioned the truck to align with the front porch and, along with his sidekick, hauled the blue-and-white striped couch from the Hayes living room up the steps and in the front door.

Following behind him, Sadie paused and motioned to Emily. "Come on, I need you to help me decide which front bedroom gets this piece."

Suspecting the request was a ploy to get her involved, Emily trailed Sadie up the curved staircase.

"Okay, it's decision time." Sadie propped her hands on her hips. "The room on the right or the one on the left?"

Emily's eyes shifted from one to the other before she strolled to the bedroom on the right. "I think this one."

Sadie motioned to Jimmy. "Okay, fellas, put it over yonder under the window." She stepped into the room behind Emily. "The couch goes good with Robert's antique sleigh bed."

Emily stroked the top of a vintage writing desk. "The moment I saw this piece, I knew Mom would love it. It's feminine, yet sturdy, like her."

"I'm glad your mama and daddy rescued this old house and turned it from a curse to a blessing. It didn't deserve to collapse into a big pile of scrap material."

"I know." Emily pointed to the empty wall above the headboard. "I want her favorite painting—the oil of a mother and daughter romping in a field of daisies—to go there."

Sadie moved beside her. "I've been thinking. You should call this the Nora suite."

"Mom talked about giving the rooms names of Georgia waterfalls."

"Nice idea, but waterfalls don't need honoring. Your parents do." Sadie nodded toward the left. "Your daddy's architectural prints are going on a wall next door, so you ought to name it the Roger suite."

The suggestion warmed and broke Emily's heart. She'd trade every ounce of effort her parents poured into transforming the Liles estate to have them back in her life. Like fingers of fog filtering out the sun, bitterness tightened her jaw.

Sadie touched Emily's arm. "Are you all right?" Her tone was tender.

"My parents should be here helping me make decisions. Instead, a drunk who didn't deserve to live sent them crashing down the side of a mountain." Moments after the words tumbled out, a knot formed in her belly. "I'm sorry, it's nothing against you ..."

"No need to apologize." Sadie paused for a long moment. "Is it okay if I give you a piece of advice?"

Emily shrugged. "I suppose."

"I understand firsthand how rage can eat away at your insides. Do you know why it's hard for me to smile? Because years ago, bitterness took hold of my heart and stole my joy."

"Regret for killing Robert?"

"Anger over what he took from me. You have to find a way to forgive and move on before hatred snatches away the happiness God wants for you."

"I don't know if I can."

Jimmy knocked on the door. "We've got a recliner out here, Miss Sadie."

"You have to for your babies' sake." She squeezed Emily's hand before joining Jimmy. "Follow me, guys, I'll show you where it goes."

Sadie's revelation haunted Emily and sent a myriad of questions spinning in her brain. Why hadn't Sadie found the strength to forgive? Even more troubling, what memories held her captive?

"Are you planning on staying in there?" Sadie stepped back in the doorway. "Or giving me a hand out here?"

"I'm coming."

An hour later, Grandpa Redding's antique desk found a home in the foyer and Sadie got to work arranging accessories and hanging pictures in the upstairs suites. After positioning a Monet *Water Lilies* framed print on the wall in her old bedroom, she strolled to the window. "Mama loved this old house. Sometimes, when Robert was gone on one of his trips, me and her would fix a fancy dinner for the two of us. Afterward, we'd sleep in one of the guest rooms and pretend we were visiting a famous celebrity's home." She closed her eyes and pinched the bridge of her nose. "It's one of the good memories."

Her comment sparked two burning questions. How many bad memories were hidden in Sadie's heart? And did they outweigh the good? Perhaps in time she'd learn the answers. Emily moved to Sadie's side and touched her shoulder. "I've been thinking, if my mother deserves a suite named for her, so does yours. Especially since she was the last woman to live here."

"What are you suggesting?"

"Naming the downstairs bedroom Carlie."

"Mama would like that." Sadie breathed deep and turned away from the window. "It looks like my work here is done."

Now's the time. Don't let it slip away. "I'm, uh, not sure how to say this, but I kind of need your help again."

Sadie's brow furrowed. "To do what? The decorating is finished."

"Here's the thing. The winery owner's son and the woman who sent me information for the newspaper article are coming to town next Saturday …"

"And …"

"They're staying here. I don't have anyone to manage this place."

Sadie held her palm toward Emily. "Hold on a minute. Are you suggesting I take the job?"

"Pepper thinks it's a good idea."

"You have to understand. She'd think it was a good idea if I ran for mayor, but it'd still be a lousy suggestion."

"Are you turning me down?"

"Let me put it to you this way. Mirabelle thinks I stole her credit card—in case you're wondering, I didn't—and half the town wants me to get my butt as far away from here as possible. So what makes you think Pepper's idea isn't slap ridiculous?"

Emily folded her arms and tapped her foot. "You know what, maybe it is the wackiest idea that ever popped into Pepper's head. Or, here's another possibility. Maybe you're too chicken to stand up and fight. Like bailing on her because a few customers gave you a hard time. Either way, I need your help, and I won't take no for an answer." Emily clasped her hand over her mouth. *Did I just harass an ex-con?*

Sadie's head tilted left. "Well, I declare, girl, you'd make one tough inmate. Except for one thing."

"What's that?"

"You got spooked too quick. See, if you're gonna have a shot of getting your way, you've got to hang in there and not back down."

"You're confusing the heck out of me."

"What I'm trying to say is, you've treated me with respect, so I'll play the role of innkeeper next week. But only until you find a qualified person to take over."

Emily sighed. "Thank you, I think."

"First thing on your list is to get some bedding for the Carlie and Nora suites. We can't have guests sleeping on bare mattresses."

"I'll take care of it tomorrow morning."

"Good, now let's get out of here before you go trying to talk me into another harebrained idea."

.

Chapter 34

Unable to concentrate on work, Rachel spun around and eyed the painting above her credenza—a panoramic view of a snow-covered mountain range, it's reflection mirrored in a crystal-clear lake. The picture normally calmed her. Not today.

Act Three—last night's date with Charlie—played in her mind. They chatted about work and vineyards during dinner at a cute little restaurant. Afterward they walked to the Alliance Theater and settled in a front-row balcony seat. Sitting close to him, breathing in the citrus scent of his cologne, stirred her emotions. He made her feel safe.

During the play, she got a kick out of watching his reactions and listening to his laugh. When the second act ended, they waited in the lobby to chat with the actors. She couldn't tell who was more charmed, him or the actors he complimented.

On the drive to her townhouse, he talked about his favorite scenes and asked her opinion about the performances. When they arrived, he walked her to the front door. She resisted the urge to invite him in and thanked him for a lovely evening.

He cupped her face in his hands, leaned close, and whispered, "Until next weekend, beautiful lady." His smile and tone both thrilled and terrified her.

Shaking off the memory, Rachel popped out of her chair and paced. Had she made a foolish mistake accepting his invitation? Were Brent and her father right about him? It wasn't too late to bow out. If she did, would it jeopardize Streetman Enterprise's relationship with a key client?

Why couldn't she come up with answers? She stopped pacing, laced her fingers behind her neck, and pressed her head forward. *What I need is another woman's opinion, someone I can trust. But who?*

The last female she considered a close friend—her college roommate—fell in love with a good-looking Italian and moved to Italy two years following graduation. Too consumed with work, Rachel hadn't taken the time or energy to replace her—and hadn't needed to. Until now.

She mentally dug deep to identify a candidate. One name filtered through the fog in her head. Nancy. She tilted her head back. Would confiding in her assistant put her in an awkward position? What if Nancy let something slip and Rachel's father found out?

If she crossed the line into friendship, would their professional relationship suffer? Did she already make the shift by divulging her desire to perform?

Rachel released her fingers and returned to her desk. Whatever happened, seeking Nancy's advice was worth the risk. She buzzed her assistant. "Do you have a minute? I need your help."

"I'm on my way, boss."

Nancy bounced into the office. "Do you want me to cover for you while you run off on a mysterious mission for a couple of hours?"

"Not today." Rachel motioned for her to take a seat on the couch.

"Hmm, are you looking for an employee-pulse update a few days ahead of schedule?"

"Not exactly." She settled beside her. "I need some specific information."

"Ask away."

"What have you heard about Charlie Bricker?"

"Besides the fact that he's good looking and seems nice, not much. I mean I'd only laid eyes on him a couple of times before he showed up to meet you. Why?"

Rachel massaged the back of her hand. "We went out—"

"I knew something was going on in your love life. Tell me what he's like. Is he charming? Did he kiss you? Are you—"

"Whoa, hold your horses, sister. I've only seen him three times."

Nancy rested her arm across the back of the couch. "Why do I get the feeling there's more to the story?"

"Because you have great instincts or you're just plain nosey." She gazed out the window and took in the view of the Peachtree Plaza Hotel. She'd come this far. She couldn't chicken out now. She took a deep breath and relayed Charlie's invitation.

"Hmm. Are you staying overnight?"

Rachel nodded. "It's a long way from Atlanta."

"Not that long. What about day two? More grapevine discussions?"

"No." Rachel uncrossed her legs. "He wants to check out Willow Falls. Something about a waterfall."

"Strictly business, of course. I take it you accepted."

"I did, but now I'm questioning if I made the right decision. I mean, he's a client's son, and my father warned me to stay away from him. And Brent ... well, you know."

Nancy pulled her knee onto the couch. "I remember my parents' first reaction when I started dating my husband. He's a Northeasterner—in their Southern-bred opinions, not good enough for their precious daughter."

"Did you listen to them?"

"Heck, no. Turns out it was the best decision I ever made." She giggled. "By the way, I'm convinced if we ever split up, Mom and Dad will ask for Robbie in the divorce settlement."

"Are you suggesting I stick to my decision?"

"I'm saying you need to forget what your father, or Brent, or anyone else thinks, and follow your heart."

"The problem is, I don't know what my heart wants."

She leaned closer and touched Rachel's arm. "Then you need to take a big leap of faith, go to Willow Falls with Charlie, and find out."

"You're right. Thank you for your advice."

"Hey, we girls have to stick together. I do have two requests."

"What?"

"First, if you and Charlie fall in love and decide to get married, you have to let me be a bridesmaid."

She thumped Nancy's arm. "Now you're getting way ahead of yourself. Oh, and about the overnight, two separate rooms."

"Your idea or his?"

"His."

"Excellent. That's one giant checkmark in the 'he's a good guy' column."

Rachel mentally added it to her list. "What's your second request?"

"When you come back to work, will you share all the fun details about your getaway weekend?"

"I don't expect I'll have much to tell. But I'm game."

Chapter 35

Emily pushed the proposal and the hotel plans across the table in the Willow Falls newspaper office. "I accept your offer, Jacob."

"Thank you, and I promise not to disappoint you."

"Now all we need is the money."

"When do you expect to hear something?"

Emily sighed. "I don't have a clue. It seems Ben Crawford's life is plagued by a long string of emergencies."

"We all have our problems." Jacob scooped up the papers and carried them to his desk. "I hear the winery owner and his girlfriend are joining you and Scott for dinner at the café Saturday night before they check into the Willow Inn."

"Actually, Charlie is the owner's son, and I think he and Rachel are business associates."

"Whatever they are, Pepper better lay in an extra supply of food, because a lot of folks are itching to show up and check the guy out."

"Why am I not surprised?"

"Because it doesn't take much to get people around here excited."

A draft of cool air swept into the office as Pepper swung the front door open.

"Your ears must be burning." Emily pulled a chair away from the table and settled down. "We were discussing the town's incurable curiosity about Charlie Bricker's visit."

"It's more like an out-of-control penchant to meddle."

Jacob shook his head. "You nailed it. What brings you to our humble headquarters this afternoon?"

"A request. With Sadie taking on a new role at the Willow Inn, I need to place an ad for a waitress job."

"Hold on," Emily said. "It's a temporary move until I find a permanent innkeeper."

"And how likely is that to happen?"

"You don't understand. Sadie doesn't want the job. She's taking it because I'm in a pinch and need her help."

Pepper pulled a chair beside Emily. "I know. But trust me when I tell you she's interested."

"That's not how she's acting."

"Because she's afraid."

"For good reason." Emily stared at the newspaper's motto engraved in a plaque, strategically placed on the wall opposite the front door. *Respect for the truth and the love of our town guides us.* "You know I asked her to take it temporarily because I value your opinion, and I was desperate. But I have no idea if she can handle the responsibilities."

"Did she tell you she managed the prison kitchen for the past ten years?"

"Which is a far cry from running an inn and taking care of guests. Even if she does do a good job, what if word gets out about her past? I mean, one credit card goes missing and half the town believes Sadie's running a nationwide theft ring. How will guests react if they find out Sadie spent thirty years in jail for killing a man?"

"I understand your concern. Frankly, their reaction worries me as well. However, like everyone else, she deserves a second chance."

"I know Sadie's like family to you and I understand you wanting to help her. But the town's future is on the line. Can we afford to risk it?"

Pepper laced her fingers and twirled her thumbs. "I hear you named three of the inn's rooms Nora, Roger, and Carlie."

"Sadie's idea, initially."

"Why not give the other three suites names of interesting people who are important to the inn or the town?"

Emily drummed her fingers on the table. "I've been toying with the idea."

"Interesting move." Jacob strolled back to the table. "To expand the idea further, you could create mini-stories about the room's namesakes and weave in snippets to promote local businesses and attractions."

Pepper nodded. "Like Scott's great grandfather, Everette Hayes."

Emily pictured the portrait hanging behind Scott's counter. "The founder of Hayes General Store."

"Exactly." Jacob locked eyes with her. "A few facts mixed with a healthy dose of fiction would send guests scurrying to its doors."

"Great news for Scott. What about the other two rooms in the main house?"

Jacob propped his hip on the corner of the table. "How about making one the Patsy Peacock suite. She's quirky as all get-out and I suspect her little gift shop would attract tourists."

"Especially the ladies." Emily shifted her gaze to Pepper. "Do you think she'll agree?"

"In a heartbeat. I have an idea for the sixth room that might solve our Sadie problem."

Emily's brow furrowed. "Name a room after her?"

"No, her nemesis."

"Are you suggesting Mirabelle?" Emily's eyes widened.

"Do you know she worked as Robert Lyles' housekeeper before Sadie and her mother moved to town?"

Did Pepper know about Mirabelle's infatuation with Robert Liles? "Is there more to the story?"

"What do you mean?"

Maybe she doesn't. "Why would I honor the woman who's making Sadie's life miserable and stirring up a hornet's nest of trouble?"

Pepper unlaced her fingers. "Think of it as a trade—celebrity status in exchange for her permanent cease-fire."

Jacob slapped the top of the table. "Pepper, I believe you're on to something."

"What makes you two think Mirabelle would go along with such a wild idea?"

Jacob guffawed. "Are you kidding? The woman clamors for attention and notoriety."

"You've got that right." Pepper pulled her phone from her purse and typed a message. "I texted her to come by here when she finishes delivering the mail, so you can present the idea."

Emily grimaced. "You mean today?"

"Why wait?" Her phone pinged. "Either Mirabelle finished early or she's taking a break, because she's on her way. I think I'll hang around and watch the show."

"You're not getting off that easy." Emily thumped Pepper's arm. "It's your idea, so you're pitching it."

"Are you telling me you're afraid of her?"

"Let's just say I'm not eager to get on her bad side."

"I'm guessing if you turn her into a celebrity," Pepper said, "she'll make you her best bud."

"I'll let you earn that status."

Jacob nodded toward the front window. "You gals better decide quick, because she's here."

Mirabelle climbed out of her mail truck, slammed the door shut, and scurried to the sidewalk. Her eyes narrowed, and her lips pinched.

Emily glanced out the window. "Uh oh, she looks like she just stepped on a rattlesnake."

She stormed in the front door. "Is this an ambush because you don't like my letter to the editor?" She jabbed her finger toward Emily. "You told me you'd get your boss to print whatever I wrote."

Jacob stood and offered Mirabelle his seat. "Calm down. We're printing it in the next edition."

"Just like I wrote it?"

"Every word."

Mirabelle plopped down and crossed her arms over her chest. "Then why did you text me to come here?"

"To run an idea by you." Pepper moved her chair beside Mirabelle. "We're considering giving every Willow Inn suite the name of a real person."

"You mean like movie stars?"

"Heck no. Any old inn can sponge off celebrity's names. We're selecting people who are important to our town. Like Nora and Roger Redding, Everette Hayes, and Patsy Peacock. It gives us the opportunity to honor them and at the same time, promote our local businesses."

"That's four rooms. Who else did you pick?"

"Carlie for one, Sadie's mother—"

"That woman?" Mirabelle gripped the edge of the table. "If Robert Liles had never married her, he'd still be alive. I suppose you're planning on plastering his killer's name on another room."

Pepper shook her head. "This may surprise you, but we're considering the Mirabelle suite."

"Now I know you're pulling my leg."

"Nope, we're dead serious."

Mirabelle's brow scrunched. "I don't understand. Why me?"

"Because, you have history with the house, as a former housekeeper." Pepper paused. "However, there is one condition."

"That figures. What do I have to do?"

"Make peace with Sadie and stop leading protests against her so our town can move on."

"But what if—"

"No what-ifs. It's all or nothing. Your name immortalized in exchange for harmony."

Mirabelle released her grip on the table. "Which room?"

Emily leaned forward. "Upstairs over the front door, next to the Nora suite. I'll even write a little story about your contributions to our town and display it in the room."

Pepper touched Mirabelle's arm. "So, what do you say? Is it a deal?"

"Can I stay overnight in it sometime?"

"Tell you what," Emily said. "You can sleep in the room before anyone else."

Mirabelle stood, moseyed across the office, and gazed out the window. "I found my missing credit card on the dryer."

Emily opened her mouth to chastise the woman.

Pepper clamped her hand on her arm and whispered, "Let it go."

"I must have laid it there after I ordered a magazine over the phone." She thrust her hands in her pants pockets. "I found it when my husband ran out of clean underwear."

Jacob laughed. "It's good he doesn't have a month's supply of skivvies, or you'd still be blaming Sadie."

"Oh yeah?" Mirabelle shook her finger at him. "Let me tell you something—"

"Hey, there's no need to get upset." Pepper snapped her fingers. "If you're ready to admit you misplaced the card, we'll give you a permanent place of honor in Georgia's finest inn."

Mirabelle snorted. "Do I have to apologize to Sadie?"

"Of course. But don't worry, she'll understand why you jumped to conclusions."

"I'll think about it and come by the café in the morning."

"Good plan. I'll make sure she's there." Pepper grinned. "In case you decide to accept our offer."

"Right now, I have to get back to my route." Mirabelle stomped out of the office and climbed into her mail truck.

"She didn't say yes, so we have no idea where we stand." Emily crossed her arms.

Pepper pushed her chair back from the table. "Believe me, she's on board."

"I won't believe it until I hear it from her lips."

Chapter 36

Emily parked in front of Patsy's Pastries and Pretties and watched the bank manager and the town's family doctor amble out of Pepper's Café. Drained from a restless night plagued with dreams about empty parking spaces, boarded-up windows, and trash strewn along Main Street, she second-guessed Pepper's decision to barter with Mirabelle. What if the woman accepted the deal but broke her end of the bargain? After all, she'd been holding tight to her resentment for more than thirty years.

The mail-delivery truck pulled into the adjacent parking space. Mirabelle stepped out with a scowl on her face. She smoothed her shirt and ambled to the sidewalk.

"It's too late to back out now." Emily reached for her purse and followed the protest leader into the café—empty except for Pepper and Sadie standing behind the counter. She pushed her sunglasses to the top of her head and pointed her thumb over her shoulder. "Another slow morning?"

"If things don't pick up during the week, I'll have to close up Monday through Thursday." Pepper poured a glass of water and slid it across the counter to Emily, then made her way to the door. She flipped the open sign to closed. "Okay, ladies, it's time to get down to business." She returned to the counter and locked eyes with Mirabelle. "Are you ready to tell Sadie what you told us the other day, about your missing credit card?"

Why was Pepper trying to paint her into a corner? Emily held her breath, hoping the situation wasn't about to get out of control. Until Mirabelle shrugged.

"I found it at my house ..."

Pepper glared. "And?"

"I know she didn't steal it." Mirabelle shifted in her seat. "But who could blame me for jumping to that conclusion? I mean, Sadie spent more than half her life in jail with a bunch of criminals. For all I knew, she'd joined up with some of them."

Pepper's face flushed. "If that's your idea of an apology—"

"Give her a break," Sadie said. "Because she's right. There are a lot of really bad people in jail who spend a lot of time planning their next crime. Most of them career criminals. But there's also good people who made big mistakes and want to turn their lives around."

She moved to a stool beside Mirabelle. "Halfway through my sentence I decided to join a Bible-study group. A bunch of us sat in a circle on cold, metal chairs in a dingy, windowless room that smelled like body odor, sweaty socks, and centuries-old mildew. During a year-long journey we came to understand that God loves us unconditionally, and we started seeing each other and ourselves through His eyes. We knew we'd face all kinds of persecution on the outside, but we decided not to judge our persecutors."

Sadie's shoulders slumped. "It turns out that was easy to say, not so easy to do." She swiveled her stool to face her nemesis. "I understand why you blamed me. If I were in your shoes, I'd have done the same thing."

Mirabelle stared at the woman she'd accused before breaking eye contact. She clasped her hands in her lap. "I guess I jumped to conclusions without thinking things through." She hesitated. "I'm sorry."

Sadie's eyes reddened as a mist of tears formed and spilled down her cheeks. She touched Mirabelle's arm. "I accept your apology and I hope we can become friends."

"Well now, this breakthrough calls for a round of caramel-apple coffee cake on the house." Pepper dashed to the kitchen and returned with the sweet offering and four plates. "Fresh from the oven."

A tingling warmth circulated through Emily's limbs as new respect for accuser and accused took hold and reignited hope for a brighter future. "Decision made. The remaining three suites will honor Patsy, Everett Hayes, and our very own Mirabelle Payne."

Sadie pulled a tissue from her pocket and dabbed her cheeks. "All good choices that will make for some interesting stories."

Mirabelle pointed her fork at Emily. "I heard about Saturday's guests. Did you hire an innkeeper?"

"Sadie agreed to fill in until I find someone."

"Huh." She swallowed a bite. "Maybe she should take the job permanently."

Sadie shook her head. "I'm not qualified. Besides, I don't expect Willow Falls residents are ready for an ex-con to mingle with tourists."

"Who knows? They might come around." Mirabelle finished her coffee cake, slid off the stool, and nudged Emily. "I've got to get to my route. Let me know when you want to talk to me about my story."

Was it possible to convince her to send a second letter to the editor, one that would bring people together? "Will tomorrow afternoon at the Willow Inn work for you?"

"Around three?"

"Works for me."

"Okay, I'll see you then."

The moment Mirabelle walked out the door, Sadie eyed Pepper. "Did you promise her a room to get her to come clean about the credit card?"

"And make nice with you."

She chuckled. "Well, I'll be ... It's just like jail. The barter system works."

"Now we have to trust Mirabelle to keep up her end of the bargain." Emily reached in her purse for her buzzing phone. "It's a call from Savannah." She answered, responded, and slipped it in her pocket. "Ben Crawford wants to call me in an hour."

"Maybe we're on a roll with good news." Pepper removed the dirty plates from the counter. "I've got to get ready in the event some people decide to show up for lunch." She nudged Sadie's arm. "How about giving me a hand in the kitchen? You're welcome to hang out here, Emily."

"Thanks, but the weather's too nice to stay inside. I think I'll wait in the park."

"Come back when the call ends and give us all the details. Oh, and on your way out, will you flip my sign to open?"

Emily tucked her purse under her arm. "Glad to." She strolled out of the café. A mother pushing a stroller on the sidewalk sparked a vision of a future afternoon when she'd walk her babies along the park's edge. She pulled her sunglasses down and crossed Main Street. The lake beckoned her, prompting her to meander across the lawn and settle on the retaining wall. She pulled her shoes off, rolled up her jeans, and dangled her feet in the cool water.

The sun's rays shimmering on the surface, like thousands of tiny diamonds, unleashed a treasure trove of memories. Swimming with friends out to the wooden platform thirty yards from the wall. Sitting beside sixteen-year-old Scott, watching him cast a fishing line, hoping he'd kiss her. Her dad teaching her how to skip pebbles across the surface of the water. She never mastered the skill.

A gentle breeze unleashed a whiff of magnolia blossoms, while a chorus of chirping birds created a symphony. A fish jumped out of the water and sent a ring of waves cascading along the surface—like consequences flowing from a single event. Maybe Ben's call signaled an end to the ripples unleashed by her parents' tragic accident. Eager to share the moment with Scott, Emily clutched her shoes, swung her legs around, and strolled to Hayes General Store.

Chapter 37

Rachel sipped a cup of coffee and proofed a proposal she'd prepared for a client. She'd managed to stay focused on work until a sentence about topography invoked an image of Charlie walking between grapevines in a lush vineyard. Although her guard was still up, she had to admit his charm and sense of humor did more than pique her interest.

Nancy stepped in. "Your father wants to see you in his office."

Would those words ever sound like anything other than a principal calling a student in for a scolding?

"Do you want me to tell him you're tied up with a client?"

"No, I don't need to rouse his suspicion." She sauntered across her office. "Tomorrow, I want to treat you to lunch to thank you for your Charlie advice. You pick the place."

"There's a new restaurant around the corner everyone's talking about."

"Sounds good. For now, I'm off to the principal's headquarters."

"To get an award or an atta-girl?"

Rachel chortled. "Fat chance." She straightened her jacket and strolled to the corner office.

Greer's assistant looked up from her work. "Go on in."

She found her father leaning back in his executive chair, carrying on a phone conversation about shooting par on the back nine. Golf was his one form of recreation. Most likely because it blended well with work. He looked up and motioned for her to take a seat.

She complied and concentrated on the wall behind him. She never understood why wealthy people dumped tons of money on paintings that, in her opinion, weren't aesthetically appealing. A pretty landscape or still life were more to her taste.

"I'll join you on the first tee a week from Sunday at nine." He ended the call and leaned forward. "Hey, Strawberry Girl, you know Brent and I are spending the weekend in Boca Raton with a new client."

She nodded. "Eighteen holes mingled with high-powered negotiations?"

"Potentially worth millions."

Like Streetman Enterprise needs more money.

"Which is why I want your help."

"To do what?"

"Take my place at a fundraising dinner Saturday night. I forgot about the invitation when I scheduled the trip."

A knot formed in the pit of her stomach. She couldn't tell him the truth, at least not all of it. Maybe she should cancel the trip with Charlie. No, she had to stand up to her father. "I wish I could help, but I already have plans for the weekend."

"What kind of plans?"

"Emily Hayes, the Willow Falls reporter who wrote the winery story, invited me to go up and have dinner with her Saturday night."

Greer's eyes narrowed. "You can postpone the trip."

"I don't think that's a good idea. I mean, going back on my commitment might cast an unfavorable light on Streetman Enterprise. Besides, the trip will give me a chance to check the town out for more development opportunities."

"I get your point." He hesitated and propped his forearms on his desk. "Is Charlie Bricker going up too?"

Rachel's pulse quickened. She didn't want to deceive him. Yet fear of her father's reaction compelled her to fudge the truth. "I didn't ask Emily if she invited anyone else." She winced at the bitter taste the words left behind.

"If he does show up—"

"There's no need to worry about me. No matter what happens, or who happens to pop in, I can take care of myself."

"I don't trust that guy to keep his hands off you." He reached for his vibrating cell phone. "I have to take this call. I'll get another associate to cover for me at the fundraiser."

"Thank you." Rachel breathed a sigh of relief and hastened from the room. Disaster diverted. Unless … Her shoulders tensed. What if her father called Charlie? She had to warn him. She rushed back to her office, gathered her courage, and pressed his number.

He answered on the second ring. "Hey, gorgeous. How about meeting me for lunch? We can try someplace new."

"Not today, way too much work is piled on my desk."

"I figured the boss's daughter had special privileges, like ditching work when the mood strikes."

"Not as much as you think. I'm calling because my father knows I'm going to Willow Falls Saturday, but not that I'm going with you."

"And you don't want Daddy to find out." Sarcasm laced his tone.

"You don't have to get all snippy. I just wanted to alert you in case you happen to talk to him."

"Look, I didn't mean to upset you. If Greer calls, I promise to keep our weekend date a secret."

Feeling like a fifth grader afraid of her domineering father, Rachel considered canceling the trip, but the thought of cowering turned her stomach.

"About Saturday, I'll pick you up at one thirty. That will give us time to walk the land before dinner."

"I'll be ready."

"Are you sure you can't sneak away for lunch?"

Even if she could, she didn't dare risk sending up more red flags. "Positive."

"I guess I have to wait a few more days to see your beautiful face."

"I think you'll survive."

After disconnecting, Rachel ran her fingers through her hair and mentally reviewed her inventory of Charlie pros and cons. She smiled and wondered which list would expand following a weekend with him.

Chapter 38

Emily scooted inside the store, disrupting a conversation between Scott and Nathan. "Hey, guys, are you discussing something important, like world peace or feeding the hungry?"

"I was telling Scott how much I miss seeing you two in church."

She dropped her shoes on the floor and laid her purse on the counter. "It's still too painful ... I hope you understand."

"Of course. We'll welcome you back with open arms as soon as you're ready. By the way, the whole town is buzzing about Saturday night. I expect another standing-room-only crowd will squeeze into Pepper's Café."

"I hope you show up to keep the peace."

"Are you worried about Mirabelle?"

She shrugged. "I think we have that situation under control." She shared the room-for-peace deal.

"Whoever came up with that idea deserves a Nobel Peace Prize."

"Pepper was the mastermind behind it."

He smiled. "I think town folks are starting to envision a brighter future."

"Their optimism will move up another notch if I get good news from Savannah. Ben Crawford is calling me." She checked her watch. "In ten minutes."

"Good, because my brother is raring to get started on the hotel. Thank you for giving him the opportunity."

"Believe me, he earned it. How's the antique and furniture business going?"

"Thanks to your purchases, this was my best month in three years, and it isn't over. In fact, I have to get back to meet an out-of-town buyer who's coming to look at some pieces you didn't buy." He took a step toward the door and hesitated. "Oh, and my wife and I will join you at Pepper's Saturday night."

"So long, Nathan." Scott pointed to Emily's bare feet and chuckled. "Did you go wading with the ducks or step in something nasty?"

"Neither, I sat on the wall and dipped my toes in the water." She plopped her purse on the counter. "Mirabelle actually apologized to Sadie."

"Which goes to prove the power of fame, even without the fortune."

"Now we have to count on her sticking to her end of the bargain."

"Underneath all the bluster, I think she's an honorable woman. It's quite a coincidence Ben decided to call the same day Mirabelle and Sadie agreed to play nice."

Emily rolled her pant legs down, slipped her feet into her shoes, and climbed onto a stool. "Maybe it means the town is in for a streak of good luck."

"Whatever happens, I hope we've seen the last of protestors parading on our sidewalks." Scott pulled two water bottles from a cooler beneath the counter. He handed one over. "Do you want to go in the back office to take the call?"

"No, I'll take it here." Emily sipped her water and remembered stories her dad shared about his college-days antics. "It's amazing Dad and Ben remained friends all these years."

"Lucky for us."

She checked her watch again. "It's past time for his call. What if another emergency summoned him? Maybe he used trips as excuses to keep from talking to me."

"Relax, already. He's likely a busy guy."

Her phone buzzed and made her jump. "It's him." She pressed the green icon. "Good morning, sir. I hope it's okay for me to put you on speaker so my husband can listen."

"I'm sorry I didn't learn about your parents in time to attend the funeral. Your dad was a great guy and friend. I hope you're okay."

"It's not easy, but I'm managing." She forced a positive tone. "Did he show you the detailed plans to finish the hotel?"

"He gave me a copy."

"Excellent, because Jacob—he worked for my parents—is ready to get the project under way."

Silence on the other end of the line stole Emily's smile. Her palms turned cold and clammy. "Mr. Crawford, did we lose you?"

"I'm here ... the thing is, a lot happened following my meeting with Roger and Nora. Unexpected personal issues put a huge financial strain on my family and my business." The angst in Ben's voice was palpable. "I've considered my situation from every possible angle, trying to find a way to honor my agreement."

Tingling attacked Emily's chest as an image of the hotel crumbling to the ground rocked her brain. She clutched the edge of the counter.

Ben cleared his throat. "I'm so sorry ... but I'm no longer in a position to invest in the hotel."

Her grip tightened.

Scott leaned close. "Mr. Crawford, we appreciate you trying to work things out. It tells us a lot about your character."

A sigh resonated through the phone. "I appreciate your comment and hope another investor will step in and fill my shoes."

"Thank you. So do we." Scott ended the call.

Emily clenched her jaw, fighting the urge to scream. Instead, she snatched her phone. "I have to call Rachel and tell her not to come."

Scott clamped his hand over hers. "Before you make any rash decisions, we need to talk this through."

"What's there to talk about? Mr. Bricker's expecting a sixty-room hotel we can't deliver."

"Look, no one knows about the call except Nathan—"

"And Pepper and Sadie."

"Okay, we'll ask all three to keep a lid on things."

She glared at him. "What's the point?"

"We need time to work something out."

"Short of robbing a bank, I can't see a solution."

"One Willow Falls ex-con is more than enough. I know it's a long shot but we have to try to find another investor." He massaged his chin and paced, then stopped and snapped his fingers. "Didn't you say Rachel works for a real-estate development firm?"

Emily nodded. "What are you thinking?"

"She'll be in town for two days, starting with dinner."

"Surrounded by nosey gawkers."

"Or, to put it another way, in the company of enthusiastic neighbors eager to turn their town into a tourist mecca. If we do a good job showcasing Willow Falls, we can follow up with a pitch."

"I don't know …"

"It's worth a shot. Besides, what do we have to lose? You go talk to Pepper and Sadie. I'll call Nathan."

"Given our luck so far, the odds are a hundred to one it won't work." Emily slid off the stool, grabbed her purse, trudged out the door, and headed down Main. The burden of finding another investor weighed heavily on her heart. Saving the town seemed hopeless. And yet, maybe Scott was right.

At the café, she dug deep to gather enough courage to walk inside and take a seat at the counter.

Sadie carried plates to a corner booth before stepping beside Emily. "At least we have two lunch customers. How'd the call go?"

"Not now," whispered Emily.

"Uh oh, must be bad news."

"I'll fill you in when the café's empty. Give Pepper a heads-up and bring me a sandwich so no one gets suspicious."

Sadie brought Emily's order from the kitchen, grabbed a damp cloth, and wiped down a vacated table.

Emily nibbled at her food and kept busy checking emails. The moment the diners left, Sadie called Pepper in from the kitchen. "From the look on your face, I assume the call didn't go well."

"The deal's off … but we don't want anyone to know. So, I'm counting on you two to keep a lid on it." She looked from one to the other. "Please tell me you didn't talk to anyone about the call."

Pepper shook her head. "I didn't."

"Me neither," Sadie said.

"Good, because we need your help."

Emily conveyed Scott's idea with a trace of enthusiasm.

Pepper pressed her palms together and touched her fingertips to her lips. "Isn't it amazing?"

"That Ben backed out?"

"No. When one door closes, another one opens."

Sadie nodded. "She's right."

"Are you both saying Scott's plan will work?"

Pepper lowered her hands. "Who else knows about Ben Crawford's call?"

"Just Nathan."

"Good, we can trust him. Now, we need to make plans. About dinner Saturday, I'll spruce up the café and create a new menu. I wish we could serve wine, but I don't have a liquor license. Maybe we can come up with an alternative."

"A lot of people are planning to show up, so you'll need Sadie to wait tables."

"I know. I'll also get Mitch to help us. That way, after we serve dinner to our out-of-town guests, she can head to the inn and assume her duties as innkeeper."

Pepper's plan planted a seed of hope in Emily's heart and reminded her how much she loved this obscure little town she called home.

Chapter 39

Emily rubbed a smudge off a silver, antique coffee urn and set it on the sideboard beside a tray of vintage cups and saucers Scott found online. She spun around to scrutinize Willow Inn's parlor. It looked warm and inviting, ready to welcome guests.

She moved to the wingback chair and breathed in the scent of chocolate from Patsy's fresh-baked cookies—a not-so-subtle form of bribery.

The front door opened, sending a shaft of light across the foyer floor. Mirabelle sauntered to the parlor entrance, a quilt draped over her arm.

Emily stood and moved toward her. "You're right on time."

"Before we talk, I want to see the room."

"The one we want to bear your name?"

"What other room would I want to look at?"

Keep your cool. "Well, okay then. Follow me." Emily led her upstairs into the suite.

Mirabelle stood in the center of the room and turned in a slow circle. "That dresser looks like one that belonged to Robert."

"Wow, you have some memory."

"I like the wall color."

"Pale rose was Mom's choice. She called this the princess room."

Mirabelle unfolded the quilt revealing pink, blue, and mint-green patterned squares and laid it across the iron bed. "The colors are perfect in here."

"It's lovely."

"My grandma made it for me. Is it all right if I leave it?"

This is promising. "By all means. Let's go back to the parlor and talk." On the way downstairs, Emily mentally prepared an opening statement.

When they sat across the coffee table from each other, Mirabelle spoke first. "I brought you something." She pulled a folded sheet of paper from her shirt pocket and handed it over.

Emily unfolded it. "Another letter to the editor?"

"Don't look so shocked." She reached for a cookie. "Go ahead and read it."

Sadie's Return, A New Perspective

Disappointment and unrealistic expectations tend to blur the line between reality and fiction. Perhaps that's what happened to our town thirty years ago. In my last letter to the editor, I claimed Sadie Liles deserved her sentence and I still believe that's true. After all, she took a life. But now she's done her time and we have a choice. Either live in the past and let anger destroy us or realize she deserves a new beginning and forgive her.

If we all choose the latter, we'll free our souls to move forward to a bright future for Willow Falls. I'm taking the first step. I invite all to join me in this act of love.

Emily sniffed back a tear. "Oh my gosh. It's beautiful. And I'm blown away by the quality of your writing."

Mirabelle picked up the pillow laying on the settee. "I bet this is hand-made, too."

"Sadie's grandmother."

"I know Robert Liles wasn't such a nice man."

Is she about to confess?

"I was fresh out of high school and dirt-poor when I went to work as his housekeeper. He made me believe he loved me." She hugged the pillow to her chest. "When he married Sadie's mother, I didn't want anyone to think he'd tossed me aside like a piece of trash. To protect what little dignity I still had, I created a giant illusion and spread all kinds of rumors. It worked." Her voice faltered. "As long as Sadie was in jail."

"And now you're seeing everything from a new perspective?"

"The truth is, I don't deserve to have a room named after me—"

"That's not true."

"Hold on. But I'm accepting it." She grabbed another cookie. "I'm turning over a new leaf, but I'm not crazy."

Emily stared at her before bursting into laughter. "Mirabelle Payne, you are one interesting woman."

"I know." She swallowed a bite. "Did Patsy make these?"

"She did."

"Are you going to join me?"

"Of course. Who can turn down Patsy's cookies?"

"Good. Because you'll need lots of energy to take notes about the story I want you to write about me."

Emily took a cookie from the plate and savored the rich taste of dark chocolate. She retrieved a notepad and pen from the coffee table. "Okay, I'm ready."

An hour later, she'd filled ten pages with a little bit of reality and a huge dose of fantasy and fudged facts. "By the time I finish tweaking your story, every guest who stays in your suite will wait with great anticipation for your mail truck to pull up outside."

"That's what I'm counting on." Mirabelle lifted off the settee and strolled to the sideboard. "I remember this coffee urn. How'd you come by so many of Robert's things?"

Emily stepped beside her and filled her in.

"Wow, that's a shock. You need to write a story for this room and include what you just told me." She turned and leaned against the sideboard. "You know what else you ought to do?"

"Don't keep me guessing."

"Call this the Sadie parlor."

Emily linked her arm with Mirabelle and grinned. "That's one fine idea, my friend."

Chapter 40

"You can do this," Rachel mumbled as she grabbed her overnight bag, forced her anxiety aside, and opened her front door. The sun forced her to squint. "You're right on time."

Charlie grinned and took her suitcase. "Your redneck carriage awaits to whisk you away." He bent his arm and held it out for her.

She grasped his muscular bicep and fell in step with him. He tossed her bag in the back seat, bowed at the waist, and held the passenger door open.

His antics made her smile. "Your choice of vehicles is perfect for a trip to the country."

"Except when we get to those winding roads in the Georgia mountains. Then I'll be wishing we were riding in a sleek Corvette with 600 horses under the hood."

"To let everyone know you're a rich guy from the big city?"

"Heck no. So I wouldn't have to drive under the speed limit around all those hairpin curves."

"It sounds like there is a little bit of daredevil in you."

"I don't know many guys who could pass up a chance to take a spin around tight curves in a road-hugging sports car." He closed the door, rounded the truck, and climbed in beside her. "Is country music okay?"

"I'd say it's appropriate for our destination."

Charlie turned the radio on and backed out of the driveway.

She dropped her purse on the floor and buckled her seat belt. "I haven't been out of the city since I was a kid."

"You're kidding. Not even for vacation?"

"Days off are for other people, not the daughter of a consummate workaholic."

Charlie pulled into traffic and drummed his fingers on the steering wheel. "I hope you don't take this the wrong way, but your old man is a piece of work."

You don't know the half of it.

"How about we treat this trip as a mini-vacation and give you a chance to relax and enjoy life before you head back to the Streetman sweat shop?"

"At least I'm well paid to work like a crazy woman."

He glanced at her. "Maybe so, but is the money worth it?"

"That's not why I stay." Rachel lowered her sunglasses from the top of her head. "You have to understand, I'm my father's only chance to pass the business on to a blood relative. If I leave, it will dash his dreams and break his heart."

"You're a good daughter. But, at some point, you have to do what makes you happy. If Greer can't accept reality, it's his problem, not yours."

His comment cut deep. "Maybe someday I'll find a reason to walk away."

"Like falling head-over-heals in love with an adventuresome guy?"

The words ignited a fluttering sensation and warmed her heart. "One thing's obvious. You're an accomplished flirt."

"Is that a yes or a no?"

"Let's call it a tentative maybe."

"Guess I'll have to work extra hard to flip it to a yes."

She folded her hands in her lap. Maybe not as hard as he thought.

"About the inn where we're staying, do you suppose it's anything like the digs in Shining or Psycho's Bates Motel?"

"You really do like thrillers."

"Only the good ones."

"I don't think knife-wielding murderers will attack you. Although you might have to worry about any snacks you find hidden in your room."

"Like Arsenic and Old Lace?"

She stared at his profile. "I'm surprised you know about that movie. It dates back to the forties."

"It was one of my mom's favorites. She had a big crush on Cary Grant. She used to tell my dad that one day she'd run away to Hollywood and marry her true love."

Rachel remembered his comment about his parents' divorce. "How did he respond?"

"He claimed Cary married five times because handsome and charming Reginald Bricker stole the best woman right out from under him." He paused for a long moment. "Little did he know, she'd go through a crazy midlife crisis and *actually* leave him."

Rachel cleared her throat. "I never knew his real name."

Charlie shrugged. "Not many people do. He says it sounds too highfalutin, hence the name Brick."

"Your dad is an interesting man."

"That's one way to describe him."

As they left the city and interstate behind, Rachel fell silent. For the past seven years, she'd spent most of her waking hours surrounded by tall buildings, with a birds-eye view of Georgia pines and lush hardwoods. Riding on a two-lane road that cut through dense woods and divided rolling farmland gave her a sense of leaving a concrete jungle and entering a green oasis. She marveled at the small towns—some too tiny for a stoplight.

Charlie reached across the console and touched her hand. "You've been quiet for a long time. What's going on in your pretty head?"

"I haven't seen a movie or live theater since we left the suburbs. I wonder what people who live in the country do for entertainment?"

"Maybe they watch TV. Or, here's a thought. They sit on their front porches and talk to their neighbors."

"I get the sense Willow Falls isn't a thriving community."

"Not yet." Charlie pulled his hand away. "According to Dad, a good-sized hotel will be open by the time the winery is up and running."

"Perhaps there are other development opportunities for Streetman Enterprise to pursue."

"Has it occurred to you that residents might not want some big company coming in and turning their town into a commercial hub?"

"What do you mean?"

"City people like to get away from the hustle and bustle to relax, unwind, and commune with nature."

Rachel spotted a wild turkey emerging from the woods. "True, but something besides a place to sleep has to attract tourists. What does Willow Falls offer?"

"There's the waterfall."

"Even with the winery, that isn't enough to create one decent paragraph for a promotional flyer."

"Maybe there are some hidden gems no one knows about."

"I hope, or they'll need a brilliant publicity professional who can make a dull town sound like a quaint village. Cabot Cove comes to mind."

"Where?"

"The fictional town in *Murder She Wrote*."

"I suppose a juicy murder would add some mystery." Charlie pulled up to a stop sign and turned right. "Get ready for some wild turns."

Rachel gasped and gripped the edge of her seat.

"What's wrong?"

"The sign read County Road. It's where the accident happened. The one that killed Emily's parents."

Charlie slowed below the speed limit. "Relax. I won't let anything happen to us."

Rachel breathed deep and focused on the dense forest enveloping the two-lane road. A deer bounded in front of them, forcing Charlie to slam on his brakes. "Two miles faster and we'd have a truck full of venison."

"Or a smashed windshield."

After a series of crazy-shaped curves and one final turn, a long stretch of straight pavement loomed ahead. "Be on the lookout on the right for an old for-sale sign nailed to a tree."

Relieved they'd made it past the snaky pavement, Rachel fixed her eyes on the road ahead.

"There it is." Charlie slowed to a stop, parked, and rushed to the passenger side to help her out. "Welcome to the future home of Willow Oaks Vineyard and Winery."

She stepped out and breathed in the fresh scent of pine. The cool air forced her to turn her jean-jacket collar up.

He held her hand, led her up a steep incline, and swept his arm in a wide arc. "Imagine all the trees and brush gone and acres of vines stretching across those hills."

"Like pictures I've seen of Napa Valley."

"Right here in Georgia." He pointed to the right. "Over there, a winding drive will lead to a European-style winery with tasting rooms and, if traffic warrants, a first-class restaurant."

"At least no one can accuse you of lacking vision."

"If I manage the project long term, I'll build a home up on that ridge. My own mini-castle overlooking the grounds."

The idea of waking up every morning, sipping a cup of coffee, and gazing at the landscape held a certain allure. Perhaps life free from stress and unrealistic demands from overbearing fathers drew people to the country. "How far are we from Willow Falls?"

"Couple of miles. We have enough time before dinner to look around." He slipped his arm around her waist and led her along the perimeter of the property.

As she listened to Charlie lay out his plans for the future and watched his face beam, a sense that Willow Falls might offer more than a weekend visit edged into her conscience. *Am I falling for this guy?*

Chapter 41

Emily chewed on her fingernail and rapid-tapped her foot on the kitchen floor. Scott tossed a dog biscuit to Cody, then pulled a chair beside her and pressed his hand against her knee. "You're gonna wear a hole in the floor."

She pushed her foot flat against the tile. "I want to go over our plans one more time."

"Anything to get you to calm down. We start with casual conversation over dinner."

"What if questions about the hotel come up?"

"We'll mention the plans you found in your parents' office."

"That works."

Scott leaned forward and propped his elbows on his knees. "Before dessert is served, Sadie will head over to the inn to prepare for our guests' arrival. When we finish dinner, we'll walk Rachel and Charlie to the hotel and show them inside."

"I hope you and Nathan got the lobby clean enough."

"You wouldn't want to eat off the floors, but it's presentable."

"Are the cobwebs gone?"

He nodded. "Along with the piles of debris. Tomorrow morning, we'll meet them back at Pepper's for breakfast. Afterward, we'll take them on a tour of Hayes General Store and give them a history lesson. And last, a trek to the waterfall."

"And based on their reaction, we'll bring up our need for investment money. Right?"

Scott tapped the tip of her nose. "You've got it."

"I hope nothing goes wrong."

"What could possibly go wrong, other than a few residents acting crazy and making fools of themselves."

"At least Mirabelle should behave herself. Do I look okay? Are slacks and a sweater appropriate or should I change into a dress?"

"You look terrific."

"Rachel and Charlie are city folks. What if they're dressed in fancy clothes?"

"Did you forget they're walking the land before joining us for dinner? It's more likely they're dressed in jeans and hiking boots."

"You're right. It's just … there's so much at stake. I want to make sure everything is perfect."

He popped up and pulled Emily to her feet. "Come on, Nervous Nellie. It's time to head to the café."

"Wait a minute. Did I remember to spray on perfume?"

Scott nuzzled her neck. "Yup. Anything else you think you're forgetting?"

"I guess not."

"Okay, then let's get this show on the road."

During the short drive, Emily clutched her purse in her lap. Questions raced through her mind at warp speed. Would big-city Rachel snub her nose at a town the size of Willow Falls? Would she find out Pepper's Café was the only restaurant in town? Was Willow Inn fancy enough for her sophisticated taste? How could a run-down hotel possibly interest Streetman Enterprise?

"It looks like every parking spot on Main is filled."

"Which means a ton of people turned out to gawk at our guests. A big crowd is bound to make everything more complicated."

"Or show our guests town folk are overloaded with enthusiasm. I'll park at the inn. Do you want me to drop you off at Pepper's first?"

She shook her head. "I'm not about to walk in there by myself."

They parked and headed up Main Street. Loud chatter from inside the café drifted out to the sidewalk.

"It sounds like a party." Scott held the door open. She stepped inside and gasped.

The simple little eatery had been magically transformed into a restaurant worthy of a mention in a Southern travel magazine. Overhead lights were dimmed. White cloths covered tables set with linen napkins and silverware. Fresh flowers and flickering candles in glass containers artfully displayed on beds of magnolia leaves served as centerpieces. On the counter, white placemats substituted for table cloths. Soft instrumental music played in the background. Delicious culinary scents floated in the air.

It appeared every seat was taken. Neighbors, who most likely arrived too late to get a seat, stood along the back wall. Above their heads hung a white vinyl sign with the words *Welcome to Willow Falls* printed in gold, sandwiched between detailed drawings of wine bottles.

Emily leaned close to Scott. "Pinch me, so I know I'm not dreaming."

He slipped his arm around her shoulders. "Pepper outdid herself, that's for darn sure."

Sadie stepped from the kitchen carrying a tray of food.

"It looks like they started serving early."

Scott nodded. "Based on the crowd, it's a good thing."

Mitch, draped in a white apron, dropped an order pad in his pocket and approached them. "I was wondering when you two would show up."

Scott punched his arm. "If you're not careful, Pepper will have you waiting tables every night."

"At least tonight our guests are in a good mood, and no one's complaining about Sadie."

"Thanks to Mirabelle's truce," Emily said. "Is she here?"

"Oh yeah." Mitch nodded toward the front booth." She and her husband were the first to show up. The way she's telling everyone about her room at the inn, you'd think she was a famous Hollywood celebrity."

"I guess I'd better enhance the story I wrote about her."

Scott snickered. "You mean add a lot more fiction."

"Whatever it takes to keep the peace. Where are you seating us, Mitch?"

"In the back-corner booth. At least it will give you a little bit of privacy."

Neighbors greeted Emily and Scott with smiles and words of encouragement as Mitch led them through the crowd. Four wine glasses, two bottles of wine—a red on the table and a white in a silver chiller sitting table side—awaited them. Emily noticed a bottle on every table. "Did Pepper get a liquor license?"

Mitch shook his head. "They're all non-alcoholic."

Emily read the label. "I never knew such a thing existed."

"At least we won't look totally unsophisticated.

"Smart move." Emily touched Scott's arm. "Will you slide in first? I want to sit on the outside in case my pregnancy bladder decides to give me fits."

He scooted across the seat facing the back wall. She slipped in beside him.

Miss Gertie, sitting with friends at the adjacent table, turned toward their booth. "Everyone's real excited about tonight."

Emily grinned. "Did you change your mind about protesting a vine-yard in our back yard?"

A smile lit up her face and deepened her wrinkles. "I decided if Jesus can turn water into wine, I can show some tolerance and welcome our newcomers with open arms."

"Good for you."

"Wait until you see the menu. Pepper has topped the charts tonight."

"What did you order?"

"I started with lobster bisque. I don't know what it is, but it sounds real fancy."

"All I can say, sweet lady, is you're in for a delicious treat." Emily reached across Scott and tossed her purse on the seat. "There's nothing Southern about lobster bisque."

"Maybe Pepper is interviewing for a job as head chef for the hotel dining room." He patted her knee.

She squeezed his hand. "I'm beginning to think everything is about to turn in our favor."

Chapter 42

Rachel clung to Charlie's arm as they made their way down the incline. "One thing's for sure, your dad picked a beautiful location to launch his dream."

"He has some peculiar ideas, but he's one smart guy."

"Are those family traits?"

"I'll let you figure that out."

When they arrived at the truck, Rachel opened the back door and reached into her overnight bag.

Charlie leaned on the passenger door. "Can I help you get something?"

"I want to change shoes before we head into town."

"Uh oh. Are you one of those women who has a different pair for every day of the year?"

"Not even close." She sat on the running board and pulled off her sneakers and socks. "I just prefer sandals for a nice dinner."

"One look at your gorgeous face and the guys will never see what's on your feet."

"I guarantee the women will."

She knocked dirt off her sneakers and tossed them on the floor. "Okay, I'm ready to go."

"Willow Falls, here we come."

He drove past a smattering of modest frame houses on lots carved out of the woods. "It looks like pickup trucks are the vehicle of choice around here, which means I'll fit right in."

"So far, I'm not seeing anything to write home about."

"Give it a break already. You're starting to sound like a narrow-minded city dweller."

"I'm just saying ..."

Charlie slowed and turned onto Main Street. The dense woods gave way to manicured lawns fronting seven Southern-style, two-story homes. Mature trees provided shade and beauty.

"Now what are you thinking?"

A squirrel darted into the street, hesitated, and scurried back to the curb.

"Pull over and stop."

"Why? The varmint got out of the way."

She pointed to a brass sign attached to the bottom of a black curbside mailbox. "See what that says? This is Naomi Jasper's home."

"And this is significant because?"

"She's a successful Southern artist. My father has one of her paintings." Rachel stepped out of the truck and stood on the sidewalk leading to the wrap-around front porch.

Charlie caught up with her. "What are you going to do, knock on her door and invite yourself in for a cup of tea?"

"She lives in Charleston, so I doubt she's here."

"Too bad she left Willow Falls. The town could use a celebrity."

"At least she didn't let the old homestead go. I want to take a look at the studio her dad built for her when she was a child prodigy."

"I'm not sure the neighbors will appreciate strangers snooping around."

Rachel shrugged. "The house next door and the one across the street look empty. Besides, they're for sale, so people are likely to think we're prospective buyers."

"I hope you're right."

She hastened down the driveway, which ended at a free-standing garage, twenty feet behind the house. To the right stood a miniature two-story, gingerbread-style structure painted pale green with pink and white accents. "Oh my gosh, it's adorable."

Rachel moved onto the porch and peered in the double window. The back of the building was two stories tall, with floor-to-ceiling windows. Easels and canvases were scattered around the room. Shelves holding artist's supplies lined a side wall. "This is where her fame and fortune started."

"It looks like the artist could walk in and start painting tomorrow. Maybe a hotel and winery will motivate her to come home."

"Which would add at least one paragraph to a publicity flyer."

They returned to the truck and eased up Main. He pulled to the curb beside Willow Inn and rolled the window down. "Is that where we're staying tonight?"

"If it is, Pepper's description didn't do it justice. It's beautiful, and based on the size, I bet someone important—"

"And rich—"

"Lived there before it was turned into a guest house."

Charlie nodded toward the white-columned estate to their right. "More good news. If either one of us comes down with a case of the flu or food poisoning, we can trudge across the street."

"It's too bad all hospitals aren't as charming as this one. If I had to go in for an operation, I'd feel like Scarlet O'Hara strolling into Tara after captivating my suitors."

"Maybe the surgeon looks like Rhett Butler."

"Which means it would be elective surgery, for sure."

"Aha. You're attracted to Southern gentlemen with skinny moustaches."

"You've obviously watched *Gone with the Wind*."

"It's required viewing for native Georgians." He inched forward and let out a long whistle. "Man, if that's the hotel Dad mentioned, it's going to take a heap of work to get it ready for tourists."

"I think it's lovely, all that ivy crawling up the walls. Speaking from a real-estate-development perspective, I'd say it has a ton of potential. If there's a ton of money to get the job done. I suspect a town this size would have a hard time coming up with the funds."

"According to Dad, they have an investor. Some guy in Savannah."

"No kidding. Maybe there's hope for this out-of-the-way piece of geography after all."

Charlie pulled forward. "It looks like something big is going on downtown. Every parking space is taken." He turned right on to Falls Street.

"Slow down a minute." She pointed to the boarded-up ticket booth and *For Rent* notice on the Willow Falls Cinema marquee.

"I wonder why it closed?"

"Several years back, I read an article about small town theaters closing up because they couldn't afford equipment to show digital film. I bet that's what happened."

"You can't stop progress." He circled the block and parked in front of the Willow Falls Post headquarters. "Not much of a newspaper office."

"How much space do you think they need to put out a biweekly?"

"I suppose not much." Charlie hopped out and opened the door for Rachel. "We're ten minutes ahead of schedule."

"Good, because I want to take a closer look at that old-fashioned general store." They crossed the street, strolled down the block, and peeked in the window. "I bet this place dates back more than a hundred years."

"It doesn't look like it's changed much."

"That's what makes it so appealing. We have to come back tomorrow, before we hike up to the waterfall."

Rachel spun around and studied Main Street. "Every little store has a different facade. And a park and lake across the street. I mean, wow. It's a perfect set for a mid-century television series."

"Looking at all those cars, I suspect someone important showed up."

Rachel thumped Charlie's arm. "See, there is a good reason I changed my shoes."

"Come on, sandal-footed woman, let's go meet the lead characters."

"Now you're talking my language." Without thinking, she linked arms with him for the block-long stroll to Pepper's Café.

Chapter 43

Emily ran her finger down the single-page menu printed under the title *Pepper's Café, Home of Fine Dining*. "Filet mignon with hollandaise sauce, pecan-crusted trout, chicken marsala? And chocolate truffle cake or peanut butter cheesecake with marshmallow topping for dessert?"

Scott pushed his menu aside. "If this doesn't impress Rachel and Charlie, I don't know what will."

"Remember, they're from Atlanta—"

"Where there are lots of fancy restaurants. I know. But I'll bet you twenty bucks they aren't expecting anything like this in Willow Falls."

Emily frowned. "Of course not. What if they find out this is a one-time thing? They'll think we're a bunch of phonies trying to pull a fast one on them."

"Hold on a minute. If your host went all out to make your experience first class, wouldn't you be impressed?"

"I see your point."

"And at the very least, they'll know we're not a bunch of bumpkins who don't know how to put on a fancy spread."

Emily caressed a pink camellia nestled on a magnolia leaf. "I admit it's amazing how Pepper pulled all this off in less than a week. Maybe I *should* recruit her as head chef for the hotel. I'm thinking Pepper's Café for breakfast and lunch and the hotel for dinner. At least at first."

"A café and a hotel restaurant? Folks around here won't know what to think."

"Mom talked about a fancy hotel dining room with white linen, fresh flowers, and candles." She snapped her fingers. "I have a great idea. We can put a piano in there and hire our high-school music teacher to play for the guests Friday and Saturday nights."

Scott propped his elbow on the table, rested his head on his knuckles, and stared at her.

"What?"

"How do you do it?"

"Do what?"

"Change from skeptic to romantic optimist in less than twenty minutes."

"Hey, I'm a female. Shifting emotional gears is in my DNA."

Scott smiled. "Did I remember to tell you how beautiful you look?"

"Yeah, but I love hearing it again." She smiled and turned her attention to Sadie approaching Gertie's table with a tray of bowls. Emily caught her eye and motioned her over.

"Are you two ready for your guests?"

"I think we are. The café looks amazing. And this menu is spectacular. Did you help Pepper pull all this together?"

"I helped with the decorating. The menu choices are all hers."

"You two make a great team."

"Thanks. Sorry I can't talk. I've got a lot of food to serve."

"We'll see you at the inn after dinner."

Sadie pivoted and rushed back to the kitchen.

"Hey, everybody, they're coming in the door." Mirabelle's voice boomed across the room.

Emily breathed deeply. "Here we go."

Chatter slowed and came to an abrupt halt—the momentary silence was broken by gasps.

"From the reaction, you'd think a pair of Martians just invaded our little town." She scooted to the edge of her seat, swung her legs to the side, and stood. Her smile vanished. Her knees buckled. She gripped the table edge to break her fall.

Scott slid behind her and gripped her shoulders. "What's going on?"

She squeezed her eyes shut and pressed her fingers against her temples. She had to be hallucinating. It was the only plausible explanation.

Chapter 44

Rachel stopped on the sidewalk beside the café and glanced in the window. "Oh my gosh. Look at all those people."

"The place is packed like sardines. Either the food's spectacular or the owner's got a two-for-one special going on."

"There's a third possibility. This really is a movie set?" Her shoulders tensed. "And we're the main attraction."

"Two out-of-town strangers? That doesn't make sense."

"Think about it. You're the guy who's going to build the winery and I'm your city-slicker sidekick."

Charlie shook his head. "If you're right, these people need a lot more forms of entertainment."

"Do I look okay?" She straightened her jacket collar. "I should have worn nicer clothes. A blouse and sweater or a tailored jacket. Maybe a skirt instead of jeans."

He clasped his hand over hers. "Relax. Did you tell anyone we were walking the land before dinner?"

"I think so. I mean, yeah."

"Okay then, no one expects you to be all dressed up. Besides, like you said, the ladies will love your fancy sandals."

She puffed her cheeks and blew out air. "Sorry for all the drama. I must sound like an egotistical, crazy woman."

"Not too much. I have an idea."

"Find a drugstore and buy a bottle of tranquillizers?"

He laughed. "Nope. Pretend you're a famous actress on tour with a Broadway show."

"Why?"

"So, you can show up and wow your adoring fans."

"Now you're talking crazy." He didn't know about the hours she stood by her office window and played imaginary leading roles. "For the past seven years, all my performances were in my head or to invisible audiences."

"What in the heck are you talking about?"

Did I say that out loud? He'll for sure think I'm a nutcase now. "Never mind."

"Okay, pretty lady. What do you want to do?"

"Buck up, go in, and enjoy dinner with our hosts."

"Good decision." Charlie held the door open. Rachel stepped inside.

Every person in the room turned in their direction. Chatter slowed, then stopped cold. Forks and glasses froze in midair.

Rachel dug her fingers into Charlie's arm. She leaned close and whispered. "Why are they all staring at us like we're aliens from outer space? Is there a big black smudge on my face? Is my shirt unbuttoned?"

"No. It's ..." He pointed toward the back corner.

Her eyes followed the direction of his finger.

A woman stood beside a booth, her mouth agape. She stumbled. Rachel watched a man grip her shoulders. "Please tell me we just crossed over into the twilight zone?"

Charlie leaned close. "We're still in Willow Falls and she's real."

Recognition filtered through the fog in Rachel's head. She covered her mouth with her hand to stifle a gasp. *How is this possible?*

"Do you want to leave?"

"I can't. I have to go meet her."

Charlie clasped his hand over hers and guided her through the sea of gaping strangers.

Chapter 45

Emily opened her eyes. She pressed her hand to her chest and watched Charlie guide Rachel through the crowd to their booth. An electrifying shock coursed through her. Here, in Pepper's Café—on an ordinary Saturday night—she stood face to face with her mirror image.

Neither woman uttered a word.

Gertie jumped from her seat. With a wide-eyed expression, she looked from one to the other. "Do you two know you look exactly alike?" She tapped Emily's arm. "Did your mama know about this? Or her mama?"

Emily struggled to find her voice. "No. I mean, I don't know."

"Well, somebody's got to know about you two. I mean a lady can't give birth to twins without noticing."

"You're right, Miss Gertie, it appears these two ladies have a lot to talk about." Scott motioned toward the booth. "Rachel, Charlie, please have a seat."

While the two couples slid into the booth, Nathan stood and tapped a utensil on his glass. "Okay, everybody, it's time to stop rubbernecking and let these folks enjoy a fine meal in peace. You'll have plenty of time to talk about everything tomorrow."

"He's one smart man," Charlie said.

Scott nodded. "He's our pastor. He's also the town's mayor and owner of a furniture store."

Emily tuned out the sounds around her and stared at Rachel. Did her dad have a child with another woman? Impossible. She couldn't imagine him cheating on her mother. What was Rachel thinking? *One of us has to say the first word.* She swallowed the lump in her throat. "We thought casual conversation would be good to start. I guess that's out the window." Her head tilted. "I can't believe we have the same hairstyle, except yours is a bit shorter."

Rachel massaged the back of her neck. "I'm thinking maybe I suffered a stroke and I'm lying on a gurney plagued with one giant illusion."

Charlie nudged her arm. "I can attest to the fact that you're sitting here in the flesh with your identical twin."

Emily pressed her hand to her chest. His comment brought back memories of her letters to Santa and pleas to God. "I spent my entire childhood begging for a sister. One of us is … oh my gosh. The envelope. The one I found in Mom and Dad's desk." She shifted to the right. "I have to go get it."

Scott put his arm around her shoulder. "I suggest you wait till we finish dinner, honey. So we don't add to the drama."

"But I have to know."

"He's right." Rachel tucked a lock of hair behind her ear. "It's best we act as normal as possible."

"Right now, I have no idea what normal looks like."

Mitch stepped up to their table and removed a bottle from the chiller. "May I start you folks off with a glass of wine? Sorry it's not the real thing. We'll have our liquor license by the time the winery is open."

"Meet Sheriff Mitch Cushman," Scott said. "His wife is the owner and chef of this fine establishment."

Charlie pushed his glass across the table. "Does everyone around here pull double duty?"

Mitch nodded. "People step up when the need arises." He uncorked the bottles and poured a round of Chardonnay. "If I may, I suggest you start with the lobster bisque, a house specialty. The white wine will compliment it nicely. Next, try the salad with raspberry vinaigrette. All three entrées are excellent, but the steak is going fast. If that's your choice, I urge you place your orders now."

Emily stared at Mitch. Did he take a crash course in a professional waiter's class? She heard something about ordering steak and managed to mumble "me too" as her mind swirled with new questions.

Scott and Charlie engaged in guy talk until Mitch returned with four bowls.

Gertie peered over her shoulder. "You'll love the soup. It's the yummiest I've ever tasted. I hear it has a touch of sherry, so eat it slow."

Charlie grinned. "Thank you for the warning, ma'am." He swallowed a spoonful. "She's right, it is delicious. This café isn't anything like my dad described it."

Scott cleared his throat. "It's gone through a recent transformation."

Rachel dipped her spoon in her bowl and locked eyes with Emily. "What's the envelope you mentioned?"

"Something I found when I was going through my parents' belongings. I thought it was old love letters."

"I have a question. Do you look like your mom or dad? Is either a redhead?"

Emily broke eye contact. At times, she'd wondered why she didn't favor either parent. "They're both taller than me. Mom's a brunette, brown eyes. Dad's hair is also dark. What about you?"

"I favor my mother." Rachel tasted the bisque. "This is exceptional." She pointed her spoon at Emily. "So, you're a writer?"

"A wannabe."

Scott laid his spoon down. "Oh, she's way beyond wannabe. She's working on her first novel. When you check into the Willow Inn, take time to read the stories she wrote about your room's namesakes. They'll give you a sense of how good she is."

Emily tilted her head. "Do you write?"

Rachel shrugged. "Boring business stuff."

Charlie scooped the last drop of bisque from his bowl. "From what she tells me, Rachel also has a creative side. She's done some acting."

"Back in my college days. Nothing since."

As they ate, the foursome dabbled in idle conversation, avoiding the giant elephant in the room. By the time she finished her steak, Emily's bladder forced her to slide out of the booth.

In the ladies' room, she leaned on the sink and stared in the mirror. Was she gazing at her own image or had Rachel magically appeared? Was her life-long yearning for a sister driven by some strange, subconscious awareness? Or was she experiencing the most far-fetched coincidence in the world. *That's not possible. We're too identical not to come from the same gene pool.*

The sealed envelope loomed large in her mind. She had to open it. At the same time, she was terrified to find out what secrets it held.

Someone tapped on the door.

"Just a minute." She washed her hands and returned to the table. Four desserts had replaced their dinner plates. She picked at her cheesecake and stole glances at Rachel. *We even wear the same shade of lipstick.*

Sadie's former nemesis wandered up to their table. "I'm Mirabelle. Nobody around here knew Emily had a twin."

Rachel pushed her plate aside. "Believe me, neither did we."

Charlie extended his hand. "It's a pleasure to meet you."

"Likewise. I hear you two are staying in the Carlie and Nora suites tonight. But you'll notice one of the rooms has my name on it."

"I take it you're someone special." Charlie released Mirabelle's hand.

Mirabelle beamed. "Years ago, Robert Liles'—he owned the house before he died—begged me to work for him. He was such a nice man. Anyway, the inn looks a lot like it did back then. There's an antique dresser—most likely worth a fortune—in the Mirabelle suite and the fancy quilt my grandma handmade. I donated it to the inn."

Rachel pushed her plate aside. "How thoughtful."

"I'm an expert on Willow Falls. Sort of a local historian. I've lived here all my life and now I head up the post office."

I really do have to spruce up her story. Emily laid her fork on the table. "Everyone in town knows Mirabelle."

"And I know everybody and everything that goes on around here. We're going to fix up that old hotel so tourists can visit your winery and stay overnight. I'm telling you, Willow Falls promises to give other Georgia tourist attractions a run for their money."

Emily fidgeted. "I'll ask Sadie to show them your room."

"And read them my story." Mirabelle tapped the table. "Are you coming in for breakfast tomorrow? I hear Pepper has another special menu all made up for you."

Emily dropped her napkin on the table. It was impossible to keep anything under wraps in this town. "That's our plan." She scooted out of her seat. "But now we need to get our guests checked in." She sensed every eye in the place followed the foursome as they made their way to the front door. Outside, she shouldered her purse and scanned the parking spaces. "Where's your car?"

Charlie nodded toward the right. "My truck is around the corner in front of the newspaper office."

"The inn's just up the street. Why don't you drive over and meet us there?"

"Good idea."

The two couples headed in the opposite direction. Emily glanced over her shoulder to confirm Charlie and Rachel were out of earshot. "Mirabelle and her big mouth."

Scott reached for her hand. "Odds are Rachel didn't pay much attention to her."

"I hope you're right."

"Do you want me to go home and get the mystery envelope?"

They crossed to the park side of Main Street. Emily recognized a young couple—one of the few who hadn't moved away—sitting on a blanket with their two children. She wondered if the scent of fresh-baked cookies wafted from their picnic basket. "I hope it really is full of love letters."

"I assume your answer is yes."

She nodded and fixed her eyes straight ahead as a frightening thought invaded her mind. What if … no. It wasn't possible.

Chapter 46

Rachel glanced over her shoulder, relieved diners weren't trailing behind them like a band of teenage groupies. *Is this what celebrities have to deal with? Gawkers and curiosity hounds?* The obscure little town she called a television set had indeed become the scene of a bizarre story. When they rounded the corner by the bank, the Willow Post headquarters came into view. She had no idea her initial encounter with Emily—a phone conversation about the winery—was the first act in a mysterious drama. "I bet we make the front page in the next edition."

"You've got that right. Instant twins would be big news, even if the town had an active movie theater." Charlie opened the passenger door.

She climbed in and tossed her purse on the floor.

He scooted to the driver's side.

When he pulled his keys from his pocket, she grasped his arm. "Don't start up yet. I need a few minutes to think."

"Take all the time you need."

She chewed on her fingernail and mentally replayed the past hour. The faces gawking at them. Charlie and Scott trying their best to carry on a neutral conversation. Emily's description of her parents. A seed of anger took root and flourished into full-blown fury. "How could he?"

"How could who do what?"

"My father." Her jaw tensed. "How could he separate us?"

"You're assuming a lot."

"You heard what Emily said about her mom and dad. She doesn't look anything like them." She reached for her wallet and extracted a photo. "You tell me if this woman looks like my mother."

He studied the picture. "Same hair color. Green eyes. There's definitely a strong resemblance."

"Believe me, she would never willingly give up one of her babies. It had to be my father and his insane one-child-per-family attitude. Why does everything have to be his way."

She dug deep into her memory. "I don't remember my mother ever talking about the day I was born." She fingered her mom's tennis bracelet. "But then, I was only eleven when she passed away." Another thought surfaced. She gripped the armrest. "Maybe she didn't know."

"That she was pregnant with twins?"

"No, that Emily survived."

"What are you suggesting?"

"It's possible she wasn't awake when we were born. My father might have told her Emily died."

"That doesn't sound logical or, for that matter, even possible."

"You have no idea what Greer Streetman is capable of when he makes up his mind."

"It's true your father is a hard-nosed business man. But I can't imagine he's coldhearted enough to give up his own flesh and blood." He handed the photo back to her.

"I admit it sounds outrageous." Rachel touched her mother's smiling face. "Mom had a heart of gold. Whatever happened, I have to get to the truth."

"Do you want to drive to Atlanta tonight?"

Rachel slipped the photo back in her wallet. "I just met a woman who looks exactly like me. The only logical explanation is Emily and I share the same DNA. There's no way I'm going to run out on her now. Besides, we have a ton to talk about."

"Okay then." He turned the key and backed out of the parking space.

She stared straight ahead and tried to imagine what was going through Emily's mind.

Chapter 47

When Scott climbed in the car and backed into the street, Emily forced her legs to carry her up the inn's porch stairs. She leaned against the porch railing, pressed her fingers to the back of her neck to release the tension, and caught sight of her reflection in the parlor window. She'd never questioned why she looked so different from her parents. Until now.

Her mind wandered back to the residents' reaction when Rachel stepped into the café. What were they thinking about the Redding family?

A vehicle pulled into the driveway and stopped. She pivoted and gripped the porch railing. Seeing her twin climb down from the truck was akin to watching a movie in which she was cast as the lead character. Except the man pulling bags from the back seat wasn't Scott. She loosened her grip and forced her mind to shift from confused sibling to hostess.

Charlie and Rachel climbed onto the porch.

Emily held the door open. "Welcome to Willow Inn."

Inside, Sadie stood beside the antique desk, holding two small gift bags—one gold, the other black. Her gaze shifted from one sister to the other. "I didn't believe it when Mitch told me you and Emily look exactly alike." She handed the gold bag to Rachel and the black to Charlie. "Welcome gifts."

Emily had looked forward to greeting their first official guests, but never in her wildest imagination could she have imagined this scenario. "Sadie will show you to your rooms."

"Miss Rachel, you're downstairs in the Carlie suite." Sadie led the way.

Emily moved to the parlor, dropped on a wingback chair, and stared at the still-life painting above the fireplace. Her pulse quickened when Scott walked into the foyer.

He tossed the envelope on the coffee table and sat in the chair beside her, "Do you want to open it now?"

"I don't know. Maybe I should wait."

"The Carlie suite is lovely." Rachel sauntered in and settled on the chocolate settee. "Sadie said it's named for her mother."

Charlie followed and sat beside her.

Under Rachel's pointed stare, Emily came to one undeniable conclusion. She'd spent the first nine months of her existence in the womb with the woman sitting across from her. Someone separated them. A fatal accident and one man's dream to start a winery brought them back together. She stared at the envelope laying on the coffee table like a shroud concealing a mysterious secret. "I have to find out what's in it."

Scott pulled a knife from his pocket and cut through the tape sealing the flap. Emily removed random sheets of paper and tossed the envelope on the floor. Flipping through the sheets, she sighed. "Mom's love letters."

"Wait." Scott reached down and retrieved the shroud. "There's something else in there." He pulled out a legal-sized envelope, removed its contents, and placed it in Emily's hands.

She read the two-page document and pressed her hand to her chest. "I don't understand why Mom and Dad didn't tell me." Her voice cracked. "I wouldn't have loved them any less." She pushed the papers across the coffee table. "Keeping my adoption a secret is one thing, but to deny me my sister—how could they?"

Rachel read through the document. "There's no mention of the birth mother or a twin. I doubt your parents knew I existed."

"How could they not know?"

Rachel reached for the pillow with the intricate floral design and traced the outline of a pink rose. "This looks handmade."

"Sadie's grandmother." A kick compelled her to press her hand to her belly. "Did I tell you I'm pregnant?"

"Not until now. Twins?"

Emily nodded. "Both girls."

"Maybe they're identical. In my wildest imagination, I could never have predicted today." Rachel tucked a lock of hair behind her ear. "I believe we were destined to find each other."

"Now I understand why I've longed for a sister all these years." Emily's voiced faltered. "I missed my other half." Elation, sprinkled with a huge dose of confusion, overwhelmed her. She pushed up, moved around the coffee table, and held her arms out.

Rachel wiped tears from her cheeks and embraced her sister. "Whatever the future holds for us, we'll face it together."

Chapter 48

Emily stood at the patio door sipping a cup of coffee, watching Cody romp in the backyard. Scott slipped up behind her and wrapped his arms around her waist. "When did you wake up?"

"Way before dawn. For as long as I live, I'll consider Nora and Roger my parents."

"Because they are."

"At the same time, I have to know why my birth mother give me away. Is there something wrong with me?"

"I guarantee there's not a thing wrong with you. Whatever the reason, I'm glad she did. Otherwise, I'd never have met you."

Emily spun around and gazed into his eyes. "And I wouldn't be carrying our babies. Maybe it's best I accept things the way they are."

"That's your decision." He glanced at his watch. "It's time to head over to Pepper's. Are you ready?"

"I suppose."

Emily fell silent during the ride downtown. Once there, she followed Scott inside and sighed. "At least the café is less crowded than last night."

They strolled to the front booth and settled across from Charlie and Rachel. "I hope you slept okay, given the circumstances."

"It took me a while to fall asleep." Rachel emptied a packet of sugar in her coffee. "I loved the story about Sadie's mother. You're a talented writer."

"Thanks. I'm writing a novel inspired by Willow Falls' history. It's based on real events and people with some interesting, quirky fictional characters thrown in the mix."

Charlie laughed. "Like some of the people we met last night."

Sadie hustled in from the kitchen. "If I may, I recommend the eggs benedict."

"You're an industrious woman, holding down two jobs." Rachel unfolded a linen napkin and laid it across her lap.

Sadie pulled an order pad from her apron pocket. "I'm helping Emily at the inn until she finds someone to fill the position."

"You should take it." Rachel smiled. "I mean, you're a great innkeeper—attentive but not obtrusive."

"Thanks." Sadie poised her pencil over the pad. "About your order, the blueberry pancakes are also a great choice."

Scott grinned. "I'll go with the pancakes."

"Me too," said Charlie.

After she and Emily opted for the eggs, Rachel leaned back and crossed her arms. "You have to come to Atlanta today."

"Why?"

"To confront our father tomorrow morning."

"We had a whole day of events planned." Emily massaged the back of her hand. Should she wait and mention their objective after breakfast? No, she had to get it out. "Here's the thing. We're hoping Streetman Enterprise will take interest in investing in our town."

Rachel leaned on the table. "Investing how?"

"The funding my parents were counting on to refurbish the hotel fell through."

"Another reason you need to go with me. I figure our father owes us big time."

The prospect of meeting the man terrified her. Somehow, for her town's sake, she had to find the courage. She nudged Scott. "Will you come too?"

"You know I will."

Emily breathed deeply. "Okay, but first I have to find someone to watch Cody."

"Who's Cody?"

"My golden retriever."

Rachel pressed her hands together and smiled. "When I was a kid, I begged my father for a dog. All I got were goldfish. You can bring Cody with you."

"Are you sure?"

"I'm positive."

"Okay, as soon as we finish breakfast, we'll pack a bag and meet you at the inn."

Two hours later, Scott pulled into the driveway and opened the passenger door. Cody jumped out and bounded up the steps to the inn's front porch. Rachel dropped to her knees and wrapped her arms around his neck. "You remind me of Brownie."

She stood and skipped down the stairs. Cody padded behind her and jumped into the truck's back seat.

Charlie strolled over to Scott's car. "I think Rachel's in love with your dog. Do you mind if he rides with us?"

Emily leaned across the console. "The question is, do you mind?"

"Not a bit."

"He's never been on a long trip before. I hope he behaves himself."

"I'm sure he will." Charlie backed out of the driveway.

Scott followed his truck up Main to County Road. Near the end of the straightaway, a yellow road sign indicating an S-shaped curve struck Emily with the force of a ten-pound sledge hammer. Someone should have done something about the dangerous road. Why didn't she wait until her parents returned home to tell them about the babies? They didn't have to die for her to find her sister.

Twenty minutes later, Scott reached across the seat and squeezed her hand. "You can relax now, we're past the danger zone."

"How'd you know?"

"Let's see, your death grip on the arm rest, your clenched jaw, your—"

"I get it. I didn't get much sleep last night. Do you mind if I take a nap?"

"As long as you don't snore loud enough to drown out the music."

"I promise." Emily reclined her seat, closed her eyes, and let the music and the car's motion lull her to sleep. A horn startled her awake.

Scott grinned. "Welcome back, sleepyhead."

"How long was I out?"

"Almost the whole trip. I got a text from Rachel. We're ten minutes from her place."

She readjusted her seat to an upright position. "I hope Cody behaved himself."

"Half the time he hung his head out the window with his jowls flapping. What is it about dogs and hurricane force wind?"

"Who knows?" A view of the Atlanta skyline conjured up memories of Emily's last trip to Atlanta with her mother. She glanced out the side window. What was Rachel doing that Saturday? What about tomorrow? Would her father toss her to the wind a second time?

Scott exited the Interstate and followed Charlie onto side streets lined with stately homes, manicured lawns, and massive trees. "Your sister lives in a ritzy part of town."

"Her father owns a business, so he's most likely rich."

Moments later, they pulled onto a driveway leading to a two-car garage on the lower level of a three-story brick townhouse.

Rachel hopped out of the truck and opened Emily's door. "I have a mind to kidnap Cody right out from under you."

She stepped out. "He does have a way to capture your heart."

"Come on. The boys will follow when they're ready." Rachel led her up the stairs, into her foyer. "I'm not much of a cook, so I'll order dinner. Would you prefer pizza or Chinese?"

"How about the latter?"

"Prepare to delight your taste buds." Rachel pointed to a door. "I imagine you're looking for the powder room."

"It was a long trip."

Emily washed her hands, checked her makeup, and joined Rachel in the kitchen. "Nice deck. All those big trees look like you're in the country, instead of a big city."

"It's my Sunday morning refuge. I'm friends with the neighborhood hawk, but the squirrels pretty much ignore me. I'm thinking we can eat out there." The guys' voices drifted in from the living room. "But first, I'll show you and Scott where to put your bags."

She followed Rachel upstairs. The guest room's warm colors and eclectic style convinced Emily she and her twin shared more than physical appearance. She pointed to a framed photo of a woman and a young girl. "You and your mother?"

"The year before she died." Rachel opened the closet and pushed clothes aside. "I hope this is enough room. The bottom dresser drawer is empty." She moved to the door. "When you're ready, come on down."

Emily nudged Scott. "Go on, honey, and enjoy their company. I don't need your help to unpack."

The moment he left, she clutched the photo in trembling hands and studied the woman's appearance. Strawberry-blond hair, green eyes. Her mouth went dry. Was she staring at the woman who brought her into this world? If so, what motivated her to keep one twin and discard the other? She placed the picture back on the dresser and poured every ounce of energy into unpacking before joining the others downstairs.

Following idle dinner conversation, Rachel carried empty containers and plates to the kitchen and returned with a platter of cookies. "This is the best I can do in the way of dessert." She leaned back and laced her fingers. "About tomorrow morning. I want to arrive at the office before anyone else, to catch our father off guard. It's the only way to force him to tell us the truth."

Emily cringed at her sister's harsh tone.

Rachel tilted her head. "From the look on your face, I'm thinking you might back out."

The urge to bail and flee back to Willow Falls gripped Emily's gut. But she couldn't bear the thought of abandoning Rachel. "I have no idea what tomorrow will bring." She reached for hand. "Whatever happens, it's comforting to know we're in this together."

Chapter 49

Rachel struggled to steady her hand as she unlocked Greer's office. She stepped inside and motioned Emily and Scott to follow.

"Welcome to my father's domain."

Emily strolled to the credenza behind Greer's desk and picked up Rachel's photo. "Why does your father keep his door locked?"

"Most likely because the artwork in here is worth a fortune. Or, here's another possibility: he has secrets he wants kept hidden."

Emily placed the photo back on the credenza. "What's your plan?"

"I want him to see us the second he walks in, to catch him by surprise."

"I hope he doesn't have a weak heart."

"Believe me, he's tough as nails." Rachel checked her watch. "He'll be here any minute." She led her twin across the room and leaned against the back of the couch, facing the door. "Are you okay?"

"If you call my heart about to burst out of my chest and my knees shaking like we're in the middle of an earthquake okay, then yeah."

Rachel grasped Emily's hand. "I understand. I didn't know my heart could beat this fast."

"Are you afraid of your father?"

"Intimidated is a better description." Rachel locked her eyes on the doorknob and gathered every ounce of courage she could muster as she watched it turn.

Greer Streetman pushed the door open, took one step, and halted. His eyes bulged. "What the …"

Rachel crossed her arms and tapped her biceps. "You didn't think we'd ever find out, did you?"

"How—"

"Willow Falls. Bricker. The vineyard. Ironic, isn't it? Your client was your undoing."

The veins in Greer's neck pulsed. He rushed past the twins and headed straight to his executive chair.

The sisters settled in two leather chairs facing his desk.

"What do you want from me?" His voice was hard, defiant.

Rachel glared. "The truth."

His jaw clenched. "What truth?"

"Why you kept me and discarded my twin."

"It's complicated." His gaze shifted from one to the other. "You look exactly alike."

"Which is what identical means."

"I didn't know."

"I don't believe you."

Greer glared at Rachel. "How dare you sneak into my office and confront me without fair warning." His head jerked toward the couch. "Who's that man?"

"Emily's husband. I demand to know why I have a twin I didn't know existed for twenty-nine years."

Greer's lip curled. He slapped his fist on the desk. "You want the truth? Well, here it is. Your mother wanted a daughter and I wanted an heir to run my business. She tried to get pregnant for seven years. Do you hear me? Seven long, tortuous years and thousands of dollars in tests. Nothing worked. It turned out she wasn't the problem."

"Are you saying—"

"Do I have to spell it out for you?"

"No, I get it."

"I didn't want anyone to know we couldn't have kids, so she secretly searched for an infant everyone would believe was hers. She even feigned pregnancy. A week before the adoption, we discovered the baby she'd selected was a twin. For nine months, we'd told everyone about one baby, not two." He loosened his tie and pulled his shirt away from his neck. "I told your mother the other infant was promised to another couple."

"Was that true?"

"No."

Rachel bolted to her feet. "All these years, you knew and you didn't tell me?"

"I wanted to protect you."

She jabbed her finger at him. "Don't lay that pile of horse manure on me. You wanted to protect your ego and manipulate my life. You robbed me of my dreams to realize yours."

Greer's brow furrowed. "What are you talking about?"

"Do you want to hear the truth? How I hate my job but stuck around because I didn't want to disappoint you and break your heart? Now I find out you're not my father. And worse, you denied me my own sister."

"I didn't mean to—"

"Oh, you meant to all right. Everything you do is intentional and calculated."

"Which is how I turned this company into what it is today. You'll appreciate my tenacity when you sit here and command this ship."

Rachel dropped back onto the chair. "Did you ever think to ask if I wanted to take command?" Her voice cracked. "No. Because you don't care." She took a deep breath. "Look, I know how much your reputation and this company means to you. And deep down, I do love you for raising me. But I can't continue to work for you."

"You can't leave me. I've invested my whole life into you."

"A week ago, I didn't have the courage to walk out. But now, everything's changed." The intensity of his glare startled her. "I'll come up with a logical reason to resign to help you save face. I'll even let you take credit for bringing Emily and me back together. If you want, you can make the announcement this morning."

"You've left me no choice." Greer laid out his plan before hustling out the door and slamming it shut.

Emily ran her fingers through her hair. "I don't know if I'm angry or relieved to find out he's not my father."

"At least now I understand the real reason he and I are nothing alike."

"What do we do now?"

"Wait for the king of the mountain to direct Act Two."

An hour later, Greer escorted Rachel to the head of the long table in the conference room packed with employees. He stood erect and held his head high. His tone dripped with arrogance as he spun a tale about his wife's inability to have a child, their decision to adopt, and his desire to keep it a secret to protect Rachel. "When I discovered she was a twin, I aimed to bring them back together." He nodded to his assistant. "Ladies and gentlemen, I want you to meet Emily Hayes."

Gasps and mumbles echoed throughout the room as she entered and made her way to Rachel's side.

"Now that I've brought them together, they've got a lot of catching up to do, and we've all got a busy week ahead. Thanks for coming in." Greer dismissed his staff with a sweep of his hand. The moment the room cleared, he swaggered out the door.

Rachel tapped her foot. "And there you have it. Greer Streetman in action."

Scott shook his head. "He's one interesting character."

"That's a major understatement." She glanced around the conference room. How many hours had she spent sitting around the massive table listening to her father drone on? "For years, I've wanted a good reason to resign. Now that I have one, I admit I'm apprehensive."

Emily touched her arm. "Fear of the unknown?"

"This is the only work I've ever done. I don't know if I have enough savings to allow me to pursue an acting career." She picked up a photo of Greer breaking ground on a new project. "I don't even know if I'm good enough to make a living in live theater."

Scott linked arms with the sisters. "I don't know about you two, but I'm starving. How about I treat the most beautiful women in Georgia to a nice breakfast?"

"Good idea. I know the perfect spot." Rachel led the way out of the building toward the Peachtree Plaza. A block from the hotel, she stopped in front of her homeless friend. "You're in a different spot today. How's it going?"

He scratched his scraggly beard and focused his rheumy eyes on Rachel. "It's you." He struggled to his feet. "I took the money you gave me over to the shelter. There's too many vets like me to keep it to myself."

Rachel pressed her hand to her chest. "What's your name, sir?"

He straightened and saluted. "Dennis Locke, Private First Class, at your service, ma'am."

"You're a good man, Private Locke." She reached into her purse and removed all the cash from her wallet. Ignoring the odor of sweat and grime, she moved close. "If you take this to the shelter right now, I'll bring you some food."

"And something for my dog?"

She stooped and patted the mutt's head. "I wouldn't leave you out." She straightened and saluted. "Thank you for your service, soldier. We all owe you a debt of gratitude." She watched his eyes gleam before he pivoted and sauntered away.

Emily's mouth dropped open. "Wow, you were way more than generous."

Rachel shrugged. "I feel sorry for the guy. Who knows what drove him to the streets."

They moved on to the hotel and found a seat in the café. When they finished breakfast, Rachel propped her forearms on the table and locked eyes with her twin. "I think we should search for the woman who brought us into this world."

Emily twisted a lock of hair around her finger and bit her lower lip.

"I take it you're not crazy about my idea."

"Maybe it's enough we found each other. I mean, what if we discover something terrible about her? Like she's an addict or a criminal. Maybe she died during childbirth."

Rachel shrugged. "True, or we might discover she gave us up because she was too young, or dirt poor. Besides, someday you might need to know your babies' genetic makeup."

Emily took a deep breath. "I suppose you're right."

"I'll make it a top priority the moment I turn in my resignation."

"Maybe you ought to hold off quitting until you have work lined up." Scott slipped his credit card in the bill folder and pushed it to the edge of the table.

"One thing about my father, he respects decisiveness. If I back out, he'll exploit my weakness and do his best to convince me to stay. I'd rather end up on the street with Private Locke than do any more battle with Greer Streetman."

"How did you manage to work for him for so many years?"

"Believe me, it wasn't easy."

The waiter returned carrying two Styrofoam containers. On the way back to the office, Rachel presented both to Dennis. "An omelet, toast and hash browns for you, bacon and eggs for your dog."

He opened the first container and sniffed. "I'm gonna share this with a friend." He stood and tipped his hat.

Rachel watched him trudge to the end of the block and disappear around the corner. "I wish I could do more to help him."

"What if our mother is a homeless woman living under a bridge or in an old beat-up car?" Emily pressed her hand to her belly. "I don't want my babies to find out something terrible about their grandmother."

Rachel planted her hands on her hips. "If we'd stumbled into a band of gypsies, tramps, and thieves, would you be expecting to find our mom in their midst?"

"I don't know. Maybe."

"I think your writer's imagination is working overtime."

Scott chuckled. "It won't be the first time."

Emily thumped his arm. "And it most likely won't be the last."

Chapter 50

Rachel tossed a stack of notes from clients in the box with the rest of her personal belongings and pushed it to the corner of her desk. She reached for her mother's photo and strolled to the window in the office she'd occupied for seven years. How many times had she stood in this spot pretending it was a stage? It was the closest she'd come to living her dream.

She stared at her mother's pretty face. "Thank you for loving me."

Nancy poked her head in. "Do you have a minute?"

"For you, absolutely. Come on over."

She moseyed to Rachel's side. "Your story about taking a leave of absence to spend time with your sister is only half true, isn't it?"

"I never could pull a fast one on you. The sister part is accurate."

"I'm curious. When your father claimed he brought you and your sister together, I watched your expression." She hesitated. "I suspect his story wasn't factual either."

"Is that the office scuttlebutt?"

Nancy shook her head.

"Good. The truth is—and you can't repeat this to anyone—Emily and I found each other by accident. My father's account was to preserve his dignity."

"You still care about him, don't you?"

Rachel watched the Skyview Ferris Wheel turn, remembering the day she climbed aboard before venturing to the Georgia Aquarium. "I've come to understand Greer loved me the best he knew how. I hope one day, his heart will soften enough to accept me for who I am."

"I suspect once you've been gone for a while, he'll miss you enough to come around."

"You once told me if I left you'd bail. I hope you change your mind, because Greer needs good people like you on his team."

"It depends."

"On what?"

"Who takes your position. What about you, are you on your way to seek fame and fortune on Broadway?"

"Right now, it's difficult to think much past today." Rachel moved to the couch.

Nancy followed and settled beside her. "What about you and Charlie Bricker? You did spend a romantic weekend together."

"The same weekend I met Emily. Believe me, there was nothing romantic about it."

"He seems like a great guy."

"He is. But it's way too early in our relationship to know where it is or isn't going."

"At least now you won't have your father or Brent—"

"Are you two talking about me?" His voice dripped with arrogance.

Nancy leaned close to Rachel and whispered, "Speak of the devil."

Brent plopped in the chair facing the couch and pointed to Rachel's desk. "It looks like you're all packed up."

"I'm getting there."

Nancy stood and headed to the door. "I'll leave you two alone to talk business."

Brent propped his ankle on his knee and glanced around the space. "Except for Greer's, this is the largest office on this floor. It's still on the QT, but he wants me to take your position until you return. I'm thinking maybe you're not coming back."

Rachel eyed Brent's smug expression. "Did he offer to adopt you or simply knight you as his heir in training?"

"What's with the attitude?"

"I have an important piece of advice for you."

"About clients?"

"No, about you."

His head tilted. "What about me?"

"If you treat employees with respect and show them appreciation, you'll serve your boss well."

"That's nuts. You know your father values grit and toughness."

"Yes, but he needs someone in a position of authority to soften his hard edges. Trust me, you'll make a great team if you play the role of good cop."

Brent fingered his sock. "I'll miss watching you butter up the troops at Cut's Steakhouse."

"That chore now belongs to you, if you can manage to check your ego at the door and follow my advice. Another thing: if you treat Nancy right, she'll be your best ally. Disrespect her and she'll leave in a heartbeat."

Brent eyed Rachel for a long moment. "Rumor is you and Charlie Bricker are an item."

"Here's the thing about rumors, you can't trust them. You know, if you don't let Greer rule your life, you'll find the right woman to ride along with you on your journey to the top."

"It could have been you. Oh, I almost forgot why I came in. Greer wants to meet with you."

Rachel waited for the highly paid messenger boy to strut out, then retrieved a file folder from her desk and strolled to the corner office one last time. Inside she found Greer staring out the window, his feet shoulder-length apart, his arms crossed over his chest. She stepped beside him and let her gaze wander toward the Fox Theater. "I'll miss this view."

"A view from the top isn't always what it's cracked up to be." He unfolded his arms, pivoted, and strode to the couch.

She settled beside him and eyed a gold gift box wrapped with a green ribbon laying on the coffee table. Beside it stood a bottle of champagne and two flutes. She tossed the file folder beside the box. "Are you expecting an important client or a VIP?"

"I have something for you." Greer placed the package in her hand. "A little going away gift."

"At least it's too big for another expensive pen." She slipped the ribbon and lid off, peeled back a layer of tissue paper, and peered inside. Stunned, she removed a framed photo of her parents—their smiles beaming—holding a baby swaddled in a pink blanket, her tiny hand gripping her father's finger.

"It was taken the day we adopted you. From the moment I first saw you, I wanted you to follow in my footsteps. So, I raised you like you were my own flesh and blood."

Rachel placed the photo back in the box.

Greer leaned forward and rested his forearms across his knees. "I wasn't completely honest with you before." He hesitated for a long moment. "The truth is, when your mother found out you had a twin, she wanted to admit she wasn't pregnant and take both of you. My pride wouldn't let her. That's why I told her another couple adopted the other baby." His voice faltered. "I was wrong to separate you and Emily. I hope you can forgive me."

A lump formed in Rachel's throat as tears trickled down her cheeks. She clasped her father's hand. "Thank you for telling me the truth." Her voice was soft. "I forgive you."

Greer pulled a handkerchief from his pocket and held it out for her. "No matter what happens, you'll always be my Strawberry Girl. And, by the way, you're the VIP I'm expecting." He twisted the cork off the champagne and filled both flutes. "The last time we toasted, it was to celebrate my plans for your life." He clinked his glass to hers. "This is to the future you choose. I hope it brings you all the happiness you deserve."

Rachel pictured the imaginary shackles around her ankles shattering into a thousand tiny pieces and blowing away in the wind. "You'll always be my father."

He patted her hand, laid his glass on the coffee table, and pointed to the file folder. "Last minute work?"

"As a matter of fact, it's something you can do for Emily and me." She sniffed, opened the file, and extracted a document. "A contract for Streetman Enterprise to invest in a hotel refurbishment in Willow Falls."

"The location of Bricker's winery."

"And the town where Emily lives. I've run the numbers and I think it's a good investment.

He nodded. "But even if it isn't, you figure I owe you."

"Yeah, you do."

"I'll get finance to cut a check and have it couriered to you tomorrow. Unless you're willing to meet me for lunch and let me give it to you personally."

"Lunch sounds delightful."

"Okay then. Noon at the Sun Dial Restaurant. Afterwards, I'll treat you to a ride on the Ferris wheel."

Rachel smiled. "Perfect."

Chapter 51

Emily moseyed into the nursery and lit a baby-powder-scented candle—a gift from her mom. She tamped down her sorrow, settled in the rocking chair, and set her computer on her lap. The Cinderella castle scene Nathan's daughter had painted on the wall made her smile. *Perfect for two little princesses.*

Cody lumbered in, sat on his haunches, and scratched behind his ear.

"When our girls are older, we have to take them to Disney World." She remembered entering the Magic Kingdom, skipping down Main Street, and gazing in awe at the castle holding center stage. The trip—her tenth birthday gift—marked the beginning of her writing experience. During the ride home, she filled a spiral notebook with a story about a princess who escaped the palace to save her village from the wicked king. Following their return from Orlando, her mom bragged about the princess story to everyone in town.

Cody yawned and stretched out in the swath of sunlight pouring in the window.

"Enough with the memories. I have to get to work." She booted her laptop, opened her manuscript, and scrolled to the end of the first chapter. One more read-through of the final paragraph convinced her she'd ended with a compelling hook. "It's time to move on to chapter two."

She closed her eyes and mentally ticked off a list of essentials for paragraph one. Identify the point-of-view. Set the scene. Establish the character's mood. So much to remember.

Doubt trickled in and paralyzed her fingers. What made her think a historical story about country folks in a small Georgia town would interest anyone outside her little world. Maybe she should write a political thriller and add some sexy scenes to appeal to the masses.

The thought sent a chill through her. "What's wrong with me? I started out wanting to write a novel to entice people to visit Willow Falls. Is my ego getting in the way? Or am I afraid of failing?"

She closed her computer, hopped up, and blew out the candle. "Come on, Cody. It's time to open the *Emily's Treasures* carton I found in my parents' closet and find out if Mom kept my story."

She found the box in the garage and carried it to the kitchen table. Inside, a treasure trove of memorabilia delighted her. Girl Scout badges. Field-day ribbons. Cards she'd made to celebrate Mother and Father's Days. A black velvet box protecting her first baby tooth.

Underneath a stack of report cards lay the notebook. She lifted it from the box and carried it to the nursery. Wearing a smile, she set the rocking chair in motion and opened to page one. An hour later, she pressed the tome to her chest. Despite the absence of professionalism, raw talent had jumped off every page.

Rachel's account of childhood plays she had created and performed for her mother came to mind. What about the stories of Naomi Jasper's father building a studio for the prodigy before she turned sixteen? Were children's interests and accomplishments inspired by God-given talent? If they were, how many recognized their gifts and carried them into adulthood?

She glanced at the glow-in-the-dark stars Scott put on the ceiling. Inspiration for dreamers. She pressed her hand to her tummy. What talents did her babies possess? How could she inspire them if she didn't accept her writing skill as a gift to respect and nurture?

Emily moved to the window. Cody wandered beside her, planted his paws on the sill, and pressed his nose to the glass. "There's a great big world out there beyond our little corner of Georgia." She spun around and headed toward the door. "And I'm going to introduce it to the most fascinating town and characters in the South. Maybe in the entire country."

Chapter 52

Rachel arrived at the Sun Dial five minutes early and followed a hostess to a reserved table. The last time she enjoyed the view from the floor-to-ceiling windows in the revolving restaurant, Charlie sat across from her. In a few minutes her father would occupy that position. *Which Greer will show up today? The father who apologized? Or the demanding boss?* She pressed her lips together, determined to face either with confidence.

She turned her attention to the view and the building that housed Streetman Enterprise. Which window was her office and her imaginary stage?

"Have you been waiting long?"

She turned toward the sound of her father's voice and pressed her hand to her chest. "Oh my gosh. Is that—"

"Brownie?" He pulled the brown-and-white stuffed puppy from under his arm and laid it on the table. "Your mother wanted to give you a real dog."

Rachel reached for the gift and choked back tears. Greer, her father, had showed up. "You have no idea how much this means to me."

He sat across from her, cleared his throat, and shifted to his comfort zone—business man. During lunch, they discussed clients and Brent's transition to her position. At least he didn't ask her to coach the man. Following his last bite of dessert, he laid his fork down, pulled an envelope from his jacket pocket, and pushed it across the table.

She opened it and removed a check. "Wow, this is more than I requested."

"I talked to Emily. Based on her description of the hotel's condition, I figured you could use the extra funds. Besides, I'm expecting a good return on my investment."

When the waiter arrived with the bill, Greer paid with cash, stepped behind Rachel, and pulled her chair away from the table. "Next stop, the Skyview Ferris Wheel."

She clung to her father's arm as the elevator descended. Outside, she donned her sunglasses. "On the way, I want to introduce you to a friend." She rounded the corner and spotted her target. "Private Dennis Locke meet my father, Greer Streetman."

Dennis stood, wiped his hand on his pants, and held it out. "Pleased to make your acquaintance, sir."

Greer's jaw dropped. "I, uh ..."

"It's okay." Rachel reached down and patted the dog's head. "Dennis is a true American hero."

He hesitated, then accepted the man's hand. "It's a pleasure to meet you as well."

"Your daughter is a mighty generous lady."

Rachel grinned. "If you give him money, he'll share it with other vets at the homeless shelter." She nudged Greer's arm. "And don't be stingy."

"Are you suggesting—"

"Open your wallet ... Dad."

Greer stared at her. His eyes moistened. "You never called me dad before."

"I hope you don't mind. So, how much are you going to give my friend?"

He removed his wallet from his back pocket and pulled out two hundred-dollar bills. "Will this do?"

Dennis stood ramrod straight and saluted. "Yes, sir, that'll help feed a whole bunch of guys." He tipped his hat to Rachel. "Thank you, ma'am, for caring."

Rachel held her breath and embraced the private. "You take good care of yourself now, you hear."

He sniffed and wiped a tear from his eye. "You too."

He scrambled down the street and turned toward the shelter.

"What makes you think he didn't fleece me?"

270

Rachel smiled. "I had a stab of doubt after giving him money a second time, so I called the shelter and found out he turned over every penny. Believe me, he's one of the good guys."

"Why is he living on the street?"

"I don't know. Maybe someday I'll find out." She linked arms with her father's. They strolled to the Ferris wheel, bought tickets, and climbed aboard.

Near the pinnacle, he clasped his hands in his lap. "I loved the woman who raised you more than you can imagine." His voice wavered. "When she died, a part of me died with her. To keep from going mad, I poured all my energy into growing Streetman Enterprise and raising you to follow in my footsteps."

"I know."

He turned toward her. "I've been wanting to ask … are you looking for your birth parents?"

Rachel stared at the ground below and spotted a red balloon escaping from a little boy's hand and drifting upward. "So far, I haven't had any luck finding them, but I'm not giving up. I was hoping you'd know something."

"It was a confidential adoption, meaning we didn't know the birth mother." He paused and shifted in his seat. "However, both parties gave consent to release the records if the need ever arose. I'll give you the name of the agency we used."

"I suspect this isn't easy for you."

"I've kept you in the dark far too long. It's time to set you free."

Rachel clutched her puppy to her chest and smiled. "Did I ever tell you my dreams about performing on Broadway?"

Chapter 53

Rachel pulled into the church parking lot and spotted one of the improv players rushing to the activities building. She tapped her fingers on the steering wheel. Maybe showing up unannounced wasn't such a good idea.

Adjusting to life away from the office had been more difficult than she expected. At least working for her father was predictable. Trying to figure out how to break into the entertainment world was difficult and more than a little disconcerting.

Afraid she'd lose her nerve, she clutched her purse and hopped out of her car. Inside the building, she approached the designated room and waited in the hall until a male concluded a prayer with a resounding amen.

The moment she stepped into the room, Alicia rushed up and embraced her. "Hey, girl, I wondered when you'd show up again. Are you here to watch or participate?"

"The jury's still out."

"Well, come on in and have a seat while you decide. We're about to get started." She moved to the center of the circle. "Tonight's performance is dramatic, unless you can figure out how to put a comedic spin on a claustrophobic stuck in an elevator. Okay, who's up first?"

The man with the Greek-theater-mask tattoo popped out of his seat. "I'll give it a whirl."

"Good for you, Thomas. The stage is all yours."

Rachel watched four players deliver top-notch performances, and a fifth fall flat at attempting comedy. Alicia finished her interpretation to the loudest round of applause. "You are all too kind." She glanced at Rachel and another woman who hadn't stepped up. "Anyone else want to give it try?"

No response.

"Okay, then. We're finished for the night. We hope to see y'all in two weeks for our crit night." She extracted two bottles of water from a cooler, sat beside Rachel, and handed one over. "I guess the jury voted no."

"It's been a long time since I've performed in front of an audience, and drama isn't my strong point. What's crit night?"

"We critique each other's work. Actors have tender egos, so for every constructive comment we give two positives. What inspired you to come back?"

"A lot has changed during the past few weeks. I'm thinking about pursuing an acting career."

"Part-time?"

She shook her head. "Full-time."

"Whew. I hope you have a lot of money saved up."

"Is it that tough?"

"Unfortunately, there are way more aspiring actors than roles. It takes a long time to build an impressive résumé, which is why many professional performers start off working two jobs."

Rachel mentally calculated her savings. She had six months, maybe a year if she scrimped.

"Before you do anything else, girlfriend, you've got to work on your confidence." Alicia glanced over her shoulder. "Just the two of us are here now. How about you step up and try your hand at performing?"

"I don't know."

"You pick the part."

She pressed her lips together. If she didn't have the courage to act here, how could she expect to audition in a room full of strangers? "Will you critique me?"

"Of course I will. I'll even give you three accolades for every suggestion."

Rachel eased up and stepped to the center of the circle. She considered doing the elevator scene until she felt her knees go wobbly. She relied on her comfort zone and launched into a scene from 42nd *Street* she'd played dozens of times to her invisible audience. Peggy Sawyer arriving in New York City.

When she finished, Alicia jumped up and applauded. "You've played that character before."

You have no idea how often. "A few times. How'd I do?"

"Your timing was spot on, and your body language superb. I was right there with you in the Big Apple. In my opinion, you're ready to stretch your wings and try something new."

"Maybe so, but not tonight."

"I understand. However, I'm not letting you off the hook the next time you join us." Alicia linked arms and led her into the hall. "I hear auditions are going on for a comedy up in Marietta. You should check it out."

"Thanks for the tip."

Back in her car, Rachel pushed her key in the ignition and paused. For the first time in seven years, she was free to choose her own path. So why was she consumed with mountains of apprehension? Fear of depleting her savings? Had her dream blown out of proportion to her talent?

What about Emily and Charlie? Did Willow Falls somehow figure in her future? "That's crazy, the town doesn't have a movie theater, much less a live-performance venue."

She turned the key, pulled out of the parking lot, and vowed to check out Alicia's recommendation.

Chapter 54

Clutching a check in her hands, Emily shoved through the Hayes General Store door and raced to the counter. "We got the money."

Scott closed the cash register and pushed a bag to Pepper. "I hope my wife didn't go crazy and rob a bank."

"Even better, Rachel came through with a contract from Streetman Enterprise." She held the check up to Scott.

"Wow. Did she ever. Have you told Jacob?"

"I will as soon as I deposit this." She hugged it to her chest and twirled around. "We're going to make Mom and Dad's dream come true after all." She stopped abruptly, her eyes wide. "What's wrong with me? No one's stepped up to replace Sadie at Willow Inn. How will I ever find someone to manage the hotel?"

Pepper laughed. "How do you do it?"

"Do what?"

"Switch from euphoria to angst in a split second?"

"Apparently it's my most accomplished talent."

"I suggest you relax. You know it'll be months before the hotel is ready, which gives you plenty of time to recruit someone and pay for training. I've checked. There are plenty of hotel management courses online."

Scott nodded. "She's right."

"Thanks for reminding me."

"I have another recommendation, if you're willing."

Emily gave Pepper a wary look. "What?"

"Make Sadie the full-time innkeeper—"

"Hold on, you know she doesn't want the job."

"That's what she says, but I'm telling you she does. The problem is she's still afraid her past will get in the way."

"Even though the Sadie uproar came to a screeching halt following Mirabelle's second editorial?"

"That helped. It's the guests she's worried about."

"She has a point."

"There's more. She doesn't feel qualified."

"Because she's not."

"True. However, Mitch and I are willing to pay for her to take one of those online courses I mentioned. Two if necessary." Pepper scooped the bag off the counter. "If you want to talk to her you can find her at the inn. She plans to spend the entire day there. Something about getting ready for a long-term guest."

Emily slipped the check in her purse. "Tell you what, as soon as I deliver the good news to Jacob, I'll run the idea by Sadie and see how she reacts."

"Thank you. I promise you won't be disappointed."

"Before I do anything, I have some banking business to take care of." Emily blew a kiss to Scott. "I'll see you tonight."

After depositing the check, Emily paused outside the bank. She ran her fingers over the vintage, cast-iron mailbox where she'd deposited childhood letters to Santa. Recent events raced through her mind at warp speed and tugged on her heartstrings. If her parents had stayed in Savannah one more hour they'd be alive ... and she wouldn't know about Rachel. *Don't you remember? That's not true. The winery would have brought us together.* Emily closed her eyes. Her hands curled into fists. *They didn't have to die.*

"Are you okay?"

Startled by Nathan's voice, she opened her eyes and uncurled her fingers. "I'm remembering ... never mind. I deposited money to finish the hotel."

He pressed his palms together. "Miracles do happen."

"Thanks to Streetman Enterprise." Regretting her harsh tone, Emily forced a smile. "I think I'm ready to come back to church Sunday."

"Perfect timing, I'm preparing a message about God's blessings in the midst of difficulties." Nathan sandwiched Emily's hands in his. "You know He never left you alone, even if you didn't feel His presence."

Deep down, she understood he spoke the truth. Yet anger still gripped her soul.

Nathan released her hand. "Have you told Jacob about the hotel?"

"I'm heading there now."

"Do you mind if I join you?"

"Not at all."

Forty minutes after breaking the news to Jacob, Emily walked into Willow Inn. She found Sadie sitting at the foyer desk, reading a magazine. "Pepper told me I'd find you here."

Sadie looked up and closed the magazine with the back cover facing up. "With Charlie Bricker checking in tomorrow, I have a lot to do."

"I hear he wants to stay for a couple of months until he finds a more permanent place to live."

"That's his plan."

Emily pulled a chair close to the desk. "Greer Streetman came through with a sizable check to finish the hotel."

"Well I declare."

"Now we can figure out how to best promote Willow Inn."

"You mean *you* can figure it out."

"No, I meant we. What are you reading?" Emily reached across the desk and flipped the magazine over. "*Institute of Hospitality.* Huh." Maybe Pepper was right. "You know, not a single person has contacted me about the innkeeper's job."

"And your point is?"

Emily propped her elbows on the desk, rested her chin on her knuckles, and studied Sadie's face. With a little bit of makeup and an updated hairstyle, she'd look years younger. Maybe she'd get Pearl to give her a makeover. "I want you to take it."

Sadie nodded toward the wall. "The wallpaper you and your mom picked out for the foyer is real close to the original." She paused. "In spite of its past, this old house will finally do good things for Willow Falls."

"Are you accepting my offer?'

She locked eyes with Emily. "You understand I don't know how to successfully manage an inn."

"Pepper and Mitch will pay for you to take some online courses. Besides, you're smart and creative—"

"And if guests find out about my past?"

"Since all the gossip about you has dropped off the grapevine, it's less likely to come up."

"It's a huge risk."

"One I'm willing to take."

Sadie laced her fingers. "Can you give me a week to think about it?"

"How about four days and you continue to manage the inn until you decide?"

"Now that's what I was talking about a few days ago. You've gotta hang in there to get what you want."

Emily reached across the desk and touched Sadie's hand. "I'm glad you came back to Willow Falls."

Chapter 55

Rachel drummed her foot on the floor and scrolled through emails, searching in vain for a response from the adoption agency Greer revealed. She shoved her laptop aside, grabbed a bottle of water from the fridge, and stepped to the glass doors leading to the deck.

She rapped her knuckles on the window. "Shoo, you pesky little squirrel. It isn't nice to sharpen your teeth on my railing."

The doorbell chime echoed through her townhouse. Hoping it was the mailman or UPS driver, she scurried to the front door and peeked through the peephole.

"Charlie." She opened the door. "I thought you were headed to Willow Falls this weekend."

"I had a few more things to take care of before heading up tomorrow." He waited. "Well, are you going to invite me in, or should I hike back to the truck and hit the road today?"

"Sorry, I'm a bit distracted." She stepped aside and motioned him to enter.

"I take it you haven't found your birth mother."

"I'm beginning to think she's a deep-cover CIA agent or hiding out in witness protection." She led him to the living room couch. "Maybe Emily was right. It's enough we found each other."

Charlie propped his feet on the coffee table. "It sounds like you're giving up."

"Not yet, but I'm getting darn close to throwing in the towel."

"Then what?"

"I'll try to figure out what to do with the rest of my life." She hugged Brownie to her chest. "I did a little acting a couple of days ago."

"With the improv group?"

"Not exactly." She hesitated." When everyone else left, I performed a familiar scene for Alicia."

"And?"

"Jumping into an improvisational character's head scared the dickens out of me. All of my acting experience involved scripts and rehearsals. Nothing off-the-cuff."

"Maybe it's time you stretched your wings and tried something new."

"I'm working on it. What about you? How's everything going with the vineyard?"

"Land clearing gets under way next week. When it's finished, we'll start setting up stakes and wires for the vines."

Rachel nodded. "I'm glad things are finally moving along."

"So is my dad. Speaking of fathers, have you talked to Greer?"

"He called a couple of times with questions about business. Nothing personal." She moved the puppy away from her chest. "I suspect he used up every ounce of emotional intelligence when he brought me Brownie and treated me to lunch. Not to mention revealing the name of the adoption agency."

Charlie stretched his arm across the back of the couch. "Maybe you're shortchanging the guy."

"What do you mean?"

"Did anyone else in the office have the information he called you about?"

"Yeah, Brent." Truth trickled in and tugged on Rachel's heart. "It's his way of reaching out to me, isn't it?"

"You catch on fast."

"Not nearly fast enough. Maybe I should call him."

"Not a good idea."

Her brow furrowed. "I don't understand. Why not?"

"I imagine Greer has a huge ego."

"Mount Everest gigantic."

"Then he needs to make the first move. Otherwise you'll paint him in a corner."

"That makes sense. Maybe he'll call with another business question." Rachel pressed her hand to her growling stomach. "It must be close to dinnertime."

"Do you want to go out?"

"I'd rather stay in. We can order a pizza and watch a movie. If you don't mind."

"I'm right there with you." He pulled his phone off his belt and pressed a number.

"You have pizza delivery on speed dial?"

"Doesn't every well-organized bachelor?"

A half-hour later, Charlie answered the door while Rachel brought an open bottle of wine and two glasses from the kitchen.

He read the label. "A Georgia winery."

"Payment from Brent for convincing your father to sign the contract."

He plopped on the floor in front of the coffee table and opened the pizza box. The scent of tomato sauce, sausage, and cheese filled the room. Rachel popped in a movie. "Have you seen *Chicago*?"

"Nope."

"It's a nice compromise for a guy who's into thrillers and a lady who likes musicals." She settled beside him, clinked her glass to his, and aimed the remote at the television.

At the end of the first act, he swallowed a bite of pizza and laughed. "A song and dance movie about two killer dames. You've gotta love it."

Before the movie was half over, the doorbell chimed.

"Sit tight, I'll get it for you." Charlie sauntered to the door and returned carrying a large envelope. "Certified mail."

"It's from the agency." Her heart pounded. "Maybe it's good news." She ripped it open and scanned the certificate. "How ..." A chill ran down her spine.

"What's wrong?"

She gave him the paper and collapsed against the couch.

"You have to call Emily and tell her."

"She was afraid we might get bad news. I have no idea how she'll respond to this." She slid the document back in the envelope and moved up to the couch. "I have to tell her in person. When did you say you're going to Willow Falls?"

"Tomorrow morning."

"Is it okay if I go with you?"

Charlie sat beside her. "It's way more than okay. Do you want to watch the rest of the show?"

"Yeah, I need the distraction."

He wrapped his arm around her shoulders and clicked the remote.

Rachel curled her legs under her, leaned against his chest, and poured every ounce of energy into focusing on the television screen.

Chapter 56

Emily and Scott slipped into the last row minutes before the service began. She didn't want people to make a fuss on her first day back to church. During the opening song, her mind wandered back to her childhood pleas for a sister. Funny how things turned out. Maybe she should try bargaining again. This time for a yes answer from Sadie. *Like you have twenty years to wait for an answer.*

Her phone rang. Two ladies in the row ahead of hers turned around to stare. Emily mouthed "sorry" and pulled the disruption from her purse. She silenced it and noticed a text from Rachel. *Charlie and I are on our way to Willow Falls. Meet us at the inn at noon?*

She responded, pocketed her phone, and tried in vain to concentrate on Nathan's message. Why the last-minute trip to town? Did Rachel have news about their mother? Or was this a pleasure visit?

When the service ended, Emily grabbed Scott's hand and scooted from her seat. Before they made it to the back door, Miss Gertie stopped them. "You look real pretty today, Emily." She chuckled. "Or are you Rachel?"

"Sometime in the future we'll have fun fooling folks." She patted her midsection. "However, for the next few months, my bulging tummy will give me away."

Sadie, Mitch, and Pepper caught up with them. "I have enough chicken parmesan left over from yesterday for the five of us if you have time to come by the house."

Scott grinned. "It sounds like you're still experimenting with new menu items."

"I'm preparing for a future influx of tourists. Plus, the white table cloths and candles come out every Friday and Saturday night."

"Thanks for the invitation." Emily glanced at her watch. "But we have to pass. I'm meeting Rachel at Willow Inn in fifteen minutes."

Sadie and Pepper exchanged glances.

"I guess we better go on over there." Scott led her through the vestibule to the front sidewalk. "When did you hear from Rachel?"

She slipped her hand in his. "During the service."

"Maybe she has good news."

"Same thing I'm thinking." A stab of doubt tensed her shoulders. "Or not."

"Do you want to take the car?"

"I'd rather walk." They turned right and headed toward the park. Families carrying blankets and baskets, settling on the grass, summoned memories of picnics with her parents. "Mom and Dad would have loved spending Sunday afternoons watching their grandbabies play." She struggled to hold back tears. "How long will it take for me to think about them without choking up?"

Scott squeezed her hand. "You have a sensitive heart, so I suspect a long time."

They passed by the hotel and climbed Willow Inn's front steps. Inside, Emily nodded toward the left. "We can wait in the parlor." She settled in a wingback chair, kicked off her right shoe, and massaged the bottom of her foot. "I love this room. It's so cozy and inviting. Mom dreamed about gathering in here with her guests for afternoon beverages, cookies, and little sandwiches. She called it Willow Falls' version of high tea."

"It can still happen." Scott sat beside her. "And afterwards, they can rush over to Hayes General Store and spend a wad of money."

"Maybe you should wear vintage clothing and give tourists a big dose of local history."

"I like the way you think." He massaged his upper lip. "Perhaps I should also grow a handle-bar moustache and carry a walking stick."

"Whatever it takes to boost sales." She slipped her shoe back on. "Sadie owes me an answer today."

"Based on Pepper's opinion, I bet she takes the position."

"I hope you're right, because I need a ton of help getting the word out about this place."

"Maybe Rachel can give you some Atlanta connections."

"She did mention something about a reporter friend." The front door swung open, sending a shaft of light dancing across the foyer floor.

Emily stood and waved to the new arrivals. "We're over here. Welcome back …" Her twin's expression spoke volumes. Emily's pulse quickened. "You found her, didn't you?"

Her twin nodded and bit her lower lip.

"Please don't tell me she died bringing us into this world."

"Oh, she's very much alive." Rachel dropped onto the settee. "I didn't want to break the news to you over the phone." She extracted a sheet of paper from a large envelope and pushed it across the coffee table. "This came in the mail yesterday.

"What is it?"

"You have to read it."

She swallowed and reached for the document. Halfway through, her hands turned cold and clammy. "How is this possible?"

"I don't know."

Emily handed the paper to Scott and collapsed against the back of the chair. "Now what do we do?"

"We have to figure something out."

Chapter 57

The moment Emily and Scott moved to the vestibule, Sadie stepped away and gripped the back of a pew.

Pepper nudged Mitch.

He smiled. "I know. You want me to wait outside so you two can talk?"

"This is why you're the sheriff. You know what's going on before it happens."

"Only when it comes to you, honey."

She patted his cheek. "We do make a good team. I'll catch up with you in a few minutes."

She stepped to Sadie's side. They moved up the side aisle to the second row from the front. "I can tell something's bothering you. What's going on?"

"I promised Emily an answer four days ago."

"And?"

"Today's the deadline."

"Have you made a decision?"

Sadie's back stiffened. "Not yet."

"I don't know why not. In my opinion, you're the best person for the job. You work hard. You know the house inside and out. You—"

"Look, I value your friendship more than you can imagine and your confidence means everything. Plus, with your help, I can learn everything there is to know about innkeeping."

"So, why the hesitation?"

Sadie picked up a bulletin laying on the seat. "It's ... the other thing that's holding me back."

Pepper scooted closer to her. "Do you think it's true?"

"You know it's possible." She pressed her hand to her chest to ease the fluttering sensation. "It would change everything."

"Perhaps for the better."

"Or it could make everything a whole lot worse."

"All I have to say is, you can't let uncertainty paralyze you. It's not fair to Emily. She needs you."

"Which is why I'm skipping lunch with you and Scott and going to the inn to talk to her."

"You know Rachel's on her way?"

She nodded.

"Do you want me to tag along for moral support?"

"No. On the way, I have to make a decision." Sadie tossed the bulletin aside. "Besides, I have to stand on my own two feet."

Pepper stood and offered her hand. "You already are, my friend."

The two women strolled through the building. Outside on the front sidewalk, Sadie embraced Pepper, then headed across the street. When she turned the corner by the bank, the hotel and Willow Inn came into view. Memories of the years she lived in Robert's home overwhelmed her. She was desperate to keep the good and erase the bad … but couldn't. Not with one giant loose end hanging over her.

A couple with a young child in tow approached from the opposite direction. The woman said hello, the little girl waved. A big change from her first day back in town. Maybe it was time to tell everyone the truth about the day she shot Robert. The thought sent a chill through her limbs. Would anyone believe her or would they consider her story a lame attempt to clear her name?

She paused outside Pepper's Café and caught sight of her reflection in the window. Prison life had taken a toll and aged her beyond her forty-eight years. She pulled the band off her ponytail and let her hair fall to her shoulders. A new style and maybe some color might help. She dismissed the idea as pointless, considering she was well beyond the age when she needed to impress people.

She crossed Falls Street, strolled toward the hospital, and noticed Charlie's truck in the inn's driveway. Did he bring Rachel from Atlanta? Did she come to town to visit Emily? Or was she here for a different reason?

Her breath quickened. She crossed the street and hesitated at the bottom of the steps. Maybe she should walk away and leave everyone alone.

No, she couldn't keep Emily waiting any longer.

Fighting the urge to flee, she climbed the inn's steps and reached for the doorknob. She forced a smile and stepped into the foyer. "Is that Charlie's truck in the driveway?"

Chapter 58

Emily jumped at the sound of Sadie's voice. Rachel turned toward the foyer.

The new arrival strolled into the parlor and halted. Her eyes darted from one twin to the other. Her smile faded. Her face paled. "It's true, isn't it?"

Scott stood and offered her his seat, then gave the document back to Emily.

She clutched it to her chest and stared at Sadie. "Did you know?"

Sadie moved to the vacated wingback and dropped as if the weight of the world pressed on her shoulders. "After I met Rachel, I considered the possibility." She hesitated. "No one, other than Pepper and Mitch, knows what I'm about to tell you. It's important for you both to hear the whole story."

She turned her head toward the still-life over the fireplace. "I felt like a princess the day I first walked into this old house. For a while, me and Mama had a fairytale life. We lived in a beautiful home, invited friends and important people over for fancy dinner parties. No worries about money. Everything was going along good, until we discovered Robert Liles' biggest weakness."

She shifted her gaze to her lap and massaged the back of her left hand. "Everyone in Willow Falls believed he was a fine, upstanding citizen. He never drank in public and he bought his liquor during his out-of-town trips. A couple of months after we moved in, he got drunk out of his mind. I'll never forget how he pushed Mama to the floor, pinned her arms over her head, and straddled her. I ran toward them and pounded on his back. Mama begged me to stop. She said 'It's okay, honey, go on to your room, he won't hurt me. He loves me.'

"After that night, whenever he started drinking, me and Mama stayed in her room behind a locked door. She said it was to protect me." She stared into space. "It's strange. She never got angry at Robert. Instead, she defended him and claimed men sometimes did things to release stress."

Sadie breathed deep. "Then, one winter, Mama got real sick with pneumonia and spent a couple of days in the hospital. The first night she was gone, I was asleep in my room." Her voice faltered and lowered to a whisper. "A hand clamped over my mouth and startled me awake. Robert stood over me. His voice slurred. He called me his special little baby doll."

Emily tensed. She clutched her chest as she watched tears pool in Sadie's eyes and spill down her cheeks.

"I smelled liquor on his breath. He claimed he wanted to show me how much he loved me. My body froze … I couldn't stop him. When he finished, guilt and shame ripped a hole in my soul."

Sadie stood and gripped the fireplace mantel. "That's the moment I understood why Mama hid from him every time he drank too much. She was desperate to protect both of us."

Rachel wiped a tear from her cheek. "Had the man ever looked at you or said anything inappropriate before that night?"

"Sometimes, when he watched me, I felt creepy. But, I never thought he was capable of … something so horrible." She turned toward the painting. "I didn't want anyone to find out what happened. So, I accepted my fate as punishment."

Rachel's brow raised. "I don't understand. Punishment for what?"

"Not fighting him off. The first month I missed a period, I tried to ignore it. Until it happened two more times. I borrowed a friend's car and drove to a nearby town to buy a pregnancy kit."

She returned to her chair and wiped her cheeks. "The next night, Robert kicked my bedroom door in—drunk. He held the test strip in front of my face before yanking me out of bed and dragging me into the hall. He demanded I get rid of the problem. Somehow, I found the courage to tell him no. His eyes were filled with so much hate and anger."

A faraway look clouded Sadie's eyes. "He shoved me to the top of the stairs and said an accidental fall would do the trick. I yanked the drawer in the console table beside the stairs open … reached in, and grabbed his loaded gun. I'll never forget how he snatched my wrist and whispered, 'You don't have the guts to shoot me, so bye-bye baby.' Something inside me snapped and made me pull the trigger."

Sadie closed her eyes and massaged her temples. "Mama raced up the stairs, screaming. She dropped to the floor and pulled Robert to her chest. Blood covered the front of her nightgown. I couldn't let the police think she'd shot her husband. When the sheriff showed up, I confessed."

Rachel's brow furrowed. "Why didn't you tell him the reason you shot your stepfather?"

"You have to understand." She opened her eyes. "Robert wasn't just a bigwig in Willow Falls. The whole county considered him important." She pointed toward the foyer. "Mama served dinner to the judge and his wife right over there. I knew there was no way anyone would believe the truth. Besides, I didn't want anyone to know I was pregnant. And I couldn't add to Mama's nightmare by telling the world what he'd done. That's why I refused a trial and accepted my fate."

Emily swallowed. "When did you find out you were carrying twins?"

"Months after I was sentenced. The prison doctors gave me two choices. Abort or give you up for adoption. You were two innocent babies growing inside me. There was no way I could destroy you. Turns out it was the best decision I ever made. The day you were born, I held you both for a brief moment"—her voice faltered—"before they took you away from me. I never saw you again."

Stunned silence seemed to draw every ounce of oxygen out of the room. Emily gasped for air as recent events raced through her mind at warp speed. She closed her eyes and pressed her fingers against her temples until Rachel's voice broke through.

"Growing up, my family went to church once a year, so I never put much stock in God." Rachel stepped around the coffee table and dropped to her knees in front of Sadie. "My heart tells me only a woman touched by the hand of the Almighty would have the courage to give up everything for her unborn babies." She grasped her mother's hands. "Thank you for sacrificing yourself to give us life."

Emily slipped out of her chair and knelt beside Rachel. "Now I understand, the three of us were destined to find each other." She wrapped her arm around her twin, rested her head in her mother's lap, and let her tears flow.

"I know you envisioned your Mama managing this lovely inn." Sadie stroked Emily's hair. "I don't want to let you down."

She lifted her head and gazed into Sadie's eyes. "Are you accepting my offer?"

"If you still want me."

"Now, more than ever ... Mama Sadie."

Chapter 59

Rachel opened the blinds in the Carlie suite to let the morning sunshine pour in and warm her cheeks. She spotted a cat stretched across the bottom step of the stairs leading to the garage apartment. Her eyes drifted up to the dormer window. Two days ago, her sister showed her the space and shared stories about her childhood. Emily had no idea how fortunate she was to have been adopted by the Redding family. Although their backgrounds were as different as salt and sugar, they had much in common—ambition, creativity, a desire to please.

She moved across the room, plopped on the loveseat, and propped her bare feet on the coffee table. Beside her lay Emily's story about the room's namesake. She picked it up and read it again. Which details were fact and which were creative conceptions from her twin's story-writing imagination? Whichever, she longed to know more about the woman she now knew as her maternal grandmother.

Rachel leaned her head back, closed her eyes, and let recent events spin through her head. One week ago, she discovered her life had begun with an unspeakable act of violence. And yet the depth of Sadie's love vanquished the shock and filled her with awe and gratitude. She smiled and hugged Carlie's story to her chest.

A tapping drew her attention. She laid the pages aside, smoothed her skirt, and opened the door.

Charlie's smile and the subtle scent of his musky cologne greeted her and sent a tingle through her limbs. "Good morning, pretty lady. Are you ready for breakfast?"

"I will be as soon as I put my shoes on."

"The go-to-church pair you bought yesterday?"

"Along with this outfit. How about I meet you in the dining room in five?"

"I'll save a seat for you." He blew her a kiss and moseyed through the foyer.

Following Sadie's revelation, his compassion expanded the pro-side of her Charlie list and further muddied her vision of the future. On the one hand, she wanted to stay in Willow Falls and spend more time with him. Yet fear of becoming trapped in his world frightened her. She valued her newfound freedom and didn't want to commit to anyone before she had a chance to test the waters and pursue her own dream.

She opened the shoebox and removed a pair of taupe heels. At three inches, they were the closest thing to stilettos available in Willow Falls. She smiled, wondering if she could adapt to living in a small town with one clothing store. Maybe when the hotel opened, enough people would move here to warrant a second. She slipped the shoes on, checked her image in the mirror, and headed to the dining room.

The mouth-watering aroma of cinnamon and the rich smell of coffee roused her appetite. Charlie stood and pulled a chair away from the table. "Our hostess is bringing in scrambled eggs, grits, and sausage."

"Why such a big breakfast?"

Sadie pushed the door open and carried a tray to the table. "Because we need plenty of protein to get us through today's unveiling."

Rachel spread a napkin across her lap. "Are you nervous?"

"A little. But not for me. I don't want anyone to think less of you and Emily. Do you mind if I say a little blessing before we begin?"

Charlie reached for Rachel's hand. "Of course we don't."

She closed her eyes and found comfort in her mother's simple, yet poignant prayer.

Following an amen, Sadie poured a cup of coffee for Rachel and settled across the table from the couple. During breakfast, the three engaged in lighthearted conversation about innkeeping and life in a small town. When they finished eating, Sadie stood to clear the table and Rachel returned to her room to freshen up.

Ten minutes later, she met Sadie and Charlie on the front porch. He held his hand out to her. "You look stunning."

"I hope I'm dressed up enough. Or am I overdressed?"

"This is the country." Sadie smiled. "You'll see everything from overalls and ballcaps to pearls and fancy hats. Besides, I doubt God pays any attention to what people wear on the outside." She tapped her chest. "It's what's in here He cares about."

"It seems I have a ton to learn about the man upstairs."

They climbed down the steps, strolled past the park, and turned the corner toward the church. As they approached the walk leading to the steps, apprehension attacked Rachel. She stopped. "Hold up a minute." She pulled her phone from her purse and tapped a text message. The response came seconds later. "Emily and Scott are on the way. I want to wait for them to arrive before we go inside."

Sadie linked arms with Rachel. "Whatever makes you comfortable."

"Thanks for understanding … Mama Sadie."

Chapter 60

Emily pressed the page-down key and typed CHAPTER 4 before shutting down her computer.

Scott stood behind her and massaged her shoulders. "You got a heck of lot done in a week."

"After Sadie … I mean Mama … agreed to manage the inn, a floodgate opened up and let the story pour through my fingers. At this pace, I'll have a first draft finished before our babies arrive."

"I can't wait to read it."

She swallowed the last drop of orange juice and glanced at her watch. "It's time to leave for church."

"Are you ready for today's big reveal?"

Emily stood and wrapped her arms around Scott's neck. "Yes, but I admit I'm nervous. I have no idea how everyone will react."

He kissed her forehead. "I suspect your story will top the gossip grapevine for at least a week."

"Maybe an entire month. Do I look okay?"

"Better than Miss America."

She inhaled deeply and exhaled. "All right then. As my sister says, it's showtime."

Scott escorted her to the car and backed out of the garage. Emily folded her hands in her lap and let her shoulders relax. Today, everyone would learn the truth. Sadie's courage had given her the strength to face what had to be done with confidence.

She responded to the incoming text from Rachel and smiled.

Scott drove past the church and pointed to the full parking lot. "It looks like the entire town showed up. Why don't you hop out and wait with your sister while I find a place to park?"

"Good idea."

He pulled up to the curb. Charlie opened the door and held his hand out to Emily.

She accepted it and stepped out of the car. The four exchanged embraces.

Sadie grinned. "My girls are prettier than angels."

Rachel stroked her cheek. "Thanks to a beautiful mother."

Emily held Sadie's hand. "Are you nervous?"

"Funny, your sister asked me the same question back at the inn. The answer is yes. For you two, not for me. I've kept the truth locked up inside for thirty years. Letting it finally come out promises to bring my smiles back."

Scott rushed around the corner and caught up with them. "Okay, folks, it's time to get this show on the road. He held Emily's hand and led the way up the steps into the vestibule.

Jacob greeted them. "Nathan has the front row reserved for you guys." He escorted them up the aisle amidst stares and whispers.

Emily slid in next to Sadie and leaned close. "By this afternoon, we'll be the biggest newsflash to hit Willow Falls since … well, you know."

Sadie patted her daughter's knee. "With one big difference. This time, it's a good story."

Mary settled at the piano and played a medley of uplifting songs. She ended with a stirring rendition of *Amazing Grace*, signaling the service to begin.

Nathan stepped up to the podium and straightened his tie. He smiled. "This is a special day for our town. One we'll remember as a testimony to God's unfailing love. In place of a typical service—with prayers, songs, and a sermon—you'll hear from three of His precious children." He motioned to the front row and stepped aside.

Emily moved into the aisle, followed by Sadie and Rachel. They stepped to the front and faced a room filled with friends and neighbors.

Swallowing the lump in her throat, Emily lifted the microphone off the podium and stepped close to the railing. "We are here to share an incredible story about sacrifice, redemption, and a mother's unselfish love. Twenty-nine years ago, heart-breaking circumstances and misguided egos separated three souls."